OXFORD WORLD'S CLASSICS

WASHINGTON SQUARE

HENRY JAMES was born in New York in 1843 of ancestry both Irish and Scottish. He received a remarkably cosmopolitan education in New York, London, Paris, and Geneva, and entered law school at Harvard in 1862. After 1869 he lived mostly in Europe, at first writing critical articles, reviews, and short stories for American periodicals. He lived in London for more than twenty years, and in 1898 moved to Rye, where his later novels were written. Under the influence of an ardent sympathy for the British cause in the First World War, Henry James was in 1915 naturalized a British subject. He died in 1916.

In his early novels, which include *Roderick Hudson* (1875), *The American* (1877), and *The Portrait of a Lady* (1881), he was chiefly concerned with the impact of the older civilization of Europe upon American life. He analysed English character with extreme subtlety in such novels as *What Maisie Knew* (1897) and *The Awkward Age* (1899). In his last three great novels, *The Wings of the Dove* (1902), *The Ambassadors* (1903), and *The Golden Bowl* (1904), he returned to the 'international' theme of the contrast of American and European character.

ADRIAN POOLE is Professor of English Literature and Fellow of Trinity College, Cambridge. He has written extensively on Henry James, and has edited *The Aspern Papers and Other Stories*, *What Maisie Knew*, and *The American* for Oxford World's Classics.

OXFORD WORLD'S CLASSICS

*For over 100 years Oxford World's Classics have brought
readers closer to the world's great literature. Now with over 700
titles—from the 4,000-year-old myths of Mesopotamia to the
twentieth century's greatest novels—the series makes available
lesser-known as well as celebrated writing.*

*The pocket-sized hardbacks of the early years contained
introductions by Virginia Woolf, T. S. Eliot, Graham Greene,
and other literary figures which enriched the experience of reading.
Today the series is recognized for its fine scholarship and
reliability in texts that span world literature, drama and poetry,
religion, philosophy, and politics. Each edition includes perceptive
commentary and essential background information to meet the
changing needs of readers.*

OXFORD WORLD'S CLASSICS

HENRY JAMES

Washington Square

Edited with an Introduction and Notes by
ADRIAN POOLE

OXFORD
UNIVERSITY PRESS

OXFORD
UNIVERSITY PRESS

Great Clarendon Street, Oxford OX2 6DP

Oxford University Press is a department of the University of Oxford.
It furthers the University's objective of excellence in research, scholarship,
and education by publishing worldwide in

Oxford New York

Auckland Cape Town Dar es Salaam Hong Kong Karachi
Kuala Lumpur Madrid Melbourne Mexico City Nairobi
New Delhi Shanghai Taipei Toronto

With offices in

Argentina Austria Brazil Chile Czech Republic France Greece
Guatemala Hungary Italy Japan Poland Portugal Singapore
South Korea Switzerland Thailand Turkey Ukraine Vietnam

Oxford is a registered trade mark of Oxford University Press
in the UK and in certain other countries

Published in the United States
by Oxford University Press Inc., New York

First published as a World's Classics paperback 1982
Reissued as an Oxford World's Classics paperback 1998
New edition 2010

British Library Cataloguing in Publication Data

Data available

Library of Congress Cataloging in Publication Data

Data available

Typeset by Glyph International, Bangalore, India
Printed in Great Britain
on acid-free paper by
Clays Ltd, St Ives plc

ISBN 978-0-19-955919-0

1 3 5 7 9 10 8 6 4 2

CONTENTS

INTRODUCTION

Readers who do not wish to learn details of the plot will prefer to treat the Introduction as an Afterword.

Washington Square is one of the most instantly appealing of James's early masterpieces, along with 'Daisy Miller', *The Europeans*, and—albeit on a different scale—*The Portrait of a Lady*. They all belong to the years of intense creative effort between 1878 and 1881 when he was making a name for himself in London, both professionally and socially. It was only in 1883, after his father's death, that he would, at the age of 40, stop signing his work 'Henry James, Jr.'.

Like all his most memorable fictions, whether early or late, *Washington Square* teases the ear with resonances of allegory, fable, and archetype. At its heart are an imprisoned daughter and a domineering father, locked in combat over the possibility of her escape from the domain that provides its very title. Yet 'Washington Square' is a real place. So too was the New York of the 1840s, the tale persuades us, with its Irish immigrants alighting at the Battery and its oyster saloon on Seventh Avenue (p. 73), its omnibuses tumbling over dislocated cobble-stones (p. 79), the pigs and chickens disporting themselves in the gutter further uptown, 'where the extension of the city began to assume a theoretic air' (p. 13). This is scarcely a realm glamorous or unearthly enough for Catherine Sloper to be its romantic heroine or her father its resident monster. Or not obviously so. Neither the conventions of 'romance' nor 'realism' provide the reader with adequate guidelines to this complex tale. Henry James Junior was experimenting, and the results are no less intriguing and disturbing than they are—one of the tale's key words—'charming'. Its first readers were not quite sure what to make of it, other than to agree that Mr James was 'clever', even perhaps at his 'cleverest'. This makes him however unnervingly close to his own cold-hearted father Dr Sloper, who is nothing if not 'clever'. What is the difference between them? The good Doctor sees the world in clear, keen, and precise terms and reaches immovable conclusions. But this is not James's vision. The world of his novel turns out to be murkier, messier, more treacherous.

Sources and Influences

Its origins can be traced to several sources, in England, France, and America. James got the plot early in 1879 in London. The previous year had been a big one for him. He had published his first book in England, *French Poets and Novelists*, and he had extended his reputation on both sides of the Atlantic with three sparkling provocative fictions, 'Daisy Miller', 'An International Episode', and—substantial enough to make a short novel—*The Europeans*. He had dined out indefatigably, he had been elected to the Reform Club, he had met literary celebrities like Alfred Lord Tennyson and George Meredith: he was turning into a celebrity himself. He enjoyed a particular intimacy with the legendary Fanny Kemble (1809–93), the now aged actress who could dispel the longueurs of English winter evenings with her stories and gossip. On 20 February she told him a tale that he scrupulously recorded in his Diary (reproduced here in Appendix 1). It was about her handsome unreliable brother Henry ('H.K.'), and his engagement to a 'dull, plain, common-place girl' with 'a handsome private fortune' ('Miss T.'), and a disapproving father who threatened to leave her not a penny of his own if she went ahead and married him. So here was a classic triangle and a grievous tussle over money and love. The girl was ready to defy her father for love, but the man was not prepared to marry her without the money, and when this seemed certain not to materialize, he was off. Sad and familiar enough in itself, but James's imagination fastened on the young woman's wound and the way she dealt with it. Coming into the money on her father's death, Miss T. determined to remain unmarried. Ten years or more later her old beau returned and renewed his suit, but she refused him. 'And yet, said Mrs K., she cared for him—and she would have married no other man. But H.K.'s selfishness had over-reached itself and this was the retribution of time.' James's first choice of phrase here had been 'the revenge of time', but on reflection he crossed it out and changed it to 'retribution'. This is a more honourable kind of justice and the fitting conclusion to a sequence that begins with the girl's 'tribulation' and her suitor's 'speculation'. James was starting to finger the keys. He was also alert to the possibilities represented by Fanny Kemble herself, who had warned the girl against her self-centred brother, and by her sister Adelaide ('Mrs S.'), who encouraged the errant man to try again. Between them these women gave James the clue for all three of his tale's sisters: Mrs Penniman, Mrs Almond, and Mrs Montgomery. But if the cast-list was developing, he still had to find the right theatre.

Meanwhile, through the spring and summer of 1879 other commitments intervened. He dashed off another short novel called *Confidence* for Scribner's; he completed a short study of Nathaniel Hawthorne which would raise all sorts of hackles back home. By mid-September he had finished the *Hawthorne* and escaped for three months to Paris, and it was here that he seems to have begun work on the Kemble story. The French surroundings may have helped him to further sources (or 'inter-texts') for his tale. Most obviously, his favoured French patron, Balzac, and his short novel, *Eugénie Grandet* (1833), the plot of which James's tale mirrors—the father, the daughter, the suitor, the money. An early review noted the similarity between them, 'with this fundamental alteration, that the story is transferred from the grimmest regions of tragedy to those of comedy'.[1] James had been introduced to Balzac's novel in Newport around 1860, and five years later, reviewing a now forgotten novel he recommended it to the author, Harriet Prescott. She should curb the wordiness of her 'ideal descriptive style' and go to school with the realists like Mérimée and Balzac; even Trollope would help.[2] Yet when it came to *Washington Square* James himself would not lavish Balzac's minute attention to detail on the interiors of his own fiction. James's realism is focused in his characters' expression, spoken and unspoken, as when Mrs Penniman reflects on Morris Townsend, that '[H]e was certainly much more imperious—she ended by calling it imperial—than Mr Penniman' (p. 27), or the Doctor sizes up the situation in the Almonds' drawing-room, 'these two young persons might confabulate, as the Doctor phrased it to himself, without attracting attention' (p. 41).

Readers of *Washington Square* have detected the influence of Balzac's French successors in the realist tradition—Zola, the Goncourts, Maupassant, Daudet—attributing to it the cool detachment that features largely though not exclusively in the narrator's voice. James certainly read and reviewed his French contemporaries

[1] *Henry James: The Contemporary Reviews*, ed. Kevin Hayes (New York, 1996), 112.
[2] Review of Harriet Elizabeth (Prescott) Spofford, *Azarian: An Episode* (1865), in *Henry James: Literary Criticism*, vol. i: *Essays on Literature, American Writers, English Writers*, ed. Leon Edel with the assistance of Mark Wilson (New York, 1984), 603–13.

with great interest. One early reviewer of *Washington Square* went so far as to accuse him of the cruelty towards his main character typical of French realism, or its sterner offspring, naturalism. It was as if James had begun 'like a spiritualized Zola with the assumption that the legitimate subject-matter of tragedy is the infliction of suffering on a human being'. Catherine Sloper's suffering made 'painful reading', as if James 'with the most admirable skill, had performed a difficult vivisection for us to witness'. The reviewer concluded that 'the piercing of live flesh in cold blood is bad art'.[3] Others have agreed in aligning James with Catherine's medical father, who can deal, we are told, 'a terribly incisive look—a look so like a surgeon's lancet' (p. 92). This would have disappointed the novelist who reviewed Zola's *Nana* in February 1880, just after finishing *Washington Square*. James deplored its lack of humour and wit, and defiantly claimed, on behalf of the English tradition, 'that we have, as a general thing, a deeper, more delicate perception of the play of character and the state of the soul'.[4]

James may have shrunk from the unbridled fancy he deplored in Miss Prescott, but he also shrank from 'the dryness, the solemnity, the air of tension and effort' he detected in Zola and his fellows.[5] A generation back, Balzac had provided a richer, more unrestrained model. Yet when it comes to the style in which the fathers express their anger, nothing could be further from Dr Sloper's feline urbanity than this tirade of Balzac's M. Grandet, at least on first hearing:

'Accursed serpent of a daughter! Oh, you bad lot, you know I love you and you take advantage of it. She's cutting her father's throat! Good Lord, you must have thrown your fortune at the feet of that good-for-nothing with his fine leather boots. By my father's pruning-hook, I can't disinherit you, by my casks! But I curse you, your cousin, and your children! . . .' He looked at his daughter, who stood there cold and silent. 'She won't budge; she won't bat an eyelid. She's more of a Grandet than I am.'[6]

More typical of Dr Sloper is the way in which he thinks to himself with amusement, in retreat from deeper feelings such as anger or compassion: 'By Jove, . . . I believe she will stick—I believe she will

   [3] *The Contemporary Reviews*, ed. Hayes, pp. 115, 116.
   [4] *Henry James: Literary Criticism*, vol. ii: *European Writers and the Prefaces*, ed. Leon Edel with the assistance of Mark Wilson (New York, 1984), 870.
   [5] Ibid. 869.
   [6] *Eugénie Grandet*, trans. Sylvia Raphael, with introduction by Christopher Prendergast (Oxford, 1990), 144–5.

stick!' (p. 90) Balzac's is not the style in which James's tyrannical fathers oppress their daughters: we might think of Gilbert Osmond and Pansy in *The Portrait of a Lady*, or even Adam Verver and Maggie in *The Golden Bowl*. Yet the possibility of such violence in word or deed haunts James's great scenes of confrontation. James did not suffer from a shortage of literary (and dramatic) models for a father's grasp on his daughter, but as Angus Wrenn has shown, Dr Sloper owes something not just to Balzac but to the less well-known contemporary French writer, the Swiss-born Victor Cherbuliez (1829–99). The classically Gothic plot of Cherbuliez's first novel, *Le Comte Kostia* (1863), revolves around the hero's rescue of an only daughter from imprisonment by the title-character, a jealously possessive widower. Like Catherine Sloper, she is made to suffer for surviving a firstborn male child who dies in infancy.[7] Nor is this the only novel by Cherbuliez that depends on such violently constrained relations between father and daughter: so too do *Paul Méré* (to which 'Daisy Miller' owes an explicit debt) and *Le Roman d'une honnête femme*.

The dramatic or melodramatic violence in Balzac, Cherbuliez, and others shadows James's restrained well-mannered fiction. The scene where it does so most vividly is far from the comforts of Washington Square. Father and daughter find themselves alone together in a steep lonely valley high up in the Alps. The reflection of the setting sun's cold, red light catches the snow-summits and lodges in the Doctor's eyes as, for the first and last time, he openly airs his rage.

The place was ugly and lonely, but the place could do her no harm. There was a kind of still intensity about her father which made him dangerous, but Catherine hardly went so far as to say to herself that it might be part of his plan to fasten his hand—the neat, fine, supple hand of a distinguished physician—in her throat. Nevertheless, she receded a step. (p. 115)

'The *place* could do her no harm', no more harm in itself than Washington Square. It is, as we say, the moment of truth when the pain they have caused each other turns into violence and inflicts injuries no less irreparable for their being a matter of words and silence, or reticence: his, hers, the narrator's. It is this last who bears witness to what Catherine 'hardly' goes so far as to say to herself, lingering with chilled fascination over 'the neat, fine, supple hand of a

[7] Angus Wrenn, *Henry James and the Second Empire* (Oxford, 1995), 86.

distinguished physician'. Earlier we were told that 'while she felt that what he said went so terribly against her, she admired his neatness and nobleness of expression' (p. 53).

The third source for this tale lay back home in America with James's great predecessor, Nathaniel Hawthorne (1804–64). There is a specific tale of his called 'Rappaccini's Daughter' that has been claimed as an inspiration for James, who we know admired it. Again there is a triangle: an oppressive father, an imprisoned daughter, and a potentially liberating lover. It is a long way from the dark fabular quality of the setting and telling to James's historically located *Washington Square* of the 1840s, but as with the other putative sources or intertexts, it is exactly the radical transformation that gives James's tale its vigour. More important than the reworking of a specific fiction, there is the provocation of the critical study that James was writing just before he moved on to the Kemble story. His *Hawthorne* was published in December 1879 in the thick of the writing of *Washington Square*, and its mixed, often hostile, reception would overshadow the novel's first readings. Writing privately to his friend and fellow-writer William Dean Howells early in 1880, James made the connection with his own tale explicit. In response to Howells's review of *Hawthorne*, James reiterated his belief that novelists—or the kind of novelist he wanted to be—thrived on 'an old civilization' (the phrases in quotation marks are from Howells's review):

It is on manners, customs, usages, habits, forms, upon all these things matured and established, that a novelist lives—they are the very stuff his work is made of; and in saying that in the absence of those 'dear and worn-out paraphernalia' which I enumerate as being wanting in American society, 'we have simply the whole of human life left,' you beg (to my sense) the question.

He goes on to speak of his own forthcoming appearance with 'a poorish story in three numbers—a tale purely American, the writing of which made me feel acutely the want of the "paraphernalia" '.[8]

It is clear that the 'purely American' tale is a response to the challenge James had himself issued in *Hawthorne*, most memorably in a well-known, even notorious passage, in which James mischievously mourns the absence in America of all the 'paraphernalia' on which

---

the traditional novelist relies. What is there to write about? Poor Hawthorne did what he could with the dark legacy of the Puritan conscience or consciousness and the 'deeper psychology'. But what of the manners, the history, the traditions, on which English and European novels fastened and feasted?

[I]t takes such an accumulation of history and custom, such a complexity of manners and types, to form a fund of suggestion for a novelist. . . . one might enumerate the items of high civilization, as it exists in other countries, which are absent from the texture of American life, until it should become a wonder to know what was left. No State, in the European sense of the word, and indeed barely a specific national name. No sovereign, no court, no personal loyalty, no aristocracy, no church, no clergy, no army, no diplomatic service, no country gentlemen, no palaces, no castles, nor manors, nor old country-houses, nor parsonages, nor thatched cottages, nor ivied ruins, no cathedrals, nor abbeys, nor little Norman churches; no great Universities, nor public schools—no Oxford, nor Eton, nor Harrow; no literature, no novels, no museums, no pictures, no political society, no sporting class—no Epsom nor Ascot!

Few of his compatriots were mollified by James's going on to say that 'The American knows that a good deal remains; what it is that remains—that is his secret, his joke, as one may say.'[9] There is much more to be said about James's own complex debts to Hawthorne, but for our purposes we can draw from this passage his sense of the 'poorish story in three numbers' as the best that could be, or could have been, done with the least undeveloped aspects of American society before 1850.

There is a further, more personal aspect to the American sources of *Washington Square*. James was born in 1843 almost forty years after Hawthorne (born in 1804), and this is the time difference to which he refers both in *Hawthorne* and *Washington Square*. It is more than the difference of generations. In James's version of history, it is the difference between innocence and experience, tantamount to a Fall.

The generation to which he [Hawthorne] belonged, that generation which grew up with the century, witnessed during a period of fifty years the immense, uninterrupted material development of the young Republic . . . [It held] a kind of superstitious faith in the grandeur of the country, its

duration, its immunity from the usual troubles of earthly empires. This faith was a simple and uncritical one . . .

The Civil War, 'that great convulsion', marked the end of an era.

It introduced into the national consciousness a certain sense of proportion and relation, of the world being a more complicated place than it had hitherto seemed, the future more treacherous, success more difficult. At the rate at which things are going, it is obvious that good Americans will be more numerous than ever; but the good American, in days to come, will be a more critical person than his complacent and confident grandfather. He has eaten of the tree of knowledge.[10]

Along with the only other fiction James deliberately set this far back in time, *The Europeans*, *Washington Square* belongs to an innocent past in which Catherine Sloper has been marooned.

Forty years back from 1880 took James to the time of his parents' marriage in 1840, his own birth in New York and earliest years. These are the times to which the narrator makes explicit reference in the 'topographical parenthesis' beginning 'I know not whether it is owing to the tenderness of early associations . . .' (p. 13). Insofar as the places dear to such relatively recent immigrants as the Jameses and Walshes could be called ancestral, New York was the city of his mother's family as Albany was of his father's. More specifically the real Washington Square in the late 1830s housed his maternal grandmother Elizabeth Walsh and her daughters Mary and Catharine (Kate): his grandmother lived there till her death in 1847 when Henry was aged 5. Henry Junior ('Harry') was born in 21 Washington Place, just round the corner, 'the most expensive and fashionable property the Jameses would ever own'.[11] The area was suffused with childhood memories, as the pages devoted to it in *The American Scene* (1907) and his late autobiographical work, *A Small Boy and Others* (1913), bear witness. Readers have been known to see in Catherine Sloper and her fate a projection of the novelist's own fears (and desires), of being left behind by the tide of history and imprisoned in some family fastness, working away like his heroine at morsels of fancy-work, a favoured metaphor of his for writing. It is true that just as the serialization

[10] Ibid. i. 426, 427–8.
[11] Paul Fisher, *House of Wits: An Intimate Portrait of the James Family* (New York, 2008), 68.

of Catherine Sloper's story in the *Cornhill* was coming to an end in November 1880, he was defending to Grace Norton his own unmarried state and intention not to marry (as his elder brother William had done the previous year).[12] But if one wants to speculate in this way, it makes more sense to consider the women to whom James was perforce closest, his mother Mary, Aunt Kate, and sister Alice. Henry and his three brothers may not have been cut out or brought up for 'business', but they still had more options than their singular sister. One can readily imagine the writer brooding on the case of his disturbed, turbulent sister Alice, but also thinking back to his mother and aunt, embroidering away in Washington Square forty years ago, as time passed and the prospect of marriage receded. James's mother Mary Walsh was born in 1810 and Aunt Kate two years later. By the time of the financial panic of 1837 they would both have been regarded by the standards of their time as near-confirmed spinsters. Until one day an attractive, unconventional, and not obviously reliable man called Henry James knocked on the door and offered one of them the prospect of liberation. Paul Fisher notes that the novelist's mother shared a number of Catherine Sloper's characteristics, including rude health and a taste for fine clothes devoid of vanity.[13] His aunt Kate—who would in due course make a calamitous short-lived marriage—virtually shared her first name. What seized the writer was of course none of these particulars. It was simply the image of any woman of respectable status with money in New York around 1840, for whom the prospect of marriage was precarious.

Place

At the end of the eighteenth century the area that would become Washington Square sported a public gallows, and in the early years of the nineteenth it served as a burial-ground for the indigent. In the late 1820s and 1830s it underwent massive changes as the middle and upper classes moved up from the tip of Manhattan and sought housing appropriate to their status. Thomas Bender describes the results as 'a revolution in urban life . . . the first instance in the city of the modern pattern of life that separates work and residence. It was

---

[12] *Letters*, ii. 314.
[13] *House of Wits*, 41, 44, 77–8.

in the region of Washington Square that an exclusively residential
housing market for middle- and upper-class commuters was created.'
Washington Square had its heyday in the 1840s, but as James's novel
notes, the tide was already sweeping further uptown, carrying with
it the Almonds and the successful branch of the Townsends. By
the time James was writing in 1880—let alone by the time Edith
Wharton in 1920 was setting *The Age of Innocence* back in the 1870s—
Washington Square had come to represent 'an eddy in the northward
flow of Manhattan life . . . the physical manifestation of collective
memory, of history'.[14]

It is an uncommon choice for a novel's title, unlike fictional venues
such as Jane Austen's Mansfield Park, Dickens's Bleak House, or
E. M. Forster's Howards End. These are country seats too for that
matter, like John Galsworthy's generic title, *The Country House*
(1907). 'Washington Square' is not so much a particular property
as an address, an address with particular attractions for a Morris
Townsend. To change the title to *The Heiress*, as Ruth and Augustus
Goetz did for their effective dramatized version (1947), and William
Wyler for the fine film based on their play (1949: see Appendix 2),
is to effect a slight shift of emphasis. When Morris confesses that
the Slopers' is 'a devilish comfortable house' (p. 80), he points to
the dream behind the title, the idea of what it means to be 'comfortable'. It is the idea by which everyone's life in this novel is regulated,
most prominently—for the idea revolves around men—the Doctor's
and Morris Townsend's. They are in total agreement about its constitution, or even, as one says of a material substance, its consistency.
It involves a good wine-cellar, for instance; here, if one likes, is
James's 'realism'. All the women pay homage to it, Aunt Penniman,
Mrs Almond, even poor straitened Mrs Montgomery. Everyone, that
is, except Catherine, at least as long as she seeks to escape. Twenty
years after *her* dream has ended, she contemplates the older Morris
with his glossy perfumed beard and concludes, 'the story of his life
defined itself in his eyes: he had made himself comfortable, and he
had never been caught' (p. 168).

I say that the idea of comfort revolves around the men, but here
James is making a historical point about the changes undergone by

<hr/>

[14] Thomas Bender, 'Washington Square in the Growing City', in Rick Beard and Leslie
Cohen Berlowitz (eds.), *Greenwich Village: Culture and Counterculture* (New Brunswick,
NJ, 1993), 28, 30.

American society between the world of the late 1870s and 'forty years ago'. The only other fiction he sets back in the past like this is *The Europeans* (1878), to which *Washington Square* is in all sorts of ways a complement. Catherine is a grimmer version of the more frankly restless Wentworth daughter, Gertrude; the Sloper mansion a more embattled urban counterpart to the airier New England country-house invaded by the Wentworths' 'charming' European cousins, Eugenia, Baroness Münster, and her brother Felix. The outcome of *The Europeans* is neatly divided between surrender and rejection—Felix gets to stay and rescue Gertrude, while Eugenia fails to land a husband and has to return whence she came. The comparative geniality of *The Europeans* is sustained by the doubling of characters (daughters, hosts, guests, suitors), whereas Dr Sloper's regime is all too dependent on a single child and her single admirer. If *The Europeans* focuses on a brother and sister who could be accused of having too much charm, then *Washington Square* asks through its homely heroine what it might mean to have not enough.

But that was then. The stories James writes in the late 1870s about *contemporary* Americans—including 'Daisy Miller', 'An International Episode', 'A Bundle of Letters', 'The Pension Beaurepas'—depict very different kinds of character and lifestyle. The idea of comfort no longer revolves around the men. They are hard at work in downtown New York, like Mr Westgate in 'An International Episode', or Ezra B. Miller (Daisy's father) back in Schenectady, unless they are worn-out wrecks like Mr Ruck in 'The Pension Beaurepas'. Meanwhile their women-folk—successors to Catherine Sloper's vigorous cousins, the Almond sisters—are at leisure in Newport, Saratoga, or Europe.

Catherine's tale takes its place in more than one sequence. The first is a series of three specifically written for the *Cornhill*, beginning with 'Daisy Miller', continuing with 'An International Episode', and concluding with 'Washington Square'. When it first appeared in Britain in volume form, *Washington Square* made part of another sequence that accentuated Catherine's distance from her liberated American successors. Though the New York firm Harper's gave it a volume all to itself, Macmillan partnered it with two shorter tales, 'The Pension Beaurepas' and 'A Bundle of Letters', to make up two volumes. If one treats this trio as a unit, the two other tales make a difference to the way one reads *Washington Square*. Seated for life in New York of the 1840s, Catherine Sloper inaugurates a series.

She marks a kind of incarceration against which her variably emancipated successors, more or less at loose in the Europe of the next three decades, are to be measured: in 'The Pension Beaurepas', Sophie Ruck and Aurora Church, and in 'A Bundle of Letters', Miranda Hope and Violet Ray. No less important is the changing balance of power between daughters and fathers. The exhausted and nerve-wracked Mr Ruck and Mr Ray are descendants of the 'over-worked men of business' who form half Dr Sloper's clientèle. Remorselessly intent on shopping, their daughters succeed in 'doing as they please' as easily as poor Catherine found it impossible. She makes a particularly poignant contrast to Isabel Archer, whose story begins appearing in the final months of 1880, exactly as Catherine Sloper's is reaching its conclusion.

Character

The four main characters are arranged with the symmetry of drama, opera, or dance (a square-dance):[15] the father, the daughter, the confidante, the suitor. Yet before we consider the principals, it is worth admiring the supporting cast, especially Mrs Almond, the Doctor's other sister. She and her large family represent a breezy prosperous 'normality' against which the pathological Sloper household asks to be measured. We are told that as a child Catherine enjoyed fraternizing with her young cousins, but the boys grow up (all seven of them) and 'settle themselves in life' (p. 14). We may faintly recall this when we read the novel's celebrated final sentence, in which Catherine is left 'seated . . .—for life, as it were'. For life, not in it. Of the two Almond daughters, one has married 'very punctually' and it is at the other's engagement party that Catherine makes the fateful acquaintance of Morris Townsend. The glimpses we get of the Almonds only serve to exacerbate Catherine's awkwardness: 'Marian Almond was a pretty little person of seventeen, with a very small figure and a very big sash, to the elegance of whose manners matrimony had nothing to add' (p. 15). Elizabeth Almond, their mother, however, is an

[15] For some suggestive reflections on the 'rhetorical square' into which the Doctor's 'controlling ironic formulations' translate the novel's situation, see Merle A. Williams, 'The American Spaces of Henry James', in Attie de Lange, Gail Fincham, Jeremy Hawthorn, and Jakob Lothe (eds.), *Literary Landscapes: From Modernism to Postcolonialism* (Basingstoke, 2008), 27–9.

important presence, her brother's confidante as Lavinia Penniman is Catherine's. She threatens or promises to become a main player, not least when she offers her niece the nearest thing Catherine will ever get to 'motherly kindness' (p. 129).

Of the four principals, Morris Townsend is the simplest. He is a gifted actor who excels at appearing—one of the novel's most loaded words—'natural': 'He liked everything to be natural' (p. 27). Our view is initially restricted to what Catherine sees *of* him (she thinks he is beautiful), and what her father sees or fails to see *in* him ('not a gentleman', 'a vulgar nature', 'a plausible coxcomb' (p. 35)). In due course we learn more about Morris from the different way he behaves when he is with the Slopers, *père et fille*, and when he is alone with Mrs Penniman, with whom he can be honest: 'I do like the money!' (p. 77) He also drops his guard, or the narrator sharply pierces it, when we hear what he says to himself, of Mrs Penniman ('The woman's an idiot' (p. 76)), and of Catherine ('Gracious Heaven, what a dull woman!' (p. 109)). What he sees in Catherine is what he sees round her, 'a devilish comfortable house' (p. 80). We get a good sense of his attraction to her and her surroundings, when he sees her alone for the first time:

He seemed more at home this time—more familiar; lounging a little in the chair, slapping a cushion that was near him with his stick, and looking round the room a good deal, and at the objects it contained, as well as at Catherine; whom, however, he also contemplated freely. (p. 27)

'However'? Does this redress the injurious implication that he contemplates Catherine as another object, or aggravate it? He is certainly remarkably free with his stick. Yet no wonder the young woman is moved by the 'smile of respectful devotion in his handsome eyes' which seems to her 'almost solemnly beautiful'. This is surely better than being simply 'solemnly beautiful', which would be a bit suspicious.

Her father sees right through the beautiful young man because they have a good deal in common. The clue to Morris, as the Doctor says in his interview with the young man's sister, Mrs Montgomery, another key supporting player, is 'the determination . . . to accept nothing of life but its pleasures, and to secure these pleasures chiefly by the aid of your complaisant sex' (p. 66). Morris is not especially devious or calculating or indeed shameless. In the decisive interview with Catherine we are told: 'He was ashamed of himself, and his shame was uncomfortable, and as he was extremely intolerant of discomfort, he felt vicious and cruel. He wanted to abuse somebody, and he began, cautiously—for he was always cautious—with himself.' (p. 133) This sentence does not quite end as one expects it to: a more vicious man would have begun, whether cautiously or not, with someone, anyone, else.

Mrs Penniman is a character of whom Jane Austen would have been proud. She was instructively popular with the novel's first readers; the reviews single her out as the best thing in the book. She is well-judged for her role in a fiction of this size and scope, beginning as an object of ridicule, then deepening and darkening into something more dangerous. Foolish, sentimental, theatrical, she is no less of an egoist than Morris or her brother Austin. She shamelessly exploits her young niece in the service of her banal romantic fictions; Morris, too, for that matter, save that she makes no impression on him. When she first glimpses the possibilities in—and for—the young man, she permits herself to think: 'That's the sort of husband I should have had!' (p. 27) By the time Catherine and her father return from Europe, Morris has turned into a surrogate son. On Catherine herself she makes an impression that is wholly baleful in fomenting the young girl's unquestioning impulse to surrender to Morris's 'beauty'. Yet although her father thinks her too stupid to see through her aunt, this is not so. By the end of the novel Catherine has developed sufficient stature and confidence to pass judgement on all three of her oppressors. Mrs Penniman receives her come-uppance in the fine climactic scene in which 'the clairvoyance of her passion'—a wonderful phrase—enables her to judge the other woman 'finally and without appeal' (p. 148). Mrs Penniman is no Madame Merle, but this is the heroine's moment of illumination, equivalent to the one in *The Portrait of a Lady* when Isabel sees finally and without appeal the older woman for who she is and what she has done.

The innermost relations of this tale however are between the Doctor, his daughter, and the narrator. At first blush Catherine seems little more than the epitome of negatives and absences, a human blank equivalent to the emptiness James had provokingly attributed to his native land. Like the America of forty years ago, Catherine appears to present nothing to write about. She is devoid of a fictional heroine's usual 'attractions' (a word on which the novel harps): all, that is, except money. Unlike Jane Austen's *Emma*, Catherine is neither handsome nor clever, but she is rich. Or to be more exact, for this calculation plays a crucial role in her 'value' to Morris, the money that her mother has left her ensures that she will be comfortably off, while the money she stands to inherit from her father will put her into the league of the super-rich. Returning to her more natural assets, we should note that when Catherine returns from Europe, Mrs Penniman, no bad judge of these things, considers her 'more positive, more mature . . . rather handsome' (p. 121). From the very start the attentive reader will not be taken in by the superficial judgements passed on Catherine: 'A dull, plain girl she was called by rigorous critics—a quiet, ladylike girl, by those of the more imaginative sort; but by neither class was she very elaborately discussed' (p. 11). Catherine has everyone else's presumptions to deal with, but her greatest burden is to carry her mother's name and not *be* the woman with the most charming eyes in the island of Manhattan, as Miss Catherine Harrington had once been. She lives with not one but two bereaved grown-ups, each of whom in their different ways, exploits her: the father who lost his beautiful, rich, intelligent wife and young son, and the aunt who knew little romance with Mr Penniman and bore no children. For all her addiction to telling the truth, Catherine learns the value of secrets—like James's greatest portrait of a growing child, the title character of *What Maisie Knew* (1897). Though infinitely less resourceful than Maisie Farange, Catherine finds like her that she can become an object of interest to herself. She discovers 'an entirely new feeling, . . . a state of expectant suspense about her own actions'. She will grow up to surprise not only herself but all three of the others closest to her.

Like his author Doctor Sloper is 'clever', 'the "brightest" doctor in the country' (p. 3). He is definite, decisive, 'incisive' (p. 92). He has a high opinion of 'reason', not least his own, but his judgement is less sure than he supposes. We are told that he has a low opinion of 'the more complicated sex', and that his beautiful dead wife was that exceptional being, 'a reasonable woman' (p. 7). Only a page previously his sister Mrs Almond has been described as 'a comely, comfortable, reasonable woman'. So, there's another exception. We meet another eminently reasonable woman in Morris's sister, Mrs Montgomery. The word recurs when the Doctor is thinking about Catherine's marriageability and the fortune she will inherit: 'a very sufficient

provision for two reasonable persons', even if one of them is penniless (p. 32). Again, he looks at Catherine 'with his cold, quiet, reasonable eye' (p. 52). However we may begin to think the balance of
power is shifting between them when she attracts this epithet on their
European tour: 'She was always her father's docile and reasonable
associate' (p. 113). Not that he will ever appreciate her 'intelligence';
he thinks her 'about as intelligent as the bundle of shawls'. In the
crucial exchange with Mrs Penniman on her return from Europe,
when Catherine declares her separation from her father, we are told
that she speaks 'reason*ingly*', before she breaks out with passionate
emotion. In the quarrel scene with Morris, he tells her he's going to
leave her until she is 'reasonable' again (p. 140). She answers back:
'I shall never be reasonable in that way!' Mrs Penniman insists that
she needs to be 'reasonable' (p. 147).

The novel exposes the limits of the Doctor's 'reason' and its
ministration to his ego. Nothing does so more insidiously than the
fine scene with Mrs Montgomery in Chapter XIV, when he twice
mistakes her meaning. Morris's sister chooses her words with care,
knowing how much depends on what she says.

> 'Nothing depends on it, for you.'
> 'I mean for—for—' and she hesitated.
> 'For your brother himself. I see!'
> 'I mean for Miss Sloper,' said Mrs Montgomery.
> The Doctor liked this; it had the accent of sincerity. (p. 64)

We do not doubt that Mrs Montgomery's capacity to think and feel
for a young woman she has never met is sincere. And yet the 'sincerity' is surely not what we most admire in her response. But then
the Doctor does not admire it; he likes it. How cruelly he goes on to
manipulate this morally imaginative woman and exploit her honesty:
'he assured her most respectfully of his regret at having so greatly
discomposed her'. Yet he extorts from her what he wants to hear,
when she exclaims (in the spirit of the woman from whose lips James
first got his clue for the story, Mrs Kemble): 'Don't let her marry
him!' (p. 69) It is something of a shock to be told that what he takes
from this is 'moral satisfaction'.

At face value, the narrator of this story is indeed far closer to
Dr Sloper than to Catherine. There are moments of overlap when
they seem to share the same valuation of the young woman, as when

the narrator speaks of her 'lively taste for dress; a lively taste is quite the expression to use. I feel as if I ought to write it very small . . .'. He speaks of 'the desire of a rather inarticulate nature to manifest itself', 'to make up for her diffidence of speech with a fine frankness of costume' (p. 11). And yet the narrator is constantly distancing himself from the Doctor. Consider the devious paragraph (p. 8), which begins with the narrator concurring with Dr Sloper's judgement of his sister Mrs Penniman. The Doctor begins shrewdly, accurately predicting her meddling role in Catherine's love-life, and all too clearly he sees through the pretensions of the young man with the moustache who will pretend to be in love with his daughter. But Catherine herself he gets totally wrong: 'Catherine won't see it, and won't believe it, fortunately for her peace of mind; poor Catherine isn't romantic' (p. 8). But she is, she is, whatever one imagines 'romantic' to stand for. What is more, her father is grossly mistaken in judging her 'a weak-minded woman'; both Mrs Penniman and Morris tell him so.

Early on we are told, of Catherine's feelings towards her father, that

Her deepest desire was to please him, and her conception of happiness was to know that she had succeeded in pleasing him. She had never succeeded beyond a certain point. Though on the whole he was very kind to her, she was perfectly aware of this, and to go beyond the point in question seemed to her really something to live for. (p. 9)

This is what her father will never permit her. Unlike the narrator— and the reader, one would hope—this man has made his mind up, and his heart too, such as it is. Both he and Mrs Penniman fail to recognize who Catherine is or could be, because they cannot 'go beyond'. 'Both she and her brother . . . exaggerated the young girl's limitations' (p. 10). This brilliant Chapter II covers Catherine's life from the age of 10 to 18, and concludes with the narrator unequivocally befriending the young woman.

People who expressed themselves roughly called her stolid. But she was irresponsive because she was shy, uncomfortably, painfully shy. This was not always understood, and she sometimes produced an impression of insensibility. In reality she was the softest creature in the world. (p. 10)

The novel tells the story of her hardening.

Once alerted to the narrator's shifty, treacherous relations with the Doctor, we can appreciate how strongly the novel tells against him.

Note the way his no less clever but more human sister Mrs Almond eventually draws away from him in dismay at the coldness of his heart. Careful readers will have kept their distance from the very start. William Veeder writes well about the subtle effects of the order in which things get said in this novel (see the Select Bibliography). At the novel's very opening, why does the narrator say that 'there flourished and practised in the city of New York a physician' (p. 3)? Shouldn't a physician practise first and flourish second? His wife's money means that he does not have to work, though of course it is to his credit that he chooses to do so. We hear that 'he passed in the best society of New York for a man of the world—which, indeed, he was, in a very sufficient degree' (p. 3). 'Indeed?' This nicely insinuates that while the best society of New York is not wholly mistaken, there are other 'best societies' elsewhere in the world. The narrative voice James creates for this tale is wonderfully subtle in its deployment of qualifying words like 'perhaps', 'on the whole', and 'almost'. To say that someone is 'half ashamed' (p. 66) withdraws half the credit for feeling the shame in the first place. Then there are negative constructions such as 'not wholly devoid of' (that is, 'containing a modicum of' (p. 56)), and hypotheses such as 'might have' (that is, 'but did not'), as in 'a voice so timidly argumentative that it might have touched him', and 'a placidity that might have been irritating' (p. 52). Or consider the twist and turn in the following short sentence: 'Her father might have pitied her, and in fact he did so; but he was sure he was right' (p. 89). We expect the accusation that her father might have pitied her but did not; we are surprised by the credit he gets for in fact doing so—only then to be perplexed by uncertainty whether to admire or deplore the stern triumph of reason, and the Doctor's refusal to go beyond it.

We have seen that at the time of writing James spoke disparagingly to friends and family of the tale as 'poorish'. This is absurdly harsh by any standards, but he had his eyes fixed on the really long fiction that would be to his former work, so he told his parents, 'as wine is unto water'.[16] This was of course to be *The Portrait of a Lady*, the first instalments of which began to appear in *Macmillan's* the following autumn. It is more of a puzzle, and a cause for some chagrin amongst James's admirers, that when he came near the end of his career to review his

---

[16] *Letters*, ii. 229, and 230, n. 3.

entire oeuvre for the New York Edition (1907–9), he chose not to include it. The other most signal omissions are *The Europeans* and *The Bostonians* (1886). James speaks in a letter of trying to read over *Washington Square*—'and I *can't*, and I fear it must go!' For him, it was one of his 'unhappy accidents'.[17] One explanation for a judgement with which most readers have not concurred is that it was a technical matter. The magisterial author of the New York Edition was intent on revising everything collected in it, and *Washington Square* was not susceptible to such treatment. The later James was determined to see and tell his stories through one (or more) of his own characters. For much of his earlier work this posed no difficulty. The tale of 'Daisy Miller', for example, had always been seen through the eyes of her anxious admirer, Winterbourne, and it was not hard to 'retouch' the tale through the point of view he already provided. This was no less true for *Roderick Hudson* (1875), *The American* (1877), *The Portrait of a Lady*, and a fair number of the early tales. But when it came to *The Europeans* and *Washington Square* it was not obvious which characters could provide such a 'coign of vantage', to use a phrase from *Macbeth*, of which James was revealingly fond. Or rather, in the case of *Washington Square* it was all too obvious that the only candidate was the Doctor. Yet to go down that road would entirely upset the tale's delicate balance of ironies and sympathies. Better to leave it alone. There are of course other possible reasons tied up with James's personal investment in the past in which the novel is set: some of the raw matter lurking beneath the surface might have been simply too painful.

Let me return in conclusion to the note struck at the start of this introduction. As a writer James never stood still, and *Washington Square* represents a specific experiment with genre, tone, extension, and depth. It was overshadowed for him by *The Portrait*, both at the time of its writing and in retrospect, and this led him to misprize this shorter masterpiece. We get a clue to his uncertainties in the revealing letter he wrote to his sternest, most intimate critic, his brother William, as the first instalments of *The Portrait* were beginning to appear:

The young man in *Washington Square* is not a portrait—he is sketched from the outside merely and not *fouillé* ['delved deeply into']. The only good thing in the story is the girl. The other book [*Portrait*] increases, I think, in merit and interest as it goes on, and being told in a more spacious,

---

[17] *Letters*, ed. Leon Edel, vol. iv, 1895–1916 (Cambridge, Mass., and London, 1984), 371.

expansive way than its predecessors, is inevitably more human, more sociable. It was the constant effort at *condensation* (which you used always to drum into my head—*àpropos* of Mérimée etc—when I was young and you bullied me) that has deprived my former things of these qualities.[18]

But William's bullying paid off, in this tale at least. For the 'effort at *condensation*' is what gives the tale its extraordinary suggestiveness. As with all James's best shorter fictions, there is a struggle between the material, the emotions, and passions that threaten to 'break out', and the demands of the form to hold them in and keep them down. Catherine Sloper's inner world is not explored at length, and that of her father hardly at all, after the shock of his double bereavement. The novel keeps reminding us that our knowledge of them is limited, but it also keeps testing our reactions to these limits and the possibility of 'going beyond' them. These limits are not stable and neatly defined, as the Doctor would wish. For we do get glances and glimpses into what lies behind and within: not much perhaps in the case of Morris Townsend and Lavinia Penniman, but something darker in the case of Austin Sloper, and something richer in that of his daughter.

At the heart of this novel is Catherine's heart. Nothing is more characteristic of its reticence—both the novel's and her heart's—than the night-scene in which she lies in misery at being cast off by her beloved father:

She lay staring at the uncomforting gloom, with her eyes filled with the movement with which her father had turned her out of his room, and of the words in which he had told her that she was a heartless daughter. Her heart was breaking. She had heart enough for that. (p. 93)

The novel grants her (and us) not only this, but also a consequent point of view. By the standards of James's longer and more complex stories it may be a simple one, but it is none the less powerful for its succinctness.

From her own point of view the great facts of her career were that Morris Townsend had trifled with her affection, and that her father had broken its spring. . . . There was something dead in her life, and her duty was to try and fill the void. (p. 157–8)

---

[18] *Letters*, ii. 316.

Nor is there no satisfaction—hers, her author's, the reader's—in the famous wording of the studied, purposive, and hence less than simply desolate ending:

Catherine, meanwhile, in the parlour, picking up her morsel of fancy-work, had seated herself with it again—for life, as it were. (p. 171)

If this is the condensation that Henry James thought brother William had bullied him into, he had no cause for complaint and nor do we.

NOTE ON THE TEXT

JAMES recorded the story he heard from Fanny Kemble on 21 February 1879 (see Appendix 1). The novel that it inspired was probably begun at some point the following autumn during the three months James spent in Paris from September to December. By the end of January 1880 he thought of it as 'a poorish story in three numbers', and two weeks later described it as 'soon to come out', though now in four numbers;[1] the *Cornhill* calculated otherwise and in due course brought it out in six instalments. James had finished it at the latest by mid-March when he left England for Italy to begin work on *The Portrait of a Lady*. It began its run in the *Cornhill Magazine* in June 1880 and concluded in November. It was accompanied by twelve illustrations by George Du Maurier (1834–96); James disliked them and even admirers of this talented artist (and late in life, successful novelist, author of the best-selling *Trilby* (1894)) have found them disappointing. This did not however impede the development of a close friendship, publicly commemorated in James's essay on Du Maurier in *Harper's New Monthly Magazine* (September 1897), where he recalled its beginnings 'on the ground of the happy accident of an injury received on either side in connection with his having consented to make drawings for a short novel that I had constructed in a crude defiance of the illustrator'.[2] The novel began in *Harper's New Monthly Magazine* one month later than in Britain, running from July to December 1880, and was first published in book form in the USA by Harper & Brothers on 1 December 1880 (both magazine and book reproduced the Du Maurier illustrations). It was first published in Britain by Macmillan & Co. (without illustrations) on 26 January 1881, in two volumes, along with 'The Pension Beaurepas' and 'A Bundle of Letters'; it was followed in August 1881 by a one-volume edition.

The current edition reprints the text of the first British edition of 1881 in two volumes by Macmillan. It makes one significant

---

[1] *Henry James Letters*, ed. Leon Edel, vol. ii, 1875–1883 (London, 1975), 268, 272.

[2] *Henry James: Literary Criticism*, vol. i: *Essays on Literature, American Writers, English Writers*, ed. Leon Edel with the assistance of Mark Wilson (New York, 1984), 879.

correction, inserting a negative present in the serial versions and required by the sense (see note to p. 132), but it retains some slightly unexpected punctuation marks 'corrected' in Harper's (see below), as well as the expression 'hoisting your flag' (p. 106) which Harper's had altered, for American readers, to 'hoisting your fly'. Single quotation marks replace double ones, and the spaces before punctuation marks (such as ';' and '?') have been closed up. Full stops have been omitted following Mr, Mrs, Dr.

In his Library of America edition, William T. Stafford reckons that between the *Cornhill* serial and the Macmillan volume there were some thirty significant alterations,[3] among which the following are the most notable (page and line references are to this Oxford World's Classics edition):

'queer corners' to 'far-away lands' (17.3)
'talkative guest' to 'anecdotical idler' (33.21)
'quiet' to 'formally submissive' (71.36)
'sadly' to 'wearily' (98.23)
'with her unexploded bomb in her hands' to 'primed, to repletion, with her apology, but unable to bring it to light' (136.26–7)
'passion' to 'passive grief' (142.1)
'grief' to 'misery' (143.4)
'some solemnity' to 'much expression' (150.15)

One might further note that the Macmillan text removes the inverted commas at 8.7 that in the *Cornhill* and Harper's had mildly ironized Catherine's 'accomplishments' (playing the piano, dancing), though it is unclear whether the irony had been directed at the sponsor of these accomplishments, Mrs Penniman, or at the social world promoting their value, or at Catherine's failure to shine in them, or all three. The Macmillan text also makes some slightly surprising alterations to punctuation marks that other editions (including Harper's) have regularized. At 137.25, the *Cornhill*'s exclamation mark ('"But I am not rich!" said Catherine') becomes a question-mark ('"But I am not rich?" said Catherine'); shortly thereafter at 139.1, Morris's '"You can afford to say that!"' turns into '"You can afford to say that?"' In the closing moments, at 171.9 the opposite move occurs

---

[3] Note on the Text, *Novels 1871–1880: Watch and Ward, Roderick Hudson, The American, The Europeans, Confidence* (Cambridge, 1983), 1238.

when instead of asking '"Is she so hard?"' Mrs Penniman exclaims '"Is she so hard!"' It is not clear whether the small shifts of intonation these changes impart are the product of authorial intention, but the present edition preserves them.

SELECT BIBLIOGRAPHY

James's Writings

THE most immediately profitable fictions to read alongside *Washington Square* are the other works James wrote between his second and third long novels, *The American* (1877) and *The Portrait of a Lady* (1881), namely: the short novels *The Europeans* and *Confidence*, and the tales 'Daisy Miller', 'Longstaff's Marriage', 'An International Episode', 'The Pension Beaurepas', 'The Diary of a Man of Fifty', and 'A Bundle of Letters'. Of the non-fiction he wrote at this time, the study of *Hawthorne* (1879) and the review of Zola's *Nana* (1880) are particularly significant (they can be found in the respective volumes of James's collected *Literary Criticism* noted below). For full details of these and other writings, see Leon Edel and Dan H. Laurence, *A Bibliography of Henry James*, 3rd edition, revised with the assistance of James Rambeau (Oxford, 1982). It is also instructive (and pleasurable) to read the works inspired by James's return to New York in 1904–5, the relevant chapters of *The American Scene* (1907) and the tales published between 1908 and 1910, 'The Jolly Corner', 'Julia Bride', 'Crapy Cornelia',' and 'A Round of Visits', and finally, the memories of his childhood included in the autobiographical work, *A Small Boy and Others* (1913). James's critical writings are collected in *Literary Criticism*, vol. i: *Essays on Literature, American Writers, English Writers*, and vol. ii: *European Writers and the Prefaces*, ed. Leon Edel with the assistance of Mark Wilson (New York, 1984). For selections of his voluminous correspondence, see *Henry James Letters*, 4 vols, ed. Leon Edel (Cambridge, Mass., and London, 1974–84); *Henry James: A Life in Letters*, ed. Philip Horne (London, 1999); and in the fullness of time, *The Complete Letters of Henry James*, ed. Pierre A. Walker and Greg W. Zacharias (Lincoln, Neb., 2006–). Michael Anesko gathers a massive amount of important material in his book, *Letters, Fictions, Lives: Henry James and William Dean Howells* (New York, 1997). There is a useful edition of *The Complete Notebooks of Henry James*, ed. with introduction and notes by Leon Edel and Lyall H. Powers (New York, 1987).

Biography

Edel, Leon, *Henry James: The Conquest of London, 1870–1883*, vol. ii of *The Life of Henry James* (London, 1962).

Fisher, Paul, *House of Wits: An Intimate Portrait of the James Family* (New York, 2008).

Kaplan, Fred, *Henry James: The Imagination of Genius* (New York, 1992).

Lewis, R. W. B., *The Jameses: A Family Narrative* (London, 1991).

Novick, Sheldon M., *Henry James: The Young Master* (New York, 1996).

Selected Criticism

Bell, Ian F. A., *Washington Square: Styles of Money* (New York, 1993).

Bell, Millicent, 'Style as Subject: *Washington Square*', *Sewanee Review*, 83.2 (1975), 19–38.

—— '"Daisy Miller" and *Washington Square*', in *Meaning in Henry James* (Cambridge, Mass., and London, 1991), 45–79.

Berlant, Lauren, 'Fancy-Work and Fancy Foot-Work: Motives for Silence in *Washington Square*', *Criticism*, 29.4 (Fall 1987), 439–58.

Chandler, Karen Michele, '"Her Ancient Faculty of Silence": Catherine Sloper's Ways of Being in James's *Washington Square* and Two Film Adaptations', in *Henry James Goes to the Movies*, ed. Susan M. Griffin (Louisville, Ky., 2002), 170–89.

Gargano, James W., '*Washington Square*: A Study in the Growth of an Inner Self', *Studies in Short Fiction*, 13.3 (Summer 1976), 355–62.

Hayes, Kevin (ed.), *Henry James: The Contemporary Reviews* (New York, 1996).

Holland, Bette, '*Washington Square*, The Family Plot', *Raritan*, 15.4 (Spring 1996), 88–110.

Hughes, Clair, 'The Ironic Dresses of *Washington Square*', in *Henry James and the Art of Dress* (Basingstoke, 2001), 29–44.

Hutchison, Stuart, '*Washington Square*: The Look of a Social History', in *Henry James: An American as Modernist* (London and Totowa, NJ, 1982, 1983), 9–23.

Klein, Marcus, '*Washington Square*: Or Downtown with Henry James', *Arizona Quarterly*, 53.4 (Winter 1997), 7–21.

Long, Robert Emmet, 'James's *Washington Square*: The Hawthorne Relation', *New England Quarterly*, 46.4 (December 1973), 573–90.

Lucas, John, '*Washington Square*', in *The Air of Reality: New Essays on Henry James*, ed. John Goode (London, 1972), 36–59.

Maini, Darshan Singh, '*Washington Square*: A Centennial Essay', *Henry James Review*, 1.1 (1979), 81–101.

Poirier, Richard, *The Comic Sense of Henry James* (London, 1960), 165–82.

Rivkin, Julie, '"Prospects of Entertainment": Film Adaptations of *Washington Square*', in *Henry James Goes to the Movies*, ed. Susan M. Griffin (Louisville, Ky., 2002), 147–69.

Rowe, John Carlos, 'For Mature Audiences: Sex, Gender and Recent Film Adaptations of Henry James's Fiction', in John R. Bradley (ed.), *Henry James on Stage and Screen* (Basingstoke, 2002), 190–211.

Swaab, Peter, 'The End of the Embroidery: From *Washington Square* to *The Heiress*', in John R. Bradley (ed.), *Henry James on Stage and Screen* (Basingstoke, 2002), 56–71.

Veeder, William, 'Style, Character, and Social Commentary', in *Henry James—The Lessons of the Master: Popular Fiction and Personal Style in the Nineteenth Century* (Chicago and London, 1975), 184–205.

Walker, Pierre A., 'The Experimental and Sentimental Novels in *Washington Square*', in *Reading Henry James in French Cultural Contexts* (Illinois, 1995), 116–25.

Williams, Merle A., 'The American Spaces of Henry James', in Attie de Lange, Gail Fincham, Jeremy Hawthorn, and Jakob Lothe, *Literary Landscapes: From Modernism to Postcolonialism* (Basingstoke, 2008), 19–37.

Zacharias, Greg W., 'Henry James' Style in *Washington Square*', *Studies in American Fiction*, 18.2 (Autumn 1990), 207–24.

Further Reading in Oxford World's Classics

Balzac, Honoré de, *Eugénie Grandet*, trans. Sylvia Raphael, introduction by Christopher Prendergast.

James, Henry, *The Ambassadors*, ed. Christopher Butler.

—— *The American*, ed. Adrian Poole.

—— *The Aspern Papers and Other Stories*, ed. Adrian Poole.

—— *The Awkward Age*, ed. Vivien Jones.

—— *The Bostonians*, ed. R. D. Gooder.

—— *Daisy Miller and Other Stories*, ed. Jean Gooder.

—— *The Europeans*, ed. Ian Campbell Ross.

—— *The Golden Bowl*, ed. Virginia Llewellyn Smith.

—— *The Portrait of a Lady*, ed. Roger Luckhurst.

—— *The Spoils of Poynton*, ed. Bernard Richards.

—— *The Turn of the Screw and Other Stories*, ed. T. J. Lustig.

—— *What Maisie Knew*, ed. Adrian Poole.

—— *The Wings of the Dove*, ed. Peter Brooks.

A CHRONOLOGY OF HENRY JAMES

COMPILED BY LEON EDEL

1843   Born 15 April at No. 21 Washington Place, New York City.

1843–4   Taken abroad by parents to Paris and London: period of residence at Windsor.

1845–55   Childhood in Albany and New York.

1855–8   Attends schools in Geneva, London, Paris, and Boulogne-sur-Mer and is privately tutored.

1858   James family settles in Newport, Rhode Island.

1859   At scientific school in Geneva. Studies German in Bonn.

1860   At school in Newport. Receives back injury on eve of Civil War while serving as volunteer fireman. Studies art briefly. Friendship with John La Farge.

1862–3   Spends term in Harvard Law School.

1864   Family settles in Boston and then in Cambridge. Early anonymous story and unsigned reviews published.

1865   First signed story published in *Atlantic Monthly*.

1869–70   Travels in England, France, and Italy. Death of his beloved cousin Minny Temple.

1870   Back in Cambridge, publishes first novel in *Atlantic*, *Watch and Ward*.

1872–4   Travels with sister Alice and aunt in Europe; writes impressionistic travel sketches for the *Nation*. Spends autumn in Paris and goes to Italy to write first large novel.

1874–5   On completion of *Roderick Hudson* tests New York City as residence; writes much literary journalism for *Nation*. First three books published: *Transatlantic Sketches*, *A Passionate Pilgrim* (tales), and *Roderick Hudson*.

1875–6   Goes to live in Paris. Meets Ivan Turgenev and through him Flaubert, Zola, Daudet, Maupassant, and Edmond de Goncourt. Writes *The American*.

1876–7   Moves to London and settles in 3 Bolton Street, Piccadilly. Revisits Paris, Florence, Rome.

1878   'Daisy Miller', published in London, establishes fame on both sides of the Atlantic. Publishes first volume of essays, *French Poets and Novelists*.

1879–82   *The Europeans, Washington Square, Confidence, The Portrait of a Lady*.

1882–3	Revisits Boston: first visit to Washington. Death of parents.
1884–6	Returns to London. Sister Alice comes to live near him. Fourteen-volume collection of novels and tales published. Writes *The Bostonians* and *The Princess Casamassima*, published in the following year.
1886	Moves to flat at 34 De Vere Gardens West.
1887	Sojourn in Italy, mainly Florence and Venice. 'The Aspern Papers', *The Reverberator*, 'A London Life'. Friendship with grand-niece of Fenimore Cooper—Constance Fenimore Woolson.
1888	*Partial Portraits* and several collections of tales.
1889–90	*The Tragic Muse*.
1890–1	Dramatizes *The American*, which has a short run. Writes four comedies, rejected by producers.
1892	Alice James dies in London.
1894	Miss Woolson commits suicide in Venice. James journeys to Italy and visits her grave in Rome.
1895	He is booed at first night of his play *Guy Domville*. Deeply depressed, he abandons the theatre.
1896–7	*The Spoils of Poynton, What Maisie Knew*.
1898	Takes long lease of Lamb House, in Rye, Sussex. *The Turn of the Screw* published.
1899–1900	*The Awkward Age, The Sacred Fount*. Friendship with Conrad and Wells.
1902–4	*The Ambassadors, The Wings of the Dove*, and *The Golden Bowl*. Friendships with H. C. Andersen and Jocelyn Persse.
1905	Revisits USA after 20-year absence, lectures on Balzac and the speech of Americans.
1906–10	*The American Scene*. Edits selective and revised 'New York Edition' of his works in 24 volumes. Friendship with Hugh Walpole.
1910	Death of brother, William James.
1913	Sargent paints his portrait as 70th birthday gift from some 300 friends and admirers. Writes autobiographies, *A Small Boy and Others*, and *Notes of a Son and Brother*.
1914	*Notes on Novelists*. Visits wounded in hospitals.
1915	Becomes a British subject.
1916	Given Order of Merit. Dies 28 February in Chelsea, aged 72. Funeral in Chelsea Old Church. Ashes buried in Cambridge, Mass., family plot.
1976	Commemorative tablet unveiled in Poets' Corner of Westminster Abbey, 17 June.

WASHINGTON SQUARE

I

DURING a portion of the first half of the present century, and more particularly during the latter part of it,* there flourished and practised in the city of New York a physician who enjoyed perhaps an exceptional share of the consideration which, in the United States, has always been bestowed upon distinguished members of the medical profession. This profession in America has constantly been held in honour, and more successfully than elsewhere has put forward a claim to the epithet of 'liberal'. In a country in which, to play a social part, you must either earn your income or make believe that you earn it, the healing art has appeared in a high degree to combine two recognized sources of credit. It belongs to the realm of the practical, which in the United States is a great recommendation; and it is touched by the light of science—a merit appreciated in a community in which the love of knowledge has not always been accompanied by leisure and opportunity. It was an element in Dr Sloper's reputation that his learning and his skill were very evenly balanced; he was what you might call a scholarly doctor, and yet there was nothing abstract in his remedies—he always ordered you to take something. Though he was felt to be extremely thorough, he was not uncomfortably theoretic, and if he sometimes explained matters rather more minutely than might seem of use to the patient, he never went so far (like some practitioners one has heard of) as to trust to the explanation alone, but always left behind him an inscrutable prescription. There were some doctors that left the prescription without offering any explanation at all: and he did not belong to that class either, which was after all the most vulgar. It will be seen that I am describing a clever man; and this is really the reason why Dr Sloper* had become a local celebrity. At the time at which we are chiefly concerned with him, he was some fifty years of age, and his popularity was at its height. He was very witty, and he passed in the best society of New York for a man of the world—which, indeed, he was, in a very sufficient degree. I hasten to add, to anticipate possible misconception, that he was not the least of a charlatan. He was a thoroughly honest man—honest in a degree of which he had perhaps lacked the opportunity to give the complete measure; and, putting aside the great good-nature of the circle in which he practised, which was rather fond of boasting that it possessed the 'brightest' doctor in the country, he daily justified his claim to the talents attributed to him by the popular voice. He was an observer, even a philosopher, and to be bright was so natural to him, and (as the popular voice said) came so easily, that he never aimed at mere effect, and had none of the little tricks and pretensions of second-rate reputations. It must be confessed that fortune had favoured him, and that he had found the path to prosperity very soft to his tread. He had married at the age of twenty-seven, for love, a very charming girl, Miss Catherine Harrington, of New York, who, in addition to her charms, had brought him a solid dowry. Mrs Sloper was amiable, graceful, accomplished, elegant, and in 1820* she had been one of the pretty girls of the small but promising capital which clustered about the Battery and overlooked the Bay, and of which the uppermost boundary was indicated by the grassy waysides of Canal Street.* Even at the age of twenty-seven Austin Sloper had made his mark sufficiently to mitigate the anomaly of his having been chosen among a dozen suitors by a young woman of high fashion, who had ten thousand dollars of income and the most charming eyes in the island of Manhattan. These eyes, and some of their accompaniments, were for about five years a source of extreme satisfaction to the young physician, who was both a devoted and a very happy husband. The fact of his having married a rich woman made no difference in the line he had traced for himself, and he cultivated his profession with as definite a purpose as if he still had no other resources than his fraction of the modest patrimony which on his father's death he had shared with his brothers and sisters. This purpose had not been preponderantly to make money—it had been rather to learn something and to do something. To learn something interesting, and to do something useful—this was, roughly speaking, the programme he had sketched, and of which the accident of his wife having an income appeared to him in no degree to modify the validity. He was fond of his practice, and of exercising a skill of which he was agreeably conscious, and it was so patent a truth that if he were not a doctor there was nothing else he could be, that a doctor he persisted in being, in the best possible conditions. Of course his easy domestic situation saved him a good deal of drudgery, and his wife's affiliation to the 'best people' brought him a good many of those patients whose symptoms are, if not more interesting in themselves than those of the lower orders, at least more consistently displayed. He desired experience, and in the course of twenty years he got a great deal. It must be added that it came to him in some forms which, whatever might have been their intrinsic value, made it the reverse of welcome. His first child, a little boy of extraordinary promise, as the Doctor, who was not addicted to easy enthusiasms, firmly believed, died at three years of age, in spite of everything that the mother's tenderness and the father's science could invent to save him. Two years later Mrs Sloper gave birth to a second infant—an infant of a sex which rendered the poor child, to the Doctor's sense, an inadequate substitute for his lamented first-born, of whom he had promised himself to make an admirable man. The little girl was a disappointment; but this was not the worst. A week after her birth the young mother, who, as the phrase is, had been doing well, suddenly betrayed alarming symptoms, and before another week had elapsed Austin Sloper was a widower.

For a man whose trade was to keep people alive he had certainly done poorly in his own family; and a bright doctor who within three years loses his wife and his little boy should perhaps be prepared to see either his skill or his affection impugned. Our friend, however, escaped criticism: that is, he escaped all criticism but his own, which was much the most competent and most formidable. He walked under the weight of this very private censure for the rest of his days, and bore for ever the scars of a castigation to which the strongest hand he knew had treated him on the night that followed his wife's death. The world, which, as I have said, appreciated him, pitied him too much to be ironical; his misfortune made him more interesting, and even helped him to be the fashion. It was observed that even medical families cannot escape the more insidious forms of disease, and that, after all, Dr Sloper had lost other patients beside the two I have mentioned; which constituted an honourable precedent. His little girl remained to him, and though she was not what he had desired, he proposed to himself to make the best of her. He had on hand a stock of unexpended authority, by which the child, in its early years, profited largely. She had been named, as a matter of course, after her poor mother, and even in her most diminutive babyhood the Doctor never called her anything but Catherine. She grew up a very robust and healthy child, and her father, as he looked at her, often said to himself that, such as she was, he at least need have no fear of losing her. I say 'such as she was', because, to tell the truth— But this is a truth of which I will defer the telling.

II

WHEN the child was about ten years old, he invited his sister, Mrs Penniman, to come and stay with him. The Miss Slopers had been but two in number, and both of them had married early in life. The younger, Mrs Almond by name, was the wife of a prosperous merchant and the mother of a blooming family. She bloomed herself, indeed, and was a comely, comfortable, reasonable woman, and a favourite with her clever brother, who, in the matter of women, even when they were nearly related to him, was a man of distinct preferences. He preferred Mrs Almond to his sister Lavinia, who had married a poor clergyman, of a sickly constitution and a flowery style of eloquence, and then, at the age of thirty-three, had been left a widow, without children, without fortune—with nothing but the memory of Mr Penniman's flowers of speech, a certain vague aroma of which hovered about her own conversation. Nevertheless, he had offered her a home under his own roof, which Lavinia accepted with the alacrity of a woman who had spent the ten years of her married life in the town of Poughkeepsie.* The Doctor had not proposed to Mrs Penniman to come and live with him indefinitely; he had suggested that she should make an asylum of his house while she looked about for unfurnished lodgings. It is uncertain whether Mrs Penniman ever instituted a search for unfurnished lodgings, but it is beyond dispute that she never found them. She settled herself with her brother and never went away, and when Catherine was twenty years old her Aunt Lavinia was still one of the most striking features of her immediate *entourage*. Mrs Penniman's own account of the matter was that she had remained to take charge of her niece's education. She had given this account, at least, to every one but the Doctor, who never asked for explanations which he could entertain himself any day with inventing. Mrs Penniman, moreover, though she had a good deal of a certain sort of artificial assurance, shrank, for indefinable reasons, from presenting herself to her brother as a fountain of instruction. She had not a high sense of humour, but she had enough to prevent her from making this mistake; and her brother, on his side, had enough to excuse her, in her situation, for laying him under contribution during a considerable part of a lifetime. He therefore assented tacitly to the proposition which Mrs Penniman had tacitly laid down, that it was of importance that the poor motherless girl should have a brilliant woman near her. His assent could only be tacit, for he had never been dazzled by his sister's intellectual lustre. Save when he fell in love with Catherine Harrington, he had never been dazzled, indeed, by any feminine characteristics whatever; and though he was to a certain extent what is called a ladies' doctor, his private opinion of the more complicated sex was not exalted. He regarded its complications as more curious than edifying, and he had an idea of the beauty of *reason*, which was on the whole meagrely gratified by what he observed in his female patients. His wife had been a reasonable woman, but she was a bright exception; among several things that he was sure of, this was perhaps the principal. Such a conviction, of course, did little either to mitigate or to abbreviate his widowhood; and it set a limit to his recognition, at the best, of Catherine's possibilities and of Mrs Penniman's ministrations. He, nevertheless, at the end of six months, accepted his sister's permanent presence as an accomplished fact, and as Catherine grew older perceived that there were in effect good reasons why she should have a companion of her own imperfect sex. He was extremely polite to Lavinia, scrupulously, formally polite; and she had never seen him in anger but once in her life, when he lost his temper in a theological discussion with her late husband. With her he never discussed theology, nor, indeed, discussed anything; he contented himself with making known, very distinctly, in the form of a lucid ultimatum, his wishes with regard to Catherine.

Once, when the girl was about twelve years old, he had said to her—

'Try and make a clever woman of her, Lavinia; I should like her to be a clever woman.'

Mrs Penniman, at this, looked thoughtful a moment. 'My dear Austin,' she then inquired, 'do you think it is better to be clever than to be good?'

'Good for what?' asked the Doctor. 'You are good for nothing unless you are clever.'

From this assertion Mrs Penniman saw no reason to dissent; she possibly reflected that her own great use in the world was owing to her aptitude for many things.

'Of course I wish Catherine to be good,' the Doctor said next day; 'but she won't be any the less virtuous for not being a fool. I am not afraid of her being wicked; she will never have the salt of malice in her character. She is as good as good bread, as the French say;* but six years hence I don't want to have to compare her to good bread and butter.'

'Are you afraid she will be insipid? My dear brother, it is I who supply the butter; so you needn't fear!' said Mrs Penniman, who had taken in hand the child's accomplishments, overlooking her at the piano, where Catherine displayed a certain talent, and going with her to the dancing-class, where it must be confessed that she made but a modest figure.

Mrs Penniman was a tall, thin, fair, rather faded woman, with a perfectly amiable disposition, a high standard of gentility, a taste for light literature, and a certain foolish indirectness and obliquity of character. She was romantic, she was sentimental, she had a passion for little secrets and mysteries—a very innocent passion, for her secrets had hitherto always been as unpractical as addled eggs. She was not absolutely veracious; but this defect was of no great consequence, for she had never had anything to conceal. She would have liked to have a lover, and to correspond with him under an assumed name in letters left at a shop; I am bound to say that her imagination never carried the intimacy farther than this. Mrs Penniman had never had a lover, but her brother, who was very shrewd, understood her turn of mind. 'When Catherine is about seventeen,' he said to himself, 'Lavinia will try and persuade her that some young man with a moustache is in love with her. It will be quite untrue; no young man, with a moustache or without, will ever be in love with Catherine. But Lavinia will take it up, and talk to her about it; perhaps, even, if her taste for clandestine operations doesn't prevail with her, she will talk to me about it. Catherine won't see it, and won't believe it, fortunately for her peace of mind; poor Catherine isn't romantic.'

She was a healthy well-grown child, without a trace of her mother's beauty. She was not ugly; she had simply a plain, dull, gentle countenance. The most that had ever been said for her was that she had a 'nice' face, and, though she was an heiress, no one had ever thought of regarding her as a belle. Her father's opinion of her moral purity was abundantly justified; she was excellently, imperturbably good; affectionate, docile, obedient, and much addicted to speaking the truth. In her younger years she was a good deal of a romp, and, though it is an awkward confession to make about one's heroine,

I must add that she was something of a glutton. She never, that I know of, stole raisins out of the pantry; but she devoted her pocket-money to the purchase of cream-cakes. As regards this, however, a critical attitude would be inconsistent with a candid reference to the early annals of any biographer. Catherine was decidedly not clever; she was not quick with her book, nor, indeed, with anything else. She was not abnormally deficient, and she mustered learning enough to acquit herself respectably in conversation with her contemporaries, among whom it must be avowed, however, that she occupied a secondary place. It is well known that in New York it is possible for a young girl to occupy a primary one. Catherine, who was extremely modest, had no desire to shine, and on most social occasions, as they are called, you would have found her lurking in the background. She was extremely fond of her father and very much afraid of him; she thought him the cleverest and handsomest and most celebrated of men. The poor girl found her account so completely in the exercise of her affections that the little tremor of fear that mixed itself with her filial passion gave the thing an extra relish rather than blunted its edge. Her deepest desire was to please him, and her conception of happiness was to know that she had succeeded in pleasing him. She had never succeeded beyond a certain point. Though on the whole he was very kind to her, she was perfectly aware of this, and to go beyond the point in question seemed to her really something to live for. What she could not know, of course, was that she disappointed him, though on three or four occasions the Doctor had been almost frank about it. She grew up peacefully and prosperously, but at the age of eighteen Mrs Penniman had not made a clever woman of her. Dr Sloper would have liked to be proud of his daughter; but there was nothing to be proud of in poor Catherine. There was nothing, of course, to be ashamed of; but this was not enough for the Doctor, who was a proud man and would have enjoyed being able to think of his daughter as an unusual girl. There would have been a fitness in her being pretty and graceful, intelligent and distinguished; for her mother had been the most charming woman of her little day, and as regards her father, of course he knew his own value. He had moments of irritation at having produced a commonplace child, and he even went so far at times as to take a certain satisfaction in the thought that his wife had not lived to find her out. He was naturally slow in making this discovery himself, and it was not till Catherine had become a young lady grown that he regarded the matter as settled. He gave her the benefit of a great many doubts; he was in no haste to conclude. Mrs Penniman frequently assured him that his daughter had a delightful nature; but he knew how to interpret this assurance. It meant, to his sense, that Catherine was not wise enough to discover that her aunt was a goose—a limitation of mind that could not fail to be agreeable to Mrs Penniman. Both she and her brother, however, exaggerated the young girl's limitations; for Catherine, though she was very fond of her aunt, and conscious of the gratitude she owed her, regarded her without a particle of that gentle dread which gave its stamp to her admiration of her father. To her mind there was nothing of the infinite about Mrs Penniman; Catherine saw her all at once, as it were, and was not dazzled by the apparition; whereas her father's great faculties seemed, as they stretched away, to lose themselves in a sort of luminous vagueness, which indicated, not that they stopped, but that Catherine's own mind ceased to follow them.

It must not be supposed that Dr Sloper visited his disappointment upon the poor girl, or ever let her suspect that she had played him a trick. On the contrary, for fear of being unjust to her, he did his duty with exemplary zeal, and recognized that she was a faithful and affectionate child. Besides, he was a philosopher; he smoked a good many cigars over his disappointment, and in the fulness of time he got used to it. He satisfied himself that he had expected nothing, though, indeed, with a certain oddity of reasoning. 'I expect nothing,' he said to himself, 'so that if she gives me a surprise, it will be all clear gain. If she doesn't, it will be no loss.' This was about the time Catherine had reached her eighteenth year; so that it will be seen her father had not been precipitate. At this time she seemed not only incapable of giving surprises; it was almost a question whether she could have received one—she was so quiet and irresponsive. People who expressed themselves roughly called her stolid. But she was irresponsive because she was shy, uncomfortably, painfully shy. This was not always understood, and she sometimes produced an impression of insensibility. In reality she was the softest creature in the world.

III

As a child she had promised to be tall, but when she was sixteen she ceased to grow, and her stature, like most other points in her composition, was not unusual. She was strong, however, and properly made, and, fortunately, her health was excellent. It has been noted that the Doctor was a philosopher, but I would not have answered for his philosophy if the poor girl had proved a sickly and suffering person. Her appearance of health constituted her principal claim to beauty, and her clear, fresh complexion, in which white and red were very equally distributed, was, indeed, an excellent thing to see. Her eye was small and quiet, her features were rather thick, her tresses brown and smooth. A dull, plain girl she was called by rigorous critics—a quiet, ladylike girl, by those of the more imaginative sort; but by neither class was she very elaborately discussed. When it had been duly impressed upon her that she was a young lady—it was a good while before she could believe it—she suddenly developed a lively taste for dress; a lively taste is quite the expression to use. I feel as if I ought to write it very small, her judgment in this matter was by no means infallible; it was liable to confusions and embarrassments. Her great indulgence of it was really the desire of a rather inarticulate nature to manifest itself; she sought to be eloquent in her garments, and to make up for her diffidence of speech by a fine frankness of costume. But if she expressed herself in her clothes it is certain that people were not to blame for not thinking her a witty person. It must be added that though she had the expectation of a fortune— Dr Sloper for a long time had been making twenty thousand dollars a year* by his profession and laying aside the half of it—the amount of money at her disposal was not greater than the allowance made to many poorer girls. In those days in New York there were still a few altar-fires flickering in the temple of Republican simplicity,* and Dr Sloper would have been glad to see his daughter present herself, with a classic grace, as a priestess of this mild faith. It made him fairly grimace, in private, to think that a child of his should be both ugly and overdressed. For himself, he was fond of the good things of life, and he made a considerable use of them; but he had a dread of vulgarity and even a theory that it was increasing in the society

that surrounded him. Moreover, the standard of luxury in the United
States thirty years ago was carried by no means so high as at present,
and Catherine's clever father took the old-fashioned view of the education of young persons. He had no particular theory on the subject;
it had scarcely as yet become a necessity of self-defence to have a collection of theories. It simply appeared to him proper and reasonable
that a well-bred young woman should not carry half her fortune on
her back. Catherine's back was a broad one, and would have carried
a good deal; but to the weight of the paternal displeasure she never
ventured to expose it, and our heroine was twenty years old before she
treated herself, for evening wear, to a red satin gown trimmed with
gold fringe;* though this was an article which, for many years, she had
coveted in secret. It made her look, when she sported it, like a woman
of thirty; but oddly enough, in spite of her taste for fine clothes, she
had not a grain of coquetry, and her anxiety when she put them on
was as to whether they, and not she, would look well. It is a point on
which history has not been explicit, but the assumption is warrant-
able; it was in the royal raiment just mentioned that she presented
herself at a little entertainment given by her aunt, Mrs Almond. The
girl was at this time in her twenty-first year, and Mrs Almond's party
was the beginning of something very important.

Some three or four years before this, Dr Sloper had moved his
household gods up town, as they say in New York. He had been living
ever since his marriage in an edifice of red brick, with granite copings
and an enormous fanlight over the door, standing in a street within
five minutes' walk of the City Hall,* which saw its best days (from
the social point of view) about 1820. After this, the tide of fashion
began to set steadily northward, as, indeed, in New York, thanks to
the narrow channel in which it flows, it is obliged to do, and the great
hum of traffic rolled farther to the right and left of Broadway. By
the time the Doctor changed his residence, the murmur of trade had
become a mighty uproar, which was music in the ears of all good citi-
zens interested in the commercial development, as they delighted to
call it, of their fortunate isle. Dr Sloper's interest in this phenomenon
was only indirect—though, seeing that, as the years went on, half his
patients came to be over-worked men of business, it might have been
more immediate—and when most of his neighbours' dwellings (also
ornamented with granite copings and large fanlights) had been converted into offices, warehouses, and shipping agencies, and otherwise

applied to the base uses of commerce, he determined to look out for a quieter home. The ideal of quiet and of genteel retirement, in 1835, was found in Washington Square,* where the doctor built himself a handsome, modern, wide-fronted house, with a big balcony before the drawing-room windows, and a flight of white marble steps ascending to a portal which was also faced with white marble. This structure, and many of its neighbours, which it exactly resembled, were supposed, forty years ago, to embody the last results of architectural science, and they remain to this day very solid and honourable dwellings. In front of them was the square, containing a considerable quantity of inexpensive vegetation, enclosed by a wooden paling, which increased its rural and accessible appearance; and round the corner was the more august precinct of the Fifth Avenue, taking its origin at this point with a spacious and confident air which already marked it for high destinies. I know not whether it is owing to the tenderness of early associations,* but this portion of New York appears to many persons the most delectable. It has a kind of established repose which is not of frequent occurrence in other quarters of the long, shrill city; it has a riper, richer, more honourable look than any of the upper ramifications of the great longitudinal thoroughfare—the look of having had something of a social history. It was here, as you might have been informed on good authority, that you had come into a world which appeared to offer a variety of sources of interest; it was here that your grandmother lived,* in venerable solitude, and dispensed a hospitality which commended itself alike to the infant imagination and the infant palate, it was here that you took your first walks abroad; following the nursery-maid with unequal step and sniffing up the strange odour of the ailantus-trees* which at that time formed the principal umbrage of the square, and diffused an aroma that you were not yet critical enough to dislike as it deserved; it was here, finally, that your first school, kept by a broad-bosomed, broad-based old lady with a ferule,* who was always having tea in a blue cup, with a saucer that didn't match, enlarged the circle both of your observations and your sensations. It was here, at any rate, that my heroine spent many years of her life; which is my excuse for this topographical parenthesis.

Mrs Almond lived much farther up town, in an embryonic street with a high number—a region where the extension of the city began to assume a theoretic air, where poplars grew beside the pavement (when there was one), and mingled their shade with the steep roofs of desultory Dutch houses, and where pigs and chickens disported themselves in the gutter. These elements of rural picturesqueness have now wholly departed from New York street scenery; but they were to be found within the memory of middle-aged persons, in quarters which now would blush to be reminded of them. Catherine had a great many cousins, and with her Aunt Almond's children, who ended by being nine in number, she lived on terms of considerable intimacy. When she was younger, they had been rather afraid of her; she was believed, as the phrase is, to be highly educated, and a person who lived in the intimacy of their Aunt Penniman had something of reflected grandeur. Mrs Penniman, among the little Almonds, was an object of more admiration than sympathy. Her manners were strange and formidable, and her mourning robes—she dressed in black for twenty years after her husband's death, and then suddenly appeared, one morning, with pink roses in her cap—were complicated in odd, unexpected places with buckles, bugles,* and pins, which discouraged familiarity. She took children too hard, both for good and for evil, and had an oppressive air of expecting subtle things of them; so that going to see her was a good deal like being taken to church and made to sit in a front pew. It was discovered after a while, however, that Aunt Penniman was but an accident in Catherine's existence, and not a part of its essence, and that when the girl came to spend a Saturday with her cousins, she was available for 'follow-my-master', and even for leap-frog. On this basis an understanding was easily arrived at, and for several years Catherine fraternized with her young kinsmen. I say young kinsmen, because seven of the little Almonds were boys, and Catherine had a preference for those games which are most conveniently played in trousers. By degrees, however, the little Almonds' trousers began to lengthen, and the wearers to disperse and settle themselves in life. The elder children were older than Catherine, and the boys were sent to college or placed in counting-rooms. Of the girls, one married very punctually, and the other as punctually became engaged. It was to celebrate this latter event that Mrs Almond gave the little party I have mentioned. Her daughter was to marry a stout young stockbroker, a boy of twenty; it was thought a very good thing.

IV

MRS PENNIMAN, with more buckles and bangles than ever, came of course to the entertainment, accompanied by her niece; the Doctor, too, had promised to look in later in the evening. There was to be a good deal of dancing, and before it had gone very far, Marian Almond came up to Catherine, in company with a tall young man. She introduced the young man as a person who had a great desire to make our heroine's acquaintance, and as a cousin of Arthur Townsend, her own intended.

Marian Almond was a pretty little person of seventeen, with a very small figure and a very big sash, to the elegance of whose manners matrimony had nothing to add. She already had all the airs of a hostess, receiving the company, shaking her fan, saying that with so many people to attend to she should have no time to dance. She made a long speech about Mr Townsend's cousin, to whom she administered a tap with her fan before turning away to other cares. Catherine had not understood all that she said; her attention was given to enjoying Marian's ease of manner and flow of ideas, and to looking at the young man, who was remarkably handsome. She had succeeded, however, as she often failed to do when people were presented to her, in catching his name, which appeared to be the same as that of Marian's little stockbroker. Catherine was always agitated by an introduction; it seemed a difficult moment, and she wondered that some people— her new acquaintance at this moment, for instance—should mind it so little. She wondered what she ought to say, and what would be the consequences of her saying nothing. The consequences at present were very agreeable. Mr Townsend, leaving her no time for embarrassment, began to talk with an easy smile, as if he had known her for a year.

'What a delightful party! What a charming house! What an interesting family! What a pretty girl your cousin is!'

These observations, in themselves of no great profundity, Mr Townsend seemed to offer for what they were worth, and as a contribution to an acquaintance. He looked straight into Catherine's eyes. She answered nothing; she only listened, and looked at him; and he, as if he expected no particular reply, went on to say many other things in the same comfortable and natural manner. Catherine, though she felt tongue-tied, was conscious of no embarrassment; it seemed proper that he should talk, and that she should simply look at him. What made it natural was that he was so handsome, or rather, as she phrased it to herself, so beautiful. The music had been silent for a while, but it suddenly began again; and then he asked her, with a deeper, intenser, smile, if she would do him the honour of dancing with him. Even to this inquiry she gave no audible assent; she simply let him put his arm round her waist—as she did so it occurred to her more vividly than it had ever done before, that this was a singular place for a gentleman's arm to be—and in a moment he was guiding her round the room in the harmonious rotation of the polka. When they paused, she felt that she was red; and then, for some moments, she stopped looking at him. She fanned herself, and looked at the flowers that were painted on her fan. He asked her if she would begin again, and she hesitated to answer, still looking at the flowers.

'Does it make you dizzy?' he asked, in a tone of great kindness.

Then Catherine looked up at him; he was certainly beautiful, and not at all red. 'Yes,' she said; she hardly knew why, for dancing had never made her dizzy.

'Ah, well, in that case,' said Mr Townsend, 'we will sit still and talk. I will find a good place to sit.'

He found a good place—a charming place; a little sofa that seemed meant only for two persons. The rooms by this time were very full; the dancers increased in number, and people stood close in front of them, turning their backs, so that Catherine and her companion seemed secluded and unobserved.

'*We* will talk,' the young man had said; but he still did all the talk-ing. Catherine leaned back in her place, with her eyes fixed upon him, smiling and thinking him very clever. He had features like young men in pictures; Catherine had never seen such features—so delicate, so chiselled and finished—among the young New Yorkers whom she passed in the streets and met at parties. He was tall and slim, but he looked extremely strong. Catherine thought he looked like a statue. But a statue would not talk like that, and, above all, would not have eyes of so rare a colour. He had never been at Mrs Almond's before; he felt very much like a stranger; and it was very kind of Catherine to take pity on him. He was Arthur Townsend's cousin—not very near; several times removed—and Arthur had brought him to present him to the family. In fact, he was a great stranger in New York. It was his native place; but he had not been there for many years. He had been knocking about the world, and living in far-away lands; he had only come back a month or two before. New York was very pleasant, only he felt lonely.

'You see, people forget you,' he said, smiling at Catherine with his delightful gaze, while he leaned forward obliquely, turning towards her, with his elbows on his knees.

It seemed to Catherine that no one who had once seen him would ever forget him; but though she made this reflection she kept it to herself, almost as you would keep something precious.

They sat there for some time. He was very amusing. He asked her about the people that were near them; he tried to guess who some of them were, and he made the most laughable mistakes. He criticized them very freely, in a positive, off-hand way. Catherine had never heard any one—especially any young man—talk just like that. It was the way a young man might talk in a novel; or better still, in a play, on the stage, close before the footlights, looking at the audience, and with every one looking at him, so that you wondered at his presence of mind. And yet Mr Townsend was not like an actor; he seemed so sincere, so natural. This was very interesting; but in the midst of it, Marian Almond came pushing through the crowd, with a little ironical cry, when she found these young people still together, which made every one turn round, and cost Catherine a conscious blush. Marian broke up their talk, and told Mr Townsend—whom she treated as if she were already married, and he had become her cousin—to run away to her mother, who had been wishing for the last half-hour to introduce him to Mr Almond.

'We shall meet again!' he said to Catherine as he left her, and Catherine thought it a very original speech.

Her cousin took her by the arm, and made her walk about. 'I needn't ask you what you think of Morris!' the young girl exclaimed.

'Is that his name?'

'I don't ask you what you think of his name, but what you think of himself,' said Marian.

'Oh, nothing particular!' Catherine answered, dissembling for the first time in her life.

'I have half a mind to tell him that!' cried Marian. 'It will do him good. He's so terribly conceited.'

'Conceited?' said Catherine, staring.

'So Arthur says, and Arthur knows about him.'

'Oh, don't tell him!' Catherine murmured imploringly.

'Don't tell him he's conceited? I have told him so a dozen times.'

At this profession of audacity, Catherine looked down at her little companion in amazement. She supposed it was because Marian was going to be married that she took so much on herself; but she wondered too, whether, when she herself should become engaged, such exploits would be expected of her.

Half an hour later she saw her aunt Penniman sitting in the embrasure of a window, with her head a little on one side, and her gold eyeglass raised to her eyes, which were wandering about the room. In front of her was a gentleman, bending forward a little, with his back turned to Catherine. She knew his back immediately, though she had never seen it; for when he left her, at Marian's instigation, he had retreated in the best order, without turning round. Morris Townsend—the name had already become very familiar to her, as if some one had been repeating it in her ear for the last half hour—Morris Townsend was giving his impressions of the company to her aunt, as he had done to herself; he was saying clever things, and Mrs Penniman was smiling, as if she approved of them. As soon as Catherine had perceived this she moved away; she would not have liked him to turn round and see her. But it gave her pleasure—the whole thing. That he should talk with Mrs Penniman, with whom she lived and whom she saw and talked with every day—that seemed to keep him near her, and to make him even easier to contemplate than if she herself had been the object of his civilities; and that Aunt Lavinia should like him, should not be shocked or startled by what he said, this also appeared to the girl a personal gain; for Aunt Lavinia's standard was extremely high, planted as it was over the grave of her late husband, in which, as she had convinced every one, the very genius of conversation was buried. One of the Almond boys, as Catherine called him, invited our heroine to dance a quadrille, and for a quarter of an hour her feet at least were occupied. This time she was not dizzy; her head was very clear. Just when the dance was over, she found herself in the crowd face to face with her father. Dr Sloper had usually a little smile, never a very big one, and with his little smile playing in his clear eyes and on his neatly-shaved lips, he looked at his daughter's crimson gown.

'Is it possible that this magnificent person is my child?' he said.

You would have surprised him if you had told him so; but it is a literal fact that he almost never addressed his daughter save in the ironical form. Whenever he addressed her he gave her pleasure; but she had to cut her pleasure out of the piece, as it were. There were portions left over, light remnants and snippets of irony, which she never knew what to do with, which seemed too delicate for her own use; and yet Catherine, lamenting the limitations of her understanding, felt that they were too valuable to waste, and had a belief that if they passed over her head they yet contributed to the general sum of human wisdom.

'I am not magnificent,' she said, mildly, wishing that she had put on another dress.

'You are sumptuous, opulent, expensive,' her father rejoined. 'You look as if you had eighty thousand a year.'

'Well, so long as I haven't—' said Catherine illogically. Her conception of her prospective wealth was as yet very indefinite.

'So long as you haven't you shouldn't look as if you had. Have you enjoyed your party?'

Catherine hesitated a moment; and then, looking away, 'I am rather tired,' she murmured. I have said that this entertainment was the beginning of something important for Catherine. For the second time in her life she made an indirect answer; and the beginning of a period of dissimulation is certainly a significant date. Catherine was not so easily tired as that.

Nevertheless, in the carriage, as they drove home, she was as quiet as if fatigue had been her portion. Dr Sloper's manner of addressing his sister Lavinia had a good deal of resemblance to the tone he had adopted towards Catherine.

'Who was the young man that was making love to you?' he presently asked.

'Oh, my good brother!' murmured Mrs Penniman, in deprecation.

'He seemed uncommonly tender. Whenever I looked at you, for half an hour, he had the most devoted air.'

'The devotion was not to me,' said Mrs Penniman. 'It was to Catherine; he talked to me of her.'

Catherine had been listening with all her ears. 'Oh, Aunt Penniman!' she exclaimed faintly.

'He is very handsome; he is very clever; he expressed himself with a great deal—a great deal of felicity,' her aunt went on.

'He is in love with this regal creature, then?' the Doctor inquired humorously.

'Oh, father,' cried the girl, still more faintly, devoutly thankful the carriage was dark.

'I don't know that; but he admired her dress.'

Catherine did not say to herself in the dark, 'My dress only?' Mrs Penniman's announcement struck her by its richness, not by its meagreness.

'You see,' said her father, 'he thinks you have eighty thousand a year.'

'I don't believe he thinks of that,' said Mrs Penniman; 'he is too refined.'

'He must be tremendously refined not to think of that!'

'Well, he is!' Catherine exclaimed, before she knew it.

'I thought you had gone to sleep,' her father answered. 'The hour has come!' he added to himself. 'Lavinia is going to get up a romance for Catherine. It's a shame to play such tricks on the girl. What is the gentleman's name?' he went on, aloud.

'I didn't catch it, and I didn't like to ask him. He asked to be introduced to me,' said Mrs Penniman, with a certain grandeur; 'but you know how indistinctly Jefferson speaks.' Jefferson was Mr Almond. 'Catherine, dear, what was the gentleman's name?'

For a minute, if it had not been for the rumbling of the carriage, you might have heard a pin drop.

'I don't know, Aunt Lavinia,' said Catherine, very softly. And, with all his irony, her father believed her.

V

HE learned what he had asked some three or four days later, after Morris Townsend, with his cousin, had called in Washington Square. Mrs Penniman did not tell her brother, on the drive home, that she had intimated to this agreeable young man, whose name she did not know, that, with her niece, she should be very glad to see him; but she was greatly pleased, and even a little flattered, when, late on a Sunday afternoon, the two gentlemen made their appearance. His coming with Arthur Townsend made it more natural and easy; the latter young man was on the point of becoming connected with the family, and Mrs Penniman had remarked to Catherine that, as he was going to marry Marian, it would be polite in him to call. These events came to pass late in the autumn, and Catherine and her aunt had been sitting together in the closing dusk, by the firelight, in the high back-parlour.

Arthur Townsend fell to Catherine's portion, while his companion placed himself on the sofa, beside Mrs Penniman. Catherine had hitherto not been a harsh critic; she was easy to please—she liked to talk with young men. But Marian's betrothed, this evening, made her feel vaguely fastidious; he sat looking at the fire and rubbing his knees with his hands. As for Catherine, she scarcely even pretended to keep up the conversation; her attention had fixed itself on the other side of the room; she was listening to what went on between the other Mr Townsend and her aunt. Every now and then he looked over at Catherine herself and smiled, as if to show that what he said was for her benefit too. Catherine would have liked to change her place, to go and sit near them, where she might see and hear him better. But she was afraid of seeming bold—of looking eager; and, besides, it would not have been polite to Marian's little suitor. She wondered why the other gentleman had picked out her aunt—how he came to have so much to say to Mrs Penniman, to whom, usually, young men were not especially devoted. She was not at all jealous of Aunt Lavinia, but she was a little envious, and above all she wondered; for Morris Townsend was an object on which she found that her imagination could exercise itself indefinitely. His cousin had been describing a house that he had taken in view of his union with Marian, and the domestic conveniences he meant to introduce into it; how Marian wanted a larger one, and Mrs Almond recommended a smaller one, and how he himself was convinced that he had got the neatest house in New York.

'It doesn't matter,' he said; 'it's only for three or four years. At the end of three or four years we'll move. That's the way to live in New York—to move every three or four years. Then you always get the last thing. It's because the city's growing so quick—you've got to keep up with it. It's going straight up town—that's where New York's going. If I wasn't afraid Marian would be lonely, I'd go up there—right up to the top—and wait for it. Only have to wait ten years—they'd all come up after you. But Marian says she wants some neighbours—she doesn't want to be a pioneer. She says that if she's got to be the first settler she had better go out to Minnesota.* I guess we'll move up little by little; when we get tired of one street we'll go higher. So you see we'll always have a new house; it's a great advantage to have a new house; you get all the latest improvements. They invent everything all over again about every five years, and it's a great thing to keep up with the new things. I always try and keep up with the new things of every kind. Don't you think that's a good motto for a young couple—to keep "going higher"? That's the name of that piece of poetry—what do they call it?—*Excelsior!*'*

Catherine bestowed on her junior visitor only just enough attention to feel that this was not the way Mr Morris Townsend had talked the other night, or that he was talking now to her fortunate aunt. But suddenly his aspiring kinsman became more interesting. He seemed to have become conscious that she was affected by his companion's presence, and he thought it proper to explain it.

'My cousin asked me to bring him, or I shouldn't have taken the liberty. He seemed to want very much to come; you know he's awfully sociable. I told him I wanted to ask you first, but he said Mrs Penniman had invited him. He isn't particular what he says when he wants to come somewhere! But Mrs Penniman seems to think it's all right.'

'We are very glad to see him,' said Catherine. And she wished to talk more about him; but she hardly knew what to say. 'I never saw him before,' she went on presently.

Arthur Townsend stared.

'Why, he told me he talked with you for over half an hour the other night.'

'I mean before the other night. That was the first time.'

'Oh, he has been away from New York—he has been all round the world. He doesn't know many people here, but he's very sociable, and he wants to know every one.'

'Every one?' said Catherine.

'Well, I mean all the good ones. All the pretty young ladies—like Mrs Penniman!' And Arthur Townsend gave a private laugh.

'My aunt likes him very much,' said Catherine.

'Most people like him—he's so brilliant.'

'He's more like a foreigner,' Catherine suggested.

'Well, I never knew a foreigner!' said young Townsend, in a tone which seemed to indicate that his ignorance had been optional.

'Neither have I,' Catherine confessed, with more humility. 'They say they are generally brilliant,' she added, vaguely.

'Well, the people of this city are clever enough for me. I know some of them that think they are too clever for me; but they ain't!'

'I suppose you can't be too clever,' said Catherine, still with humility.

'I don't know. I know some people that call my cousin too clever.'

Catherine listened to this statement with extreme interest, and a feeling that if Morris Townsend had a fault it would naturally be that one. But she did not commit herself, and in a moment she asked:—'Now that he has come back, will he stay here always?'

'Ah,' said Arthur, 'if he can get something to do.'

'Something to do?'

'Some place or other; some business.'

'Hasn't he got any?' said Catherine, who had never heard of a young man—of the upper class—in this situation.

'No; he's looking round. But he can't find anything.'

'I am very sorry,' Catherine permitted herself to observe.

'Oh, he doesn't mind,' said young Townsend. 'He takes it easy—he isn't in a hurry. He is very particular.'

Catherine thought he naturally would be, and gave herself up for some moments to the contemplation of this idea, in several of its bearings.

'Won't his father take him into his business—his office?' she at last inquired.

'He hasn't got any father—he has only got a sister. Your sister can't help you much.'

It seemed to Catherine that if she were his sister she would disprove this axiom. 'Is she—is she pleasant?' she asked in a moment.

'I don't know—I believe she's very respectable,' said young Townsend. And then he looked across to his cousin and began to laugh. 'Look here, we are talking about you,' he added.

Morris Townsend paused in his conversation with Mrs Penniman, and stared, with a little smile. Then he got up, as if he were going.

'As far as you are concerned, I can't return the compliment,' he said to Catherine's companion. 'But as regards Miss Sloper, it's another affair.'

Catherine thought this little speech wonderfully well turned; but she was embarrassed by it, and she also got up. Morris Townsend stood looking at her and smiling; he put out his hand for farewell. He was going, without having said anything to her; but even on these terms she was glad to have seen him.

'I will tell her what you have said—when you go!' said Mrs Penniman, with an insinuating laugh.

Catherine blushed, for she felt almost as if they were making sport of her. What in the world could this beautiful young man have said? He looked at her still, in spite of her blush; but very kindly and respectfully.

'I have had no talk with you,' he said, 'and that was what I came for. But it will be a good reason for coming another time; a little pretext—if I am obliged to give one. I am not afraid of what your aunt will say when I go.'

With this the two young men took their departure; after which Catherine, with her blush still lingering, directed a serious and interrogative eye to Mrs Penniman. She was incapable of elaborate artifice, and she resorted to no jocular device—to no affectation of the belief that she had been maligned—to learn what she desired.

'What did you say you would tell me?' she asked.

Mrs Penniman came up to her, smiling and nodding a little, looked at her all over, and gave a twist to the knot of ribbon in her neck. 'It's a great secret, my dear child; but he is coming a-courting!'

Catherine was serious still. 'Is that what he told you?'

'He didn't say so exactly. But he left me to guess it. I'm a good guesser.'

'Do you mean a-courting me?'

'Not me, certainly, miss; though I must say he is a hundred times more polite to a person who has no longer extreme youth to recommend her than most of the young men. He is thinking of some one else.' And Mrs Penniman gave her niece a delicate little kiss. 'You must be very gracious to him.'

Catherine stared—she was bewildered. 'I don't understand you,' she said; 'he doesn't know me.'

'Oh yes, he does; more than you think. I have told him all about you.'

'Oh, Aunt Penniman!' murmured Catherine, as if this had been a breach of trust. 'He is a perfect stranger—we don't know him.' There was infinite modesty in the poor girl's 'we'.

Aunt Penniman, however, took no account of it; she spoke even with a touch of acrimony. 'My dear Catherine, you know very well that you admire him!'

'Oh, Aunt Penniman!' Catherine could only murmur again. It might very well be that she admired him—though this did not seem to her a thing to talk about. But that this brilliant stranger—this sudden apparition, who had barely heard the sound of her voice—took that sort of interest in her that was expressed by the romantic phrase of which Mrs Penniman had just made use: this could only be a figment of the restless brain of Aunt Lavinia, whom every one knew to be a woman of powerful imagination.

VI

MRS PENNIMAN even took for granted at times that other people had as much imagination as herself; so that when, half an hour later, her brother came in, she addressed him quite on this principle.

'He has just been here, Austin; it's such a pity you missed him.'

'Whom in the world have I missed?' asked the Doctor.

'Mr Morris Townsend; he has made us such a delightful visit.'

'And who in the world is Mr Morris Townsend?'

'Aunt Penniman means the gentleman—the gentleman whose name I couldn't remember,' said Catherine.

'The gentleman at Elizabeth's party who was so struck with Catherine,' Mrs Penniman added.

'Oh, his name is Morris Townsend, is it? And did he come here to propose to you?'

'Oh, father,' murmured the girl for all answer, turning away to the window, where the dusk had deepened to darkness.

'I hope he won't do that without your permission,' said Mrs Penniman, very graciously.

'After all, my dear, he seems to have yours,' her brother answered.

Lavinia simpered, as if this might not be quite enough, and Catherine, with her forehead touching the window-panes, listened to this exchange of epigrams as reservedly as if they had not each been a pin-prick in her own destiny.

'The next time he comes,' the Doctor added, 'you had better call me. He might like to see me.'

Morris Townsend came again, some five days afterwards; but Dr Sloper was not called, as he was absent from home at the time. Catherine was with her aunt when the young man's name was brought in, and Mrs Penniman, effacing herself and protesting, made a great point of her niece's going into the drawing-room alone.

'This time it's for you—for you only,' she said. 'Before, when he talked to me, it was only preliminary—it was to gain my confidence. Literally, my dear, I should not have the *courage* to show myself to-day.'

And this was perfectly true. Mrs Penniman was not a brave woman, and Morris Townsend had struck her as a young man of great force of character, and of remarkable powers of satire; a keen, resolute, brilliant nature, with which one must exercise a great deal of tact. She said to herself that he was 'imperious', and she liked the word and the idea. She was not the least jealous of her niece, and she had been perfectly happy with Mr Penniman, but in the bottom of her heart she permitted herself the observation: 'That's the sort of husband I should have had!' He was certainly much more imperious—she ended by calling it imperial—than Mr Penniman.

So Catherine saw Mr Townsend alone, and her aunt did not come in even at the end of the visit. The visit was a long one; he sat there—in the front parlour, in the biggest arm-chair—for more than an hour. He seemed more at home this time—more familiar; lounging a little in the chair, slapping a cushion that was near him with his stick, and looking round the room a good deal, and at the objects it contained, as well as at Catherine; whom, however, he also contemplated freely. There was a smile of respectful devotion in his handsome eyes which seemed to Catherine almost solemnly beautiful; it made her think of a young knight in a poem. His talk, however, was not particularly knightly; it was light and easy and friendly; it took a practical turn, and he asked a number of questions about herself—what were her tastes—if she liked this and that—what were her habits. He said to her, with his charming smile, 'Tell me about yourself; give me a little sketch.' Catherine had very little to tell, and she had no talent for sketching; but before he went she had confided to him that she had a secret passion for the theatre, which had been but scantily gratified, and a taste for operatic music—that of Bellini and Donizetti,* in especial (it must be remembered in extenuation of this primitive young woman that she held these opinions in an age of general darkness)—which she rarely had an occasion to hear, except on the hand-organ. She confessed that she was not particularly fond of literature. Morris Townsend agreed with her that books were tiresome things; only, as he said, you had to read a good many before you found it out. He had been to places that people had written books about, and they were not a bit like the descriptions. To see for yourself—that was the great thing; he always tried to see for himself. He had seen all the principal actors—he had been to all the best theatres in London and Paris. But the actors were always like the authors—they always exaggerated. He liked everything to be natural. Suddenly he stopped, looking at Catherine with his smile.

'That's what I like you for; you are so natural! Excuse me,' he added; 'you see I am natural myself!'

And before she had time to think whether she excused him or not—which afterwards, at leisure, she became conscious that she did—he began to talk about music, and to say that it was his greatest pleasure in life. He had heard all the great singers in Paris and London—Pasta and Rubini and Lablache*—and when you had done that, you could say that you knew what singing was.

'I sing a little myself,' he said; 'some day I will show you. Not to-day, but some other time.'

And then he got up to go; he had omitted, by accident, to say that he would sing to her if she would play to him. He thought of this after he got into the street; but he might have spared his compunction, for Catherine had not noticed the lapse. She was thinking only that 'some other time' had a delightful sound; it seemed to spread itself over the future.

This was all the more reason, however, though she was ashamed and uncomfortable, why she should tell her father that Mr Morris Townsend had called again. She announced the fact abruptly, almost violently, as soon as the Doctor came into the house; and having done so—it was her duty—she took measures to leave the room. But she could not leave it fast enough; her father stopped her just as she reached the door.

'Well, my dear, did he propose to you to-day?' the Doctor asked.

This was just what she had been afraid he would say; and yet she had no answer ready. Of course she would have liked to take it as a joke—as her father must have meant it; and yet she would have liked, also, in denying it, to be a little positive, a little sharp; so that he would perhaps not ask the question again. She didn't like it—it made her unhappy. But Catherine could never be sharp; and for a moment she only stood, with her hand on the door-knob, looking at her satiric parent, and giving a little laugh.

'Decidedly,' said the Doctor to himself, 'my daughter is not brilliant!'

But he had no sooner made this reflection than Catherine found something; she had decided on the whole to take the thing as a joke.

'Perhaps he will do it the next time!' she exclaimed, with a repetition of her laugh. And she quickly got out of the room.

The Doctor stood staring; he wondered whether his daughter were serious. Catherine went straight to her own room, and by the time she reached it she bethought herself that there was something else—something better—she might have said. She almost wished, now, that her father would ask his question again, so that she might reply: 'Oh yes, Mr Morris Townsend proposed to me, and I refused him!'

The Doctor, however, began to put his questions elsewhere; it naturally having occurred to him that he ought to inform himself properly about this handsome young man who had formed the habit of running in and out of his house. He addressed himself to the elder of his sisters, Mrs Almond*—not going to her for the purpose; there was no such hurry as that—but having made a note of the matter for the first opportunity. The Doctor was never eager, never impatient nor nervous; but he made notes of everything, and he regularly consulted his notes. Among them the information he obtained from Mrs Almond about Morris Townsend took its place.

'Lavinia has already been to ask me,' she said. 'Lavinia is most excited; I don't understand it. It's not, after all, Lavinia that the young man is supposed to have designs upon. She is very peculiar.'

'Ah, my dear,' the Doctor replied, 'she has not lived with me these twelve years without my finding it out!'

'She has got such an artificial mind,' said Mrs Almond, who always enjoyed an opportunity to discuss Lavinia's peculiarities with her brother. 'She didn't want me to tell you that she had asked me about Mr Townsend; but I told her I would. She always wants to conceal everything.'

'And yet at moments no one blurts things out with such crudity. She is like a revolving lighthouse; pitch darkness alternating with a dazzling brilliancy! But what did you tell her?' the Doctor asked.

'What I tell you; that I know very little of him.'

'Lavinia must have been disappointed at that,' said the Doctor; 'she would prefer him to have been guilty of some romantic crime. However, we must make the best of people. They tell me our gentleman is the cousin of the little boy to whom you are about to entrust the future of your little girl.'

'Arthur is not a little boy; he is a very old man; you and I will never be so old. He is a distant relation of Lavinia's *protégé*. The name is the same, but I am given to understand that there are Townsends and Townsends. So Arthur's mother tells me; she talked about "branches"—younger branches, elder branches, inferior branches—as if it were a royal house. Arthur, it appears, is of the reigning line, but poor Lavinia's young man is not. Beyond this, Arthur's mother knows very little about him; she has only a vague story that he has been "wild". But I know his sister a little, and she is a very nice woman. Her name is Mrs Montgomery; she is a widow, with a little property and five children. She lives in the Second Avenue.'

'What does Mrs Montgomery say about him?'

'That he has talents by which he might distinguish himself.'

'Only he is lazy, eh?'

'She doesn't say so.'

'That's family pride,' said the Doctor. 'What is his profession?'

'He hasn't got any; he is looking for something. I believe he was once in the Navy.'

'Once? What is his age?'

'I suppose he is upwards of thirty. He must have gone into the Navy very young. I think Arthur told me that he inherited a small property—which was perhaps the cause of his leaving the Navy—and that he spent it all in a few years. He travelled all over the world, lived abroad, amused himself. I believe it was a kind of system, a theory he had. He has lately come back to America, with the intention, as he tells Arthur, of beginning life in earnest.'

'Is he in earnest about Catherine, then?'

'I don't see why you should be incredulous,' said Mrs Almond. 'It seems to me that you have never done Catherine justice. You must remember that she has the prospect of thirty thousand a year.'

The Doctor looked at his sister a moment, and then, with the slightest touch of bitterness: 'You at least appreciate her,' he said.

Mrs Almond blushed.

'I don't mean that is her only merit; I simply mean that it is a great one. A great many young men think so; and you appear to me never to have been properly aware of that. You have always had a little way of alluding to her as an unmarriageable girl.'

'My allusions are as kind as yours, Elizabeth,' said the Doctor, frankly. 'How many suitors has Catherine had, with all her expectations—how much attention has she ever received? Catherine is not unmarriageable, but she is absolutely unattractive. What other reason is there for Lavinia being so charmed with the idea that there is a lover in the house? There has never been one before, and Lavinia, with her sensitive, sympathetic nature, is not used to the idea.

It affects her imagination. I must do the young men of New York the justice to say that they strike me as very disinterested. They prefer pretty girls—lively girls—girls like your own. Catherine is neither pretty nor lively.'

'Catherine does very well; she has a style of her own—which is more than my poor Marian has, who has no style at all,' said Mrs Almond. 'The reason Catherine has received so little attention is that she seems to all the young men to be older than themselves. She is so large, and she dresses—so richly. They are rather afraid of her, I think; she looks as if she had been married already, and you know they don't like married women. And if our young men appear disinterested,' the Doctor's wiser sister went on, 'it is because they marry, as a general thing, so young, before twenty-five, at the age of innocence and sincerity, before the age of calculation. If they only waited a little, Catherine would fare better.'

'As a calculation? Thank you very much,' said the Doctor.

'Wait till some intelligent man of forty comes along, and he will be delighted with Catherine,' Mrs Almond continued.

'Mr Townsend is not old enough, then; his motives may be pure.'

'It is very possible that his motives are pure; I should be very sorry to take the contrary for granted. Lavinia is sure of it, and, as he is a very prepossessing youth, you might give him the benefit of the doubt.'

Dr Sloper reflected a moment.

'What are his present means of subsistence?'

'I have no idea. He lives, as I say, with his sister.'

'A widow, with five children? Do you mean he lives *upon* her?'

Mrs Almond got up, and with a certain impatience: 'Had you not better ask Mrs Montgomery herself?' she inquired.

'Perhaps I may come to that,' said the Doctor. 'Did you say the Second Avenue?' He made a note of the Second Avenue.

VII

HE was, however, by no means so much in earnest as this might seem
to indicate; and, indeed, he was more than anything else amused with
the whole situation. He was not in the least in a state of tension or of
vigilance, with regard to Catherine's prospects; he was even on his
guard against the ridicule that might attach itself to the spectacle of
a house thrown into agitation by its daughter and heiress receiving
attentions unprecedented in its annals. More than this, he went so far
as to promise himself some entertainment from the little drama—if
drama it was—of which Mrs Penniman desired to represent the
ingenious Mr Townsend as the hero. He had no intention, as yet, of
regulating the *dénouement*. He was perfectly willing, as Elizabeth had
suggested, to give the young man the benefit of every doubt. There
was no great danger in it; for Catherine, at the age of twenty-two,
was after all a rather mature blossom, such as could be plucked from
the stem only by a vigorous jerk. The fact that Morris Townsend was
poor—was not of necessity against him; the Doctor had never made
up his mind that his daughter should marry a rich man. The fortune
she would inherit struck him as a very sufficient provision for two
reasonable persons, and if a penniless swain who could give a good
account of himself should enter the lists, he should be judged quite
upon his personal merits. There were other things besides. The
Doctor thought it very vulgar to be precipitate in accusing people of
mercenary motives, inasmuch as his door had as yet not been in the
least besieged by fortune-hunters; and, lastly, he was very curious to
see whether Catherine might really be loved for her moral worth. He
smiled as he reflected that poor Mr Townsend had been only twice to
the house, and he said to Mrs Penniman that the next time he should
come she must ask him to dinner.

He came very soon again, and Mrs Penniman had of course great
pleasure in executing this mission. Morris Townsend accepted her
invitation with equal good grace, and the dinner took place a few days
later. The Doctor had said to himself, justly enough, that they must
not have the young man alone; this would partake too much of the
nature of encouragement. So two or three other persons were invited;
but Morris Townsend, though he was by no means the ostensible,

was the real, occasion of the feast. There is every reason to suppose that he desired to make a good impression; and if he fell short of this result, it was not for want of a good deal of intelligent effort. The Doctor talked to him very little during dinner; but he observed him attentively, and after the ladies had gone out he pushed him the wine and asked him several questions. Morris was not a young man who needed to be pressed, and he found quite enough encouragement in the superior quality of the claret. The Doctor's wine was admirable, and it may be communicated to the reader that while he sipped it Morris reflected that a cellar-full of good liquor—there was evidently a cellar-full here—would be a most attractive idiosyncrasy in a father-in-law. The Doctor was struck with his appreciative guest; he saw that he was not a commonplace young man. 'He has ability,' said Catherine's father, 'decided ability; he has a very good head if he chooses to use it. And he is uncommonly well turned out; quite the sort of figure that pleases the ladies. But I don't think I like him.' The Doctor, however, kept his reflections to himself, and talked to his visitors about foreign lands, concerning which Morris offered him more information than he was ready, as he mentally phrased it, to swallow. Dr Sloper had travelled but little, and he took the liberty of not believing everything this anecdotical idler narrated. He prided himself on being something of a physiognomist,* and while the young man, chatting with easy assurance, puffed his cigar and filled his glass again, the Doctor sat with his eyes quietly fixed on his bright, expressive face. 'He has the assurance of the devil himself,' said Morris's host; 'I don't think I ever saw such assurance. And his powers of invention are most remarkable. He is very knowing; they were not so knowing as that in my time. And a good head, did I say? I should think so—after a bottle of Madeira, and a bottle and a half of claret?'

After dinner Morris Townsend went and stood before Catherine, who was standing before the fire in her red satin gown.

'He doesn't like me—he doesn't like me at all!' said the young man.

'Who doesn't like you?' asked Catherine.

'Your father; extraordinary man!'

'I don't see how you know,' said Catherine, blushing.

'I feel; I am very quick to feel.'

'Perhaps you are mistaken.'

'Ah, well; you ask him and you will see.'

'I would rather not ask him, if there is any danger of his saying what you think.'

Morris looked at her with an air of mock melancholy.

'It wouldn't give you any pleasure to contradict him?'

'I never contradict him,' said Catherine.

'Will you hear me abused without opening your lips in my defence?'

'My father won't abuse you. He doesn't know you enough.'

Morris Townsend gave a loud laugh, and Catherine began to blush again.

'I shall never mention you,' she said, to take refuge from her confusion.

'That is very well; but it is not quite what I should have liked you to say. I should have liked you to say: "If my father doesn't think well of you, what does it matter?"'

'Ah, but it would matter; I couldn't say that!' the girl exclaimed.

He looked at her for a moment, smiling a little; and the Doctor, if he had been watching him just then, would have seen a gleam of fine impatience in the sociable softness of his eye. But there was no impatience in his rejoinder—none, at least, save what was expressed in a little appealing sigh. 'Ah, well, then, I must not give up the hope of bringing him round!'

He expressed it more frankly to Mrs Penniman, later in the evening. But before that he sang two or three songs at Catherine's timid request; not that he flattered himself that this would help to bring her father round. He had a sweet, light tenor voice, and when he had finished, every one made some exclamation—every one, that is, save Catherine, who remained intensely silent. Mrs Penniman declared that his manner of singing was 'most artistic', and Dr Sloper said it was 'very taking—very taking indeed', speaking loudly and distinctly, but with a certain dryness.

'He doesn't like me—he doesn't like me at all,' said Morris Townsend, addressing the aunt in the same manner as he had done the niece. 'He thinks I'm all wrong.'

Unlike her niece, Mrs Penniman asked for no explanation. She only smiled very sweetly, as if she understood everything; and, unlike Catherine too, she made no attempt to contradict him. 'Pray, what does it matter?' she murmured softly.

'Ah, you say the right thing!' said Morris, greatly to the gratification of Mrs Penniman, who prided herself on always saying the right thing.

The Doctor, the next time he saw his sister Elizabeth, let her know that he had made the acquaintance of Lavinia's *protégé*.

'Physically,' he said, 'he's uncommonly well set up. As an anatomist, it is really a pleasure to me to see such a beautiful structure; although, if people were all like him, I suppose there would be very little need for doctors.'

'Don't you see anything in people but their bones?' Mrs Almond rejoined. 'What do you think of him as a father?'

'As a father? Thank Heaven I am not his father!'

'No; but you are Catherine's. Lavinia tells me she is in love.'

'She must get over it. He is not a gentleman.'

'Ah, take care! Remember that he is a branch of the Townsends.'

'He is not what I call a gentleman. He has not the soul of one. He is extremely insinuating; but it's a vulgar nature. I saw through it in a minute. He is altogether too familiar—I hate familiarity. He is a plausible coxcomb.'*

'Ah, well,' said Mrs Almond; 'if you make up your mind so easily, it's a great advantage.'

'I don't make up my mind easily. What I tell you is the result of thirty years of observation; and in order to be able to form that judgment in a single evening, I have had to spend a lifetime in study.'

'Very possibly you are right. But the thing is for Catherine to see it.'

'I will present her with a pair of spectacles!' said the Doctor.

VIII

IF it were true that she was in love, she was certainly very quiet about it; but the Doctor was of course prepared to admit that her quietness might mean volumes. She had told Morris Townsend that she would not mention him to her father, and she saw no reason to retract this vow of discretion. It was no more than decently civil, of course, that after having dined in Washington Square, Morris should call there again; and it was no more than natural that, having been kindly received on this occasion, he should continue to present himself. He had had plenty of leisure on his hands; and thirty years ago, in New York, a young man of leisure had reason to be thankful for aids to self-oblivion. Catherine said nothing to her father about these visits, though they had rapidly become the most important, the most absorbing thing in her life. The girl was very happy. She knew not as yet what would come of it; but the present had suddenly grown rich and solemn. If she had been told she was in love, she would have been a good deal surprised; for she had an idea that love was an eager and exacting passion, and her own heart was filled in these days with the impulse of self-effacement and sacrifice. Whenever Morris Townsend had left the house, her imagination projected itself, with all its strength, into the idea of his soon coming back; but if she had been told at such a moment that he would not return for a year, or even that he would never return, she would not have complained nor rebelled, but would have humbly accepted the decree, and sought for consolation in thinking over the times she had already seen him, the words he had spoken, the sound of his voice, of his tread, the expression of his face. Love demands certain things as a right; but Catherine had no sense of her rights; she had only a consciousness of immense and unexpected favours. Her very gratitude for these things had hushed itself; for it seemed to her that there would be something of impudence in making a festival of her secret. Her father suspected Morris Townsend's visits, and noted her reserve. She seemed to beg pardon for it; she looked at him constantly in silence, as if she meant to say that she said nothing because she was afraid of irritating him. But the poor girl's dumb eloquence irritated him more than anything else would have done, and he caught himself murmuring more than once that it was a grievous pity his only child was a simpleton. His murmurs, however, were inaudible; and for a while he said nothing to any one. He would have liked to know exactly how often young Townsend came; but he had determined to ask no questions of the girl herself—to say nothing more to her that would show that he watched her. The Doctor had a great idea of being largely just: he wished to leave his daughter her liberty, and interfere only when the danger should be proved. It was not in his manner to obtain information by indirect methods, and it never even occurred to him to question the servants. As for Lavinia, he hated to talk to her about the matter; she annoyed him with her mock romanticism. But he had to come to this. Mrs Penniman's convictions as regards the relations of her niece and the clever young visitor who saved appearances by coming ostensibly for both the ladies—Mrs Penniman's convictions had passed into a riper and richer phase. There was to be no crudity in Mrs Penniman's treatment of the situation; she had become as uncommunicative as Catherine herself. She was tasting of the sweets of concealment; she had taken up the line of mystery. 'She would be enchanted to be able to prove to herself that she is persecuted,' said the Doctor; and when at last he questioned her, he was sure she would contrive to extract from his words a pretext for this belief.

'Be so good as to let me know what is going on in the house,' he said to her, in a tone which, under the circumstances, he himself deemed genial.

'Going on, Austin?' Mrs Penniman exclaimed. 'Why, I am sure I don't know! I believe that last night the old gray cat had kittens?'

'At her age?' said the Doctor. 'The idea is startling—almost shocking. Be so good as to see that they are all drowned. But what else has happened?'

'Ah, the dear little kittens!' cried Mrs Penniman. 'I wouldn't have them drowned for the world!'

Her brother puffed his cigar a few moments in silence. 'Your sympathy with kittens, Lavinia,' he presently resumed, 'arises from a feline element in your own character.'

'Cats are very graceful, and very clean,' said Mrs Penniman, smiling.

'And very stealthy. You are the embodiment both of grace and of neatness; but you are wanting in frankness.'

'You certainly are not, dear brother.'

'I don't pretend to be graceful, though I try to be neat. Why haven't you let me know that Mr Morris Townsend is coming to the house four times a week?'

Mrs Penniman lifted her eyebrows. 'Four times a week?'

'Five times, if you prefer it. I am away all day, and I see nothing. But when such things happen, you should let me know.'

Mrs Penniman, with her eyebrows still raised, reflected intently. 'Dear Austin,' she said at last, 'I am incapable of betraying a confidence. I would rather suffer anything.'

'Never fear; you shall not suffer. To whose confidence is it you allude? Has Catherine made you take a vow of eternal secrecy?'

'By no means. Catherine has not told me as much as she might. She has not been very trustful.'

'It is the young man, then, who has made you his confidant? Allow me to say that it is extremely indiscreet of you to form secret alliances with young men. You don't know where they may lead you.'

'I don't know what you mean by an alliance,' said Mrs Penniman. 'I take a great interest in Mr Townsend; I won't conceal that. But that's all.'

'Under the circumstances, that is quite enough. What is the source of your interest in Mr Townsend?'

'Why,' said Mrs Penniman, musing, and then breaking into her smile, 'that he is so interesting!'

The Doctor felt that he had need of his patience. 'And what makes him interesting?—his good looks?'

'His misfortunes, Austin.'

'Ah, he has had misfortunes? That, of course, is always interesting. Are you at liberty to mention a few of Mr Townsend's?'

'I don't know that he would like it,' said Mrs Penniman. 'He has told me a great deal about himself—he has told me, in fact, his whole history. But I don't think I ought to repeat those things. He would tell them to you, I am sure, if he thought you would listen to him kindly. With kindness you may do anything with him.'

The Doctor gave a laugh. 'I shall request him very kindly, then, to leave Catherine alone.'

'Ah!' said Mrs Penniman, shaking her forefinger at her brother, with her little finger turned out, 'Catherine has probably said something to him kinder than that!'

'Said that she loved him? Do you mean that?'

Mrs Penniman fixed her eyes on the floor. 'As I tell you, Austin, she doesn't confide in me.'

'You have an opinion, I suppose, all the same. It is that I ask you for; though I don't conceal from you that I shall not regard it as conclusive.'

Mrs Penniman's gaze continued to rest on the carpet; but at last she lifted it, and then her brother thought it very expressive.

'I think Catherine is very happy; that is all I can say.'

'Townsend is trying to marry her—is that what you mean?'

'He is greatly interested in her.'

'He finds her such an attractive girl?'

'Catherine has a lovely nature, Austin,' said Mrs Penniman, 'and Mr Townsend has had the intelligence to discover that.'

'With a little help from you, I suppose. My dear Lavinia,' cried the Doctor, 'you are an admirable aunt!'

'So Mr Townsend says,' observed Lavinia, smiling.

'Do you think he is sincere?' asked her brother.

'In saying that?'

'No; that's of course. But in his admiration for Catherine?'

'Deeply sincere. He has said to me the most appreciative, the most charming things about her. He would say them to you, if he were sure you would listen to him—gently.'

'I doubt whether I can undertake it. He appears to require a great deal of gentleness.'

'He is a sympathetic, sensitive nature,' said Mrs Penniman.

Her brother puffed his cigar again in silence. 'These delicate qualities have survived his vicissitudes, eh? All this while you haven't told me about his misfortunes.'

'It is a long story,' said Mrs Penniman, 'and I regard it as a sacred trust. But I suppose there is no objection to my saying that he has been wild—he frankly confesses that. But he has paid for it.'

'That's what has impoverished him, eh?'

'I don't mean simply in money. He is very much alone in the world.'

'Do you mean that he has behaved so badly that his friends have given him up?'

'He has had false friends, who have deceived and betrayed him.'

'He seems to have some good ones too. He has a devoted sister, and half a dozen nephews and nieces.'

Mrs Penniman was silent a minute. 'The nephews and nieces are children, and the sister is not a very attractive person.'

'I hope he doesn't abuse her to you,' said the Doctor; 'for I am told he lives upon her.'

'Lives upon her?'

'Lives with her, and does nothing for himself; it is about the same thing.'

'He is looking for a position—most earnestly,' said Mrs Penniman. 'He hopes every day to find one.'

'Precisely. He is looking for it here—over there in the front parlour. The position of husband of a weak-minded woman with a large fortune would suit him to perfection!'

Mrs Penniman was truly amiable, but she now gave signs of temper. She rose with much animation, and stood for a moment looking at her brother. 'My dear Austin,' she remarked, 'if you regard Catherine as a weak-minded woman, you are particularly mistaken!' And with this she moved majestically away.

IX

It was a regular custom with the family in Washington Square to go and spend Sunday evening at Mrs Almond's. On the Sunday after the conversation I have just narrated, this custom was not intermitted; and on this occasion, towards the middle of the evening, Dr Sloper found reason to withdraw to the library, with his brother-in-law, to talk over a matter of business. He was absent some twenty minutes, and when he came back into the circle, which was enlivened by the presence of several friends of the family, he saw that Morris Townsend had come in and had lost as little time as possible in seating himself on a small sofa, beside Catherine. In the large room, where several different groups had been formed, and the hum of voices and of laughter was loud, these two young persons might confabulate, as the Doctor phrased it to himself, without attracting attention. He saw in a moment, however, that his daughter was painfully conscious of his own observation. She sat motionless, with her eyes bent down, staring at her open fan, deeply flushed, shrinking together as if to minimize the indiscretion of which she confessed herself guilty.

The Doctor almost pitied her. Poor Catherine was not defiant; she had no genius for bravado; and as she felt that her father viewed her companion's attentions with an unsympathizing eye, there was nothing but discomfort for her in the accident of seeming to challenge him. The Doctor felt, indeed, so sorry for her that he turned away, to spare her the sense of being watched; and he was so intelligent a man that, in his thoughts, he rendered a sort of poetic justice to her situation.

'It must be deucedly pleasant for a plain, inanimate girl like that to have a beautiful young fellow come and sit down beside her and whisper to her that he is her slave—if that is what this one whispers. No wonder she likes it, and that she thinks me a cruel tyrant; which of course she does, though she is afraid—she hasn't the animation necessary—to admit it to herself. Poor old Catherine!' mused the Doctor; 'I verily believe she is capable of defending me when Townsend abuses me!'

And the force of this reflection, for the moment, was such in making him feel the natural opposition between his point of view and that of an infatuated child, that he said to himself that he was perhaps after all taking things too hard and crying out before he was hurt. He must not condemn Morris Townsend unheard. He had a great aversion to taking things too hard; he thought that half the discomfort and many of the disappointments of life come from it; and for an instant he asked himself whether, possibly, he did not appear ridiculous to this intelligent young man, whose private perception of incongruities he suspected of being keen. At the end of a quarter of an hour Catherine had got rid of him, and Townsend was now standing before the fireplace in conversation with Mrs Almond.

'We will try him again,' said the Doctor. And he crossed the room and joined his sister and her companion, making her a sign that she should leave the young man to him. She presently did so, while Morris looked at him, smiling, without a sign of evasiveness in his affable eye.

'He's amazingly conceited!' thought the Doctor; and then he said aloud: 'I am told you are looking out for a position.'

'Oh, a position is more than I should presume to call it,' Morris Townsend answered. 'That sounds so fine. I should like some quiet work—something to turn an honest penny.'

'What sort of thing should you prefer?'

'Do you mean what am I fit for? Very little, I am afraid. I have nothing but my good right arm, as they say in the melodramas.'

'You are too modest,' said the Doctor. 'In addition to your good right arm, you have your subtle brain. I know nothing of you but what I see; but I see by your physiognomy that you are extremely intelligent.'

'Ah,' Townsend murmured, 'I don't know what to answer when you say that! You advise me, then, not to despair?'

And he looked at his interlocutor as if the question might have a double meaning. The Doctor caught the look and weighed it a moment before he replied. 'I should be very sorry to admit that a robust and well-disposed young man need ever despair. If he doesn't succeed in one thing, he can try another. Only, I should add, he should choose his line with discretion.'

'Ah, yes, with discretion,' Morris Townsend repeated, sympathetically. 'Well, I have been indiscreet, formerly; but I think I have got over it. I am very steady now.' And he stood a moment, looking down at his remarkably neat shoes. Then at last, 'Were you kindly intending to propose something for my advantage?' he inquired, looking up and smiling.

'Damn his impudence!' the Doctor exclaimed, privately. But in a moment he reflected that he himself had, after all, touched first upon this delicate point, and that his words might have been construed as an offer of assistance. 'I have no particular proposal to make,' he presently said; 'but it occurred to me to let you know that I have you in my mind. Sometimes one hears of opportunities. For instance—should you object to leaving New York—to going to a distance?'

'I am afraid I shouldn't be able to manage that. I must seek my fortune here or nowhere. You see,' added Morris Townsend, 'I have ties—I have responsibilities here. I have a sister, a widow, from whom I have been separated for a long time, and to whom I am almost everything. I shouldn't like to say to her that I must leave her. She rather depends upon me, you see.'

'Ah, that's very proper; family feeling is very proper,' said Dr Sloper. 'I often think there is not enough of it in our city. I think I have heard of your sister.'

'It is possible, but I rather doubt it; she lives so very quietly.'

'As quietly, you mean,' the Doctor went on, with a short laugh, 'as a lady may do who has several young children.'

'Ah, my little nephews and nieces—that's the very point! I am helping to bring them up,' said Morris Townsend. 'I am a kind of amateur tutor; I give them lessons.'

'That's very proper, as I say; but it is hardly a career.'

'It won't make my fortune!' the young man confessed.

'You must not be too much bent on a fortune,' said the Doctor. 'But I assure you I will keep you in mind; I won't lose sight of you!'

'If my situation becomes desperate I shall perhaps take the liberty of reminding you!' Morris rejoined, raising his voice a little, with a brighter smile, as his interlocutor turned away.

Before he left the house the Doctor had a few words with Mrs Almond.

'I should like to see his sister,' he said. 'What do you call her? Mrs Montgomery. I should like to have a little talk with her.'

'I will try and manage it,' Mrs Almond responded. 'I will take the first opportunity of inviting her, and you shall come and meet her. Unless, indeed,' Mrs Almond added, 'she first takes it into her head to be sick and to send for you.'

'Ah no, not that; she must have trouble enough without that. But it would have its advantages, for then I should see the children. I should like very much to see the children.'

'You are very thorough. Do you want to catechize them about their uncle?'

'Precisely. Their uncle tells me he has charge of their education, that he saves their mother the expense of school-bills. I should like to ask them a few questions in the commoner branches.'

'He certainly has not the cut of a schoolmaster!' Mrs Almond said to herself a short time afterwards, as she saw Morris Townsend in a corner bending over her niece, who was seated.

And there was, indeed, nothing in the young man's discourse at this moment that savoured of the pedagogue.

'Will you meet me somewhere to-morrow or next day?' he said, in a low tone, to Catherine.

'Meet you?' she asked, lifting her frightened eyes.

'I have something particular to say to you—very particular.'

'Can't you come to the house? Can't you say it there?'

Townsend shook his head gloomily. 'I can't enter your doors again!'

'Oh, Mr Townsend!' murmured Catherine. She trembled as she wondered what had happened, whether her father had forbidden it.

'I can't in self-respect,' said the young man. 'Your father has insulted me.'

'Insulted you?'

'He has taunted me with my poverty.'

'Oh, you are mistaken—you misunderstood him!' Catherine spoke with energy, getting up from her chair.

'Perhaps I am too proud—too sensitive. But would you have me otherwise?' he asked, tenderly.

'Where my father is concerned, you must not be sure. He is full of goodness,' said Catherine.

'He laughed at me for having no position! I took it quietly; but only because he belongs to you.'

'I don't know,' said Catherine; 'I don't know what he thinks. I am sure he means to be kind. You must not be too proud.'

'I will be proud only of you,' Morris answered. 'Will you meet me in the Square in the afternoon?'

A great blush on Catherine's part had been the answer to the declaration I have just quoted. She turned away, heedless of his question.

'Will you meet me?' he repeated. 'It is very quiet there; no one need see us—toward dusk?'

'It is you who are unkind, it is you who laugh, when you say such things as that.'

'My dear girl!' the young man murmured.

'You know how little there is in me to be proud of. I am ugly and stupid.'

Morris greeted this remark with an ardent murmur, in which she recognized nothing articulate but an assurance that she was his own dearest.

But she went on. 'I am not even—I am not even—' And she paused a moment.

'You are not what?'

'I am not even brave.'

'Ah, then, if you are afraid, what shall we do?'

She hesitated awhile; then at last—'You must come to the house,' she said; 'I am not afraid of that.'

'I would rather it were in the Square,' the young man urged. 'You know how empty it is, often. No one will see us.'

'I don't care who sees us! But leave me now.'

He left her resignedly; he had got what he wanted. Fortunately he was ignorant that half an hour later, going home with her father and feeling him near, the poor girl, in spite of her sudden declaration of courage, began to tremble again. Her father said nothing; but she had an idea his eyes were fixed upon her in the darkness. Mrs Penniman also was silent; Morris Townsend had told her that her niece preferred, unromantically, an interview in a chintz-covered parlour to a sentimental tryst beside a fountain sheeted with dead leaves, and she was lost in wonderment at the oddity—almost the perversity—of the choice.

X

CATHERINE received the young man the next day on the ground she had chosen—amid the chaste upholstery of a New York drawing-room furnished in the fashion of fifty years ago. Morris had swallowed his pride and made the effort necessary to cross the threshold of her too derisive parent—an act of magnanimity which could not fail to render him doubly interesting.

'We must settle something—we must take a line,' he declared, passing his hand through his hair and giving a glance at the long narrow mirror which adorned the space between the two windows, and which had at its base a little gilded bracket covered by a thin slab of white marble, supporting in its turn a backgammon board folded together in the shape of two volumes, two shining folios inscribed in letters of greenish gilt, *History of England*. If Morris had been pleased to describe the master of the house as a heartless scoffer, it is because he thought him too much on his guard, and this was the easiest way to express his own dissatisfaction—a dissatisfaction which he had made a point of concealing from the Doctor. It will probably seem to the reader, however, that the Doctor's vigilance was by no means excessive, and that these two young people had an open field. Their intimacy was now considerable, and it may appear that for a shrinking and retiring person our heroine had been liberal of her favours. The young man, within a few days, had made her listen to things for which she had not supposed that she was prepared; having a lively foreboding of difficulties, he proceeded to gain as much ground as possible in the present. He remembered that fortune favours the brave, and even if he had forgotten it, Mrs Penniman would have remembered it for him. Mrs Penniman delighted of all things in a drama, and she flattered herself that a drama would now be enacted. Combining as she did the zeal of the prompter with the impatience of the spectator, she had long since done her utmost to pull up the curtain. She, too, expected to figure in the performance—to be the confidant, the Chorus, to speak the epilogue. It may even be said that there were times when she lost sight altogether of the modest heroine of the play, in the contemplation of certain great passages which would naturally occur between the hero and herself.

What Morris had told Catherine at last was simply that he loved her, or rather adored her. Virtually, he had made known as much already—his visits had been a series of eloquent intimations of it. But now he had affirmed it in lover's vows, and, as a memorable sign of it, he had passed his arm round the girl's waist and taken a kiss. This happy certitude had come sooner than Catherine expected, and she had regarded it, very naturally, as a priceless treasure. It may even be doubted whether she had ever definitely expected to possess it; she had not been waiting for it, and she had never said to herself that at a given moment it must come. As I have tried to explain, she was not eager and exacting; she took what was given her from day to day; and if the delightful custom of her lover's visits, which yielded her a happiness in which confidence and timidity were strangely blended, had suddenly come to an end, she would not only not have spoken of herself as one of the forsaken, but she would not have thought of herself as one of the disappointed. After Morris had kissed her, the last time he was with her, as a ripe assurance of his devotion, she begged him to go away, to leave her alone, to let her think. Morris went away, taking another kiss first. But Catherine's meditations had lacked a certain coherence. She felt his kisses on her lips and on her cheeks for a long time afterwards; the sensation was rather an obstacle than an aid to reflection. She would have liked to see her situation all clearly before her, to make up her mind what she should do if, as she feared, her father should tell her that he disapproved of Morris Townsend. But all that she could see with any vividness was that it was terribly strange that any one should disapprove of him; that there must in that case be some mistake, some mystery, which in a little while would be set at rest. She put off deciding and choosing; before the vision of a conflict with her father she dropped her eyes and sat motionless, holding her breath and waiting. It made her heart beat, it was intensely painful. When Morris kissed her and said these things—that also made her heart beat; but this was worse, and it frightened her. Nevertheless, to-day, when the young man spoke of settling something, taking a line, she felt that it was the truth, and she answered very simply and without hesitating.

'We must do our duty,' she said; 'we must speak to my father. I will do it to-night; you must do it to-morrow.'

'It is very good of you to do it first,' Morris answered. 'The young man—the happy lover—generally does that. But just as you please!'

It pleased Catherine to think that she should be brave for his sake, and in her satisfaction she even gave a little smile. 'Women have more tact,' she said; 'they ought to do it first. They are more conciliating; they can persuade better.'

'You will need all your powers of persuasion. But after all,' Morris added, 'you are irresistible.'

'Please don't speak that way—and promise me this. Tomorrow, when you talk with father, you will be very gentle and respectful.'

'As much so as possible,' Morris promised. 'It won't be much use, but I shall try. I certainly would rather have you easily than have to fight for you.'

'Don't talk about fighting; we shall not fight.'

'Ah, we must be prepared,' Morris rejoined; 'you especially, because for you it must come hardest. Do you know the first thing your father will say to you?'

'No, Morris; please tell me.'

'He will tell you I am mercenary.'

'Mercenary?'

'It's a big word; but it means a low thing. It means that I am after your money.'

'Oh!' murmured Catherine, softly.

The exclamation was so deprecating and touching that Morris indulged in another little demonstration of affection. 'But he will be sure to say it,' he added.

'It will be easy to be prepared for that,' Catherine said. 'I shall simply say that he is mistaken—that other men may be that way, but that you are not.'

'You must make a great point of that, for it will be his own great point.'

Catherine looked at her lover a minute, and then she said, 'I shall persuade him. But I am glad we shall be rich,' she added.

Morris turned away, looking into the crown of his hat. 'No, it's a misfortune,' he said at last. 'It is from that our difficulty will come.'

'Well, if it is the worst misfortune, we are not so unhappy. Many people would not think it so bad. I will persuade him, and after that we shall be very glad we have money.'

Morris Townsend listened to this robust logic in silence. 'I will leave my defence to you; it's a charge that a man has to stoop to defend himself from.'

Catherine on her side was silent for a while; she was looking at him while he looked, with a good deal of fixedness, out of the window. 'Morris,' she said, abruptly, 'are you very sure you love me?'

He turned round, and in a moment he was bending over her. 'My own dearest, can you doubt it?'

'I have only known it five days,' she said; 'but now it seems to me as if I could never do without it.'

'You will never be called upon to try!' And he gave a little tender, reassuring laugh. Then, in a moment, he added, 'There is something you must tell me, too.' She had closed her eyes after the last word she uttered, and kept them closed; and at this she nodded her head, without opening them. 'You must tell me', he went on, 'that if your father is dead against me, if he absolutely forbids our marriage, you will still be faithful.'

Catherine opened her eyes, gazing at him, and she could give no better promise than what he read there.

'You will cleave to me?'* said Morris. 'You know you are your own mistress—you are of age.'

'Ah, Morris!' she murmured, for all answer. Or rather not for all; for she put her hand into his own. He kept it awhile, and presently he kissed her again. This is all that need be recorded of their conversation; but Mrs Penniman, if she had been present, would probably have admitted that it was as well it had not taken place beside the fountain in Washington Square.

XI

CATHERINE listened for her father when he came in that evening, and she heard him go to his study. She sat quiet, though her heart was beating fast, for nearly half an hour; then she went and knocked at his door—a ceremony without which she never crossed the threshold of this apartment. On entering it now she found him in his chair beside the fire, entertaining himself with a cigar and the evening paper.

'I have something to say to you,' she began very gently; and she sat down in the first place that offered.

'I shall be very happy to hear it, my dear,' said her father. He waited—waited, looking at her, while she stared, in a long silence, at the fire. He was curious and impatient, for he was sure she was going to speak of Morris Townsend; but he let her take her own time, for he was determined to be very mild.

'I am engaged to be married!' Catherine announced at last, still staring at the fire.

The Doctor was startled; the accomplished fact was more than he had expected. But he betrayed no surprise. 'You do right to tell me,' he simply said. 'And who is the happy mortal whom you have honoured with your choice?'

'Mr Morris Townsend.' And as she pronounced her lover's name, Catherine looked at him. What she saw was her father's still gray eye and his clearcut, definite smile. She contemplated these objects for a moment, and then she looked back at the fire; it was much warmer.

'When was this arrangement made?' the Doctor asked.

'This afternoon—two hours ago.'

'Was Mr Townsend here?'

'Yes, father; in the front parlour.' She was very glad that she was not obliged to tell him that the ceremony of their betrothal had taken place out there under the bare ailantus-trees.

'Is it serious?' said the Doctor.

'Very serious, father.'

Her father was silent a moment. 'Mr Townsend ought to have told me.'

'He means to tell you to-morrow.'

'After I know all about it from you? He ought to have told me before. Does he think I didn't care—because I left you so much liberty?'

'Oh, no,' said Catherine; 'he knew you would care. And we have been so much obliged to you for—for the liberty.'

The Doctor gave a short laugh. 'You might have made a better use of it, Catherine.'

'Please don't say that, father,' the girl urged, softly, fixing her dull and gentle eyes upon him.

He puffed his cigar awhile, meditatively. 'You have gone very fast,' he said at last.

'Yes,' Catherine answered simply; 'I think we have.'

Her father glanced at her an instant, removing his eyes from the fire. 'I don't wonder Mr Townsend likes you. You are so simple and so good.'

'I don't know why it is—but he *does* like me. I am sure of that.'

'And are you very fond of Mr Townsend?'

'I like him very much, of course—or I shouldn't consent to marry him.'

'But you have known him a very short time, my dear.'

'Oh,' said Catherine, with some eagerness, 'it doesn't take long to like a person—when once you begin.'

'You must have begun very quickly. Was it the first time you saw him—that night at your aunt's party?'

'I don't know, father,' the girl answered. 'I can't tell you about that.'

'Of course; that's your own affair. You will have observed that I have acted on that principle. I have not interfered, I have left you your liberty, I have remembered that you are no longer a little girl— that you have arrived at years of discretion.'

'I feel very old—and very wise,' said Catherine, smiling faintly.

'I am afraid that before long you will feel older and wiser yet. I don't like your engagement.'

'Ah!' Catherine exclaimed, softly, getting up from her chair.

'No, my dear. I am sorry to give you pain; but I don't like it. You should have consulted me before you settled it. I have been too easy with you, and I feel as if you had taken advantage of my indulgence. Most decidedly, you should have spoken to me first.'

Catherine hesitated a moment, and then—'It was because I was afraid you wouldn't like it!' she confessed.

'Ah, there it is! You had a bad conscience.'

'No, I have not a bad conscience, father!' the girl cried out, with considerable energy. 'Please don't accuse me of anything so dreadful.' These words, in fact, represented to her imagination something very terrible indeed, something base and cruel, which she associated with malefactors and prisoners. 'It was because I was afraid—afraid—' she went on.

'If you were afraid, it was because you had been foolish!'

'I was afraid you didn't like Mr Townsend.'

'You were quite right. I don't like him.'

'Dear father, you don't know him,' said Catherine, in a voice so timidly argumentative that it might have touched him.

'Very true; I don't know him intimately. But I know him enough. I have my impression of him. You don't know him either.'

She stood before the fire, with her hands lightly clasped in front of her; and her father, leaning back in his chair and looking up at her, made this remark with a placidity that might have been irritating.

I doubt, however, whether Catherine was irritated, though she broke into a vehement protest. 'I don't know him?' she cried. 'Why, I know him—better than I have ever known any one!'

'You know a part of him—what he has chosen to show you. But you don't know the rest.'

'The rest? What is the rest?'

'Whatever it may be. There is sure to be plenty of it.'

'I know what you mean,' said Catherine, remembering how Morris had forewarned her. 'You mean that he is mercenary.'

Her father looked up at her still, with his cold, quiet, reasonable eye. 'If I meant it, my dear, I should say it! But there is an error I wish particularly to avoid—that of rendering Mr Townsend more interesting to you by saying hard things about him.'

'I won't think them hard, if they are true,' said Catherine.

'If you don't, you will be a remarkably sensible young woman!'

'They will be your reasons, at any rate, and you will want me to hear your reasons.'

The Doctor smiled a little. 'Very true. You have a perfect right to ask for them.' And he puffed his cigar a few moments. 'Very well, then, without accusing Mr Townsend of being in love only with your fortune—and with the fortune that you justly expect—I will say that there is every reason to suppose that these good things have entered into his calculation more largely than a tender solicitude for your happiness strictly requires. There is, of course, nothing impossible in an intelligent young man entertaining a disinterested affection for you. You are an honest, amiable girl, and an intelligent young man might easily find it out. But the principal thing that we know about this young man—who is, indeed, very intelligent—leads us to suppose that, however much he may value your personal merits, he values your money more. The principal thing we know about him is that he has led a life of dissipation, and has spent a fortune of his own in doing so. That is enough for me, my dear. I wish you to marry a young man with other antecedents—a young man who could give positive guarantees. If Morris Townsend has spent his own fortune in amusing himself, there is every reason to believe that he would spend yours.'

The Doctor delivered himself of these remarks slowly, deliberately, with occasional pauses and prolongations of accent, which made no great allowance for poor Catherine's suspense as to his conclusion. She sat down at last, with her head bent and her eyes still fixed upon him; and strangely enough—I hardly know how to tell it—even while she felt that what he said went so terribly against her, she admired his neatness and nobleness of expression. There was something hopeless and oppressive in having to argue with her father; but she too, on her side, must try to be clear. He was so quiet; he was not at all angry; and she, too, must be quiet. But her very effort to be quiet made her tremble.

'That is not the principal thing we know about him,' she said; and there was a touch of her tremor in her voice. 'There are other things— many other things. He has very high abilities—he wants so much to do something. He is kind, and generous, and true,' said poor Catherine, who had not suspected hitherto the resources of her eloquence. 'And his fortune—his fortune that he spent—was very small!'

'All the more reason he shouldn't have spent it,' cried the Doctor, getting up with a laugh. Then as Catherine, who had also risen to her feet again, stood there in her rather angular earnestness, wishing so much and expressing so little, he drew her towards him and kissed her. 'You won't think me cruel?' he said, holding her a moment.

This question was not reassuring; it seemed to Catherine, on the contrary, to suggest possibilities which made her feel sick. But she answered coherently enough—'No, dear father; because if you knew

how I feel—and you must know, you know everything—you would be
so kind, so gentle.'

'Yes, I think I know how you feel,' the Doctor said. 'I will be very
kind—be sure of that. And I will see Mr Townsend to-morrow.
Meanwhile, and for the present, be so good as to mention to no one
that you are engaged.'

XII

ON the morrow, in the afternoon, he stayed at home, awaiting Mr Townsend's call—a proceeding by which it appeared to him (justly perhaps, for he was a very busy man) that he paid Catherine's suitor great honour, and gave both these young people so much the less to complain of. Morris presented himself with a countenance sufficiently serene—he appeared to have forgotten the 'insult' for which he had solicited Catherine's sympathy two evenings before, and Dr Sloper lost no time in letting him know that he had been prepared for his visit.

'Catherine told me yesterday what has been going on between you,' he said. 'You must allow me to say that it would have been becoming of you to give me notice of your intentions before they had gone so far.'

'I should have done so,' Morris answered, 'if you had not had so much the appearance of leaving your daughter at liberty. She seems to me quite her own mistress.'

'Literally, she is. But she has not emancipated herself morally quite so far, I trust, as to choose a husband without consulting me. I have left her at liberty, but I have not been in the least indifferent. The truth is that your little affair has come to a head with a rapidity that surprises me. It was only the other day that Catherine made your acquaintance.'

'It was not long ago, certainly,' said Morris, with great gravity. 'I admit that we have not been slow to—to arrive at an understanding. But that was very natural, from the moment we were sure of ourselves—and of each other. My interest in Miss Sloper began the first time I saw her.'

'Did it not by chance precede your first meeting?' the Doctor asked.

Morris looked at him an instant. 'I certainly had already heard that she was a charming girl.'

'A charming girl—that's what you think her?'

'Assuredly. Otherwise I should not be sitting here.'

The Doctor meditated a moment. 'My dear young man,' he said at last, 'you must be very susceptible. As Catherine's father, I have,

I trust, a just and tender appreciation of her many good qualities; but I don't mind telling you that I have never thought of her as a charming girl, and never expected any one else to do so.'

Morris Townsend received this statement with a smile that was not wholly devoid of deference. 'I don't know what I might think of her if I were her father. I can't put myself in that place. I speak from my own point of view.'

'You speak very well,' said the Doctor; 'but that is not all that is necessary. I told Catherine yesterday that I disapproved of her engagement.'

'She let me know as much, and I was very sorry to hear it. I am greatly disappointed.' And Morris sat in silence awhile, looking at the floor.

'Did you really expect I would say I was delighted, and throw my daughter into your arms?'

'Oh, no; I had an idea you didn't like me.'

'What gave you the idea?'

'The fact that I am poor.'

'That has a harsh sound,' said the Doctor, 'but it is about the truth—speaking of you strictly as a son-in-law. Your absence of means, of a profession, of visible resources or prospects, places you in a category from which it would be imprudent for me to select a husband for my daughter, who is a weak young woman with a large fortune. In any other capacity I am perfectly prepared to like you. As a son-in-law, I abominate you!'

Morris Townsend listened respectfully. 'I don't think Miss Sloper is a weak woman,' he presently said.

'Of course you must defend her—it's the least you can do. But I have known my child twenty years, and you have known her six weeks. Even if she were not weak, however, you would still be a penniless man.'

'Ah, yes; that is *my* weakness! And therefore, you mean, I am mercenary—I only want your daughter's money.'

'I don't say that. I am not obliged to say it; and to say it, save under stress of compulsion, would be very bad taste. I say simply that you belong to the wrong category.'

'But your daughter doesn't marry a category,' Townsend urged, with his handsome smile. 'She marries an individual—an individual whom she is so good as to say she loves.'

'An individual who offers so little in return!'

'Is it possible to offer more than the most tender affection and a lifelong devotion?' the young man demanded.

'It depends how we take it. It is possible to offer a few other things besides, and not only is it possible, but it's usual. A lifelong devotion is measured after the fact; and meanwhile it is customary in these cases to give a few material securities. What are yours? A very handsome face and figure, and a very good manner. They are excellent as far as they go, but they don't go far enough.'

'There is one thing you should add to them,' said Morris; 'the word of a gentleman!'

'The word of a gentleman that you will always love Catherine? You must be a very fine gentleman to be sure of that.'

'The word of a gentleman that I am not mercenary; that my affection for Miss Sloper is as pure and disinterested a sentiment as was ever lodged in a human breast! I care no more for her fortune than for the ashes in that grate.'

'I take note—I take note,' said the Doctor. 'But having done so, I turn to our category again. Even with that solemn vow on your lips, you take your place in it. There is nothing against you but an accident, if you will; but with my thirty years' medical practice, I have seen that accidents may have far-reaching consequences.'

Morris smoothed his hat—it was already remarkably glossy—and continued to display a self-control which, as the Doctor was obliged to admit, was extremely creditable to him. But his disappointment was evidently keen.

'Is there nothing I can do to make you believe in me?'

'If there were I should be sorry to suggest it, for—don't you see?—I don't want to believe in you!' said the Doctor, smiling.

'I would go and dig in the fields.'

'That would be foolish.'

'I will take the first work that offers, to-morrow.'

'Do so by all means—but for your own sake, not for mine.'

'I see; you think I am an idler!' Morris exclaimed, a little too much in the tone of a man who has made a discovery. But he saw his error immediately and blushed.

'It doesn't matter what I think, when once I have told you I don't think of you as a son-in-law.'

But Morris persisted. 'You think I would squander her money.'

The Doctor smiled. 'It doesn't matter, as I say; but I plead guilty to that.'

'That's because I spent my own, I suppose,' said Morris. 'I frankly confess that. I have been wild. I have been foolish. I will tell you every crazy thing I ever did, if you like. There were some great follies among the number—I have never concealed that. But I have sown my wild oats. Isn't there some proverb about a reformed rake?* I was not a rake, but I assure you I have reformed. It is better to have amused oneself for a while and have done with it. Your daughter would never care for a milksop; and I will take the liberty of saying that you would like one quite as little. Besides, between my money and hers there is a great difference. I spent my own; it was because it was my own that I spent it. And I made no debts; when it was gone I stopped. I don't owe a penny in the world.'

'Allow me to inquire what you are living on now—though I admit,' the Doctor added, 'that the question, on my part, is inconsistent.'

'I am living on the remnants of my property,' said Morris Townsend.

'Thank you!' the Doctor gravely replied.

Yes, certainly, Morris's self-control was laudable. 'Even admitting I attach an undue importance to Miss Sloper's fortune,' he went on, 'would not that be in itself an assurance that I should take good care of it?'

'That you should take too much care would be quite as bad as that you should take too little. Catherine might suffer as much by your economy as by your extravagance.'

'I think you are very unjust!' The young man made this declaration decently, civilly, without violence.

'It is your privilege to think so, and I surrender my reputation to you! I certainly don't flatter myself I gratify you.'

'Don't you care a little to gratify your daughter? Do you enjoy the idea of making her miserable?'

'I am perfectly resigned to her thinking me a tyrant for a twelvemonth.'

'For a twelvemonth!' exclaimed Morris, with a laugh.

'For a lifetime, then! She may as well be miserable in that way as in the other.'

Here at last Morris lost his temper. 'Ah, you are not polite, sir!' he cried.

'You push me to it—you argue too much.'

'I have a great deal at stake.'

'Well, whatever it is,' said the Doctor, 'you have lost it!'

'Are you sure of that?' asked Morris; 'are you sure your daughter will give me up?'

'I mean, of course, you have lost it as far as I am concerned. As for Catherine's giving you up—no, I am not sure of it. But as I shall strongly recommend it, as I have a great fund of respect and affection in my daughter's mind to draw upon, and as she has the sentiment of duty developed in a very high degree, I think it extremely possible.'

Morris Townsend began to smooth his hat again. 'I too, have a fund of affection to draw upon!' he observed at last.

The Doctor at this point showed his own first symptoms of irritation. 'Do you mean to defy me?'

'Call it what you please, sir! I mean not to give your daughter up.'

The Doctor shook his head. 'I haven't the least fear of your pining away your life. You are made to enjoy it.'

Morris gave a laugh. 'Your opposition to my marriage is all the more cruel, then! Do you intend to forbid your daughter to see me again?'

'She is past the age at which people are forbidden, and I am not a father in an old-fashioned novel. But I shall strongly urge her to break with you.'

'I don't think she will,' said Morris Townsend.

'Perhaps not. But I shall have done what I could.'

'She has gone too far,' Morris went on.

'To retreat? Then let her stop where she is.'

'Too far to stop, I mean.'

The Doctor looked at him a moment; Morris had his hand on the door. 'There is a great deal of impertinence in your saying it.'

'I will say no more, sir!' Morris answered; and, making his bow, he left the room.

XIII

IT may be thought the Doctor was too positive, and Mrs Almond intimated as much. But as he said, he had his impression; it seemed to him sufficient, and he had no wish to modify it. He had passed his life in estimating people (it was part of the medical trade), and in nineteen cases out of twenty he was right.

'Perhaps Mr Townsend is the twentieth case,' Mrs Almond suggested.

'Perhaps he is, though he doesn't look to me at all like a twentieth case. But I will give him the benefit of the doubt, and, to make sure, I will go and talk with Mrs Montgomery. She will almost certainly tell me I have done right; but it is just possible that she will prove to me that I have made the greatest mistake of my life. If she does, I will beg Mr Townsend's pardon. You needn't invite her to meet me, as you kindly proposed; I will write her a frank letter, telling her how matters stand, and asking leave to come and see her.'

'I am afraid the frankness will be chiefly on your side. The poor little woman will stand up for her brother, whatever he may be.'

'Whatever he may be? I doubt that. People are not always so fond of their brothers.'

'Ah,' said Mrs Almond, 'when it's a question of thirty thousand a year coming into a family—'

'If she stands up for him on account of the money, she will be a humbug. If she is a humbug I shall see it. If I see it, I won't waste time with her.'

'She is not a humbug—she is an exemplary woman. She will not wish to play her brother a trick simply because he is selfish.'

'If she is worth talking to, she will sooner play him a trick than that he should play Catherine one. Has she seen Catherine, by the way— does she know her?'

'Not to my knowledge. Mr Townsend can have had no particular interest in bringing them together.'

'If she is an exemplary woman, no. But we shall see to what extent she answers your description.'

'I shall be curious to hear her description of you!' said Mrs Almond, with a laugh. 'And, meanwhile, how is Catherine taking it?'

'As she takes everything—as a matter of course.'

'Doesn't she make a noise? Hasn't she made a scene?'*

'She is not scenic.'

'I thought a love-lorn maiden was always scenic.'

'A fantastic widow is more so. Lavinia has made me a speech: she thinks me very arbitrary.'*

'She has a talent for being in the wrong,' said Mrs Almond. 'But I am very sorry for Catherine, all the same.'

'So am I. But she will get over it.'

'You believe she will give him up?'

'I count upon it. She has such an admiration for her father.'

'Oh, we know all about that! But it only makes me pity her the more. It makes her dilemma the more painful, and the effort of choosing between you and her lover almost impossible.'

'If she can't choose, all the better.'

'Yes, but he will stand there entreating her to choose, and Lavinia will pull on that side.'

'I am glad she is not on my side; she is capable of ruining an excellent cause. The day Lavinia gets into your boat it capsizes. But she had better be careful,' said the Doctor. 'I will have no treason in my house!'

'I suspect she will be careful; for she is at bottom very much afraid of you.'

'They are both afraid of me—harmless as I am!' the Doctor answered. 'And it is on that that I build—on the salutary terror I inspire!'

XIV

HE wrote his frank letter to Mrs Montgomery, who punctually answered it, mentioning an hour at which he might present himself in the Second Avenue. She lived in a neat little house of red brick, which had been freshly painted, with the edges of the bricks very sharply marked out in white. It has now disappeared, with its companions, to make room for a row of structures more majestic. There were green shutters upon the windows, without slats, but pierced with little holes, arranged in groups; and before the house was a diminutive yard, ornamented with a bush of mysterious character, and surrounded by a low wooden paling, painted in the same green as the shutters. The place looked like a magnified babyhouse, and might have been taken down from a shelf in a toy-shop. Dr Sloper, when he went to call, said to himself, as he glanced at the objects I have enumerated, that Mrs Montgomery was evidently a thrifty and self-respecting little person—the modest proportions of her dwelling seemed to indicate that she was of small stature—who took a virtuous satisfaction in keeping herself tidy, and had resolved that, since she might not be splendid, she would at least be immaculate. She received him in a little parlour, which was precisely the parlour he had expected: a small unspeckled bower, ornamented with a desultory foliage of tissue-paper, and with clusters of glass drops, amid which—to carry out the analogy—the temperature of the leafy season was maintained by means of a cast-iron stove, emitting a dry blue flame, and smelling strongly of varnish. The walls were embellished with engravings swathed in pink gauze, and the tables ornamented with volumes of extracts from the poets, usually bound in black cloth stamped with florid designs in jaundiced gilt. The Doctor had time to take cognizance of these details; for Mrs Montgomery, whose conduct he pronounced under the circumstances inexcusable, kept him waiting some ten minutes before she appeared. At last, however, she rustled in, smoothing down a stiff poplin* dress, with a little frightened flush in a gracefully rounded cheek.

She was a small, plump, fair woman, with a bright, clear eye, and an extraordinary air of neatness and briskness. But these qualities were evidently combined with an unaffected humility, and the Doctor gave her his esteem as soon as he had looked at her. A brave little person, with lively perceptions, and yet a disbelief in her own talent for social, as distinguished from practical, affairs—this was his rapid mental *résumé* of Mrs Montgomery, who, as he saw, was flattered by what she regarded as the honour of his visit. Mrs Montgomery, in her little red house in the Second Avenue, was a person for whom Dr Sloper was one of the great men, one of the fine gentlemen of New York; and while she fixed her agitated eyes upon him, while she clasped her mittened hands together in her glossy poplin lap, she had the appearance of saying to herself that he quite answered her idea of what a distinguished guest would naturally be. She apologized for being late; but he interrupted her.

'It doesn't matter,' he said; 'for while I sat here I had time to think over what I wish to say to you, and to make up my mind how to begin.'

'Oh, do begin!' murmured Mrs Montgomery.

'It is not so easy,' said the Doctor, smiling. 'You will have gathered from my letter that I wish to ask you a few questions, and you may not find it very comfortable to answer them.'

'Yes; I have thought what I should say. It is not very easy.'

'But you must understand my situation—my state of mind. Your brother wishes to marry my daughter, and I wish to find out what sort of a young man he is. A good way to do so seemed to be to come and ask you; which I have proceeded to do.'

Mrs Montgomery evidently took the situation very seriously; she was in a state of extreme moral concentration. She kept her pretty eyes, which were illumined by a sort of brilliant modesty, attached to his own countenance, and evidently paid the most earnest attention to each of his words. Her expression indicated that she thought his idea of coming to see her a very superior conception, but that she was really afraid to have opinions on strange subjects.

'I am extremely glad to see you,' she said, in a tone which seemed to admit, at the same time, that this had nothing to do with the question.

The doctor took advantage of this admission. 'I didn't come to see you for your pleasure; I came to make you say disagreeable things— and you can't like that. What sort of a gentleman is your brother?'

Mrs Montgomery's illuminated gaze grew vague, and began to wander. She smiled a little, and for some time made no answer, so that the Doctor at last became impatient. And her answer, when it came, was not satisfactory. 'It is difficult to talk about one's brother.'

'Not when one is fond of him, and when one has plenty of good to say.'

'Yes, even then, when a good deal depends on it,' said Mrs Montgomery.

'Nothing depends on it, for you.'

'I mean for—for—' and she hesitated.

'For your brother himself. I see!'

'I mean for Miss Sloper,' said Mrs Montgomery.

The Doctor liked this; it had the accent of sincerity. 'Exactly; that's the point. If my poor girl should marry your brother, everything—as regards her happiness—would depend on his being a good fellow. She is the best creature in the world, and she could never do him a grain of injury. He, on the other hand, if he should not be all that we desire, might make her very miserable. That is why I want you to throw some light upon his character, you know. Of course, you are not bound to do it. My daughter, whom you have never seen, is nothing to you; and I, possibly, am only an indiscreet and impertinent old man. It is perfectly open to you to tell me that my visit is in very bad taste and that I had better go about my business. But I don't think you will do this; because I think we shall interest you, my poor girl and I. I am sure that if you were to see Catherine, she would interest you very much. I don't mean because she is interesting in the usual sense of the word, but because you would feel sorry for her. She is so soft, so simple-minded, she would be such an easy victim! A bad husband would have remarkable facilities for making her miserable; for she would have neither the intelligence nor the resolution to get the better of him, and yet she would have an exaggerated power of suffering. I see,' added the Doctor, with his most insinuating, his most professional laugh, 'you are already interested!'

'I have been interested from the moment he told me he was engaged,' said Mrs Montgomery.

'Ah! he says that—he calls it an engagement?'

'Oh, he has told me you didn't like it.'

'Did he tell you that I don't like *him*?'

'Yes, he told me that too. I said I couldn't help it!' added Mrs Montgomery.

'Of course you can't. But what you can do is to tell me I am right—to give me an attestation, as it were.' And the Doctor accompanied this remark with another professional smile.

Mrs Montgomery, however, smiled not at all; it was obvious that she could not take the humorous view of his appeal. 'That is a good deal to ask,' she said at last.

'There can be no doubt of that; and I must, in conscience, remind you of the advantages a young man marrying my daughter would enjoy. She has an income of ten thousand dollars in her own right, left her by her mother; if she marries a husband I approve, she will come into almost twice as much more at my death.'

Mrs Montgomery listened in great earnestness to this splendid financial statement; she had never heard thousands of dollars so familiarly talked about. She flushed a little with excitement. 'Your daughter will be immensely rich,' she said softly.

'Precisely—that's the bother of it.'

'And if Morris should marry her, he—he—' And she hesitated timidly.

'He would be master of all that money? By no means. He would be master of the ten thousand a year that she has from her mother; but I should leave every penny of my own fortune, earned in the laborious exercise of my profession, to public institutions.'

Mrs Montgomery dropped her eyes at this, and sat for some time gazing at the straw matting which covered her floor.

'I suppose it seems to you,' said the Doctor, laughing, 'that in so doing I should play your brother a very shabby trick.'

'Not at all. That is too much money to get possession of so easily, by marrying. I don't think it would be right.'

'It's right to get all one can. But in this case your brother wouldn't be able. If Catherine marries without my consent, she doesn't get a penny from my own pocket.'

'Is that certain?' asked Mrs Montgomery, looking up.

'As certain as that I sit here!'

'Even if she should pine away?'

'Even if she should pine to a shadow, which isn't probable.'

'Does Morris know this?'

'I shall be most happy to inform him!' the Doctor exclaimed.

Mrs Montgomery resumed her meditations, and her visitor, who was prepared to give time to the affair, asked himself whether, in spite of her little conscientious air, she was not playing into her brother's hands. At the same time he was half ashamed of the ordeal to which he had subjected her, and was touched by the gentleness with which she bore it. 'If she were a humbug,' he said, 'she would get angry; unless she be very deep indeed. It is not probable that she is as deep as that.'

'What makes you dislike Morris so much?' she presently asked, emerging from her reflections.

'I don't dislike him in the least as a friend, as a companion. He seems to me a charming fellow, and I should think he would be excellent company. I dislike him, exclusively, as a son-in-law. If the only office of a son-in-law were to dine at the paternal table, I should set a high value upon your brother. He dines capitally. But that is a small part of his function, which, in general, is to be a protector, and caretaker of my child, who is singularly ill-adapted to take care of herself. It is there that he doesn't satisfy me. I confess I have nothing but my impression to go by; but I am in the habit of trusting my impression. Of course you are at liberty to contradict it flat. He strikes me as selfish and shallow.'

Mrs Montgomery's eyes expanded a little, and the Doctor fancied he saw the light of admiration in them. 'I wonder you have discovered he is selfish!' she exclaimed.

'Do you think he hides it so well?'

'Very well indeed,' said Mrs Montgomery. 'And I think we are all rather selfish,' she added quickly.

'I think so too; but I have seen people hide it better than he. You see I am helped by a habit I have of dividing people into classes, into types. I may easily be mistaken about your brother as an individual, but his type is written on his whole person.'

'He is very good-looking,' said Mrs Montgomery.

The Doctor eyed her a moment. 'You women are all the same! But the type to which your brother belongs was made to be the ruin of you, and you were made to be its handmaids and victims. The sign of the type in question is the determination—sometimes terrible in its quiet intensity—to accept nothing of life but its pleasures, and to secure these pleasures chiefly by the aid of your complaisant sex. Young men of this class never do anything for themselves that they can get other people to do for them, and it is the infatuation, the devotion, the superstition of others, that keeps them going. These others in ninety-nine cases out of a hundred are women. What our young friends chiefly insist upon is that some one else shall suffer for them; and women do that sort of thing, as you must know, wonderfully well.' The Doctor paused a moment, and then he added abruptly, 'You have suffered immensely for your brother!'

This exclamation was abrupt, as I say, but it was also perfectly calculated. The Doctor had been rather disappointed at not finding his compact and comfortable little hostess surrounded in a more visible degree by the ravages of Morris Townsend's immorality; but he had said to himself that this was not because the young man had spared her, but because she had contrived to plaster up her wounds. They were aching there, behind the varnished stove, the festooned engravings, beneath her own neat little poplin bosom; and if he could only touch the tender spot, she would make a movement that would betray her. The words I have just quoted were an attempt to put his finger suddenly upon the place; and they had some of the success that he looked for. The tears sprang for a moment to Mrs Montgomery's eyes, and she indulged in a proud little jerk of the head.

'I don't know how you have found that out!' she exclaimed.

'By a philosophic trick—by what they call induction. You know you have always your option of contradicting me. But kindly answer me a question. Don't you give your brother money? I think you ought to answer that.'

'Yes, I have given him money,' said Mrs Montgomery.

'And you have not had much to give him?'

She was silent a moment. 'If you ask me for a confession of poverty, that is easily made. I am very poor.'

'One would never suppose it from your—your charming house,' said the Doctor. 'I learned from my sister that your income was moderate, and your family numerous.'

'I have five children,' Mrs Montgomery observed; 'but I am happy to say I can bring them up decently.'

'Of course you can—accomplished and devoted as you are! But your brother has counted them over, I suppose?'

'Counted them over?'

'He knows there are five, I mean. He tells me it is he that brings them up.'

Mrs Montgomery stared a moment, and then quickly—'Oh, yes; he teaches them—Spanish.'

The Doctor laughed out. 'That must take a great deal off your hands! Your brother also knows, of course, that you have very little money.'

'I have often told him so!' Mrs Montgomery exclaimed, more unreservedly than she had yet spoken. She was apparently taking some comfort in the Doctor's clairvoyance.

'Which means that you have often occasion to, and that he often sponges on you. Excuse the crudity of my language; I simply express a fact. I don't ask you how much of your money he has had, it is none of my business. I have ascertained what I suspected—what I wished.' And the Doctor got up, gently smoothing his hat. 'Your brother lives on you,' he said as he stood there.

Mrs Montgomery quickly rose from her chair, following her visitor's movements with a look of fascination. But then, with a certain inconsequence—'I have never complained of him!' she said.

'You needn't protest—you have not betrayed him. But I advise you not to give him any more money.'

'Don't you see it is in my interest that he should marry a rich person?' she asked. 'If, as you say, he lives on me, I can only wish to get rid of him, and to put obstacles in the way of his marrying is to increase my own difficulties.'

'I wish very much you would come to me with your difficulties,' said the Doctor. 'Certainly, if I throw him back on your hands, the least I can do is to help you to bear the burden. If you will allow me to say so, then, I shall take the liberty of placing in your hands, for the present, a certain fund for your brother's support.'

Mrs Montgomery stared; she evidently thought he was jesting; but she presently saw that he was not, and the complication of her feelings became painful. 'It seems to me that I ought to be very much offended with you,' she murmured.

'Because I have offered you money? That's a superstition,' said the Doctor. 'You must let me come and see you again, and we will talk about these things. I suppose that some of your children are girls.'

'I have two little girls,' said Mrs Montgomery.

'Well, when they grow up, and begin to think of taking husbands, you will see how anxious you will be about the moral character of these gentlemen. Then you will understand this visit of mine!'

'Ah, you are not to believe that Morris's moral character is bad!'

The Doctor looked at her a little, with folded arms. 'There is something I should greatly like—as a moral satisfaction. I should like to hear you say—"He is abominably selfish!"'

The words came out with the grave distinctness of his voice, and they seemed for an instant to create, to poor Mrs Montgomery's troubled vision, a material image. She gazed at it an instant, and then she turned away. 'You distress me, sir!' she exclaimed. 'He is, after all, my brother, and his talents, his talents—' On these last words her voice quavered, and before he knew it she had burst into tears.

'His talents are first-rate!' said the Doctor. 'We must find the proper field for them!' And he assured her most respectfully of his regret at having so greatly discomposed her. 'It's all for my poor Catherine,' he went on. 'You must know her, and you will see.'

Mrs Montgomery brushed away her tears and blushed at having shed them. 'I should like to know your daughter,' she answered; and then, in an instant—'Don't let her marry him!'

Dr Sloper went away with the words gently humming in his ears— 'Don't let her marry him!' They gave him the moral satisfaction of which he had just spoken, and their value was the greater that they had evidently cost a pang to poor little Mrs Montgomery's family pride.

XV

HE had been puzzled by the way that Catherine carried herself; her attitude at this sentimental crisis seemed to him unnaturally passive. She had not spoken to him again after that scene in the library, the day before his interview with Morris; and a week had elapsed without making any change in her manner. There was nothing in it that appealed for pity, and he was even a little disappointed at her not giving him an opportunity to make up for his harshness by some manifestation of liberality which should operate as a compensation. He thought a little of offering to take her for a tour in Europe; but he was determined to do this only in case she should seem mutely to reproach him. He had an idea that she would display a talent for mute reproaches, and he was surprised at not finding himself exposed to these silent batteries. She said nothing, either tacitly, or explicitly, and as she was never very talkative, there was now no especial eloquence in her reserve. And poor Catherine was not sulky—a style of behaviour for which she had too little histrionic talent; she was simply very patient. Of course she was thinking over her situation, and she was apparently doing so in a deliberate and unimpassioned manner, with a view of making the best of it.

'She will do as I have bidden her,' said the Doctor, and he made the further reflection that his daughter was not a woman of a great spirit. I know not whether he had hoped for a little more resistance for the sake of a little more entertainment; but he said to himself, as he had said before, that though it might have its momentary alarms, paternity was, after all, not an exciting vocation.

Catherine meanwhile had made a discovery of a very different sort; it had become vivid to her that there was a great excitement in trying to be a good daughter. She had an entirely new feeling, which may be described as a state of expectant suspense about her own actions. She watched herself as she would have watched another person, and wondered what she would do. It was as if this other person, who was both herself and not herself, had suddenly sprung into being, inspiring her with a natural curiosity as to the performance of untested functions.

'I am glad I have such a good daughter,' said her father, kissing her, after the lapse of several days.

'I am trying to be good,' she answered, turning away, with a conscience not altogether clear.

'If there is anything you would like to say to me, you know you must not hesitate. You needn't feel obliged to be so quiet. I shouldn't care that Mr Townsend should be a frequent topic of conversation, but whenever you have anything particular to say about him I shall be very glad to hear it.'

'Thank you,' said Catherine; 'I have nothing particular at present.'

He never asked her whether she had seen Morris again, because he was sure that if this had been the case she would tell him. She had in fact not seen him, she had only written him a long letter. The letter at least was long for her; and, it may be added, that it was long for Morris; it consisted of five pages, in a remarkably neat and handsome hand. Catherine's handwriting was beautiful, and she was even a little proud of it; she was extremely fond of copying, and possessed volumes of extracts which testified to this accomplishment; volumes which she had exhibited one day to her lover, when the bliss of feeling that she was important in his eyes was exceptionally keen. She told Morris in writing that her father had expressed the wish that she should not see him again, and that she begged he would not come to the house until she should have 'made up her mind'. Morris replied with a passionate epistle, in which he asked to what, in Heaven's name, she wished to make up her mind. Had not her mind been made up two weeks before, and could it be possible that she entertained the idea of throwing him off? Did she mean to break down at the very beginning of their ordeal, after all the promises of fidelity she had both given and extracted? And he gave an account of his own interview with her father—an account not identical at all points with that offered in these pages. 'He was terribly violent,' Morris wrote; 'but you know my self-control. I have need of it all when I remember that I have it in my power to break in upon your cruel captivity.' Catherine sent him in answer to this, a note of three lines. 'I am in great trouble; do not doubt of my affection, but let me wait a little and think.' The idea of a struggle with her father, of setting up her will against his own, was heavy on her soul, and it kept her formally submissive, as a great physical weight keeps us motionless. It never entered into her mind to throw her lover off; but from the first she tried to assure herself that there would be a peaceful way out of their difficulty.

The assurance was vague, for it contained no element of positive conviction that her father would change his mind. She only had an idea that if she should be very good, the situation would in some mysterious manner improve. To be good, she must be patient, respectful, abstain from judging her father too harshly, and from committing any act of open defiance. He was perhaps right, after all, to think as he did; by which Catherine meant not in the least that his judgment of Morris's motives in seeking to marry her was perhaps a just one, but that it was probably natural and proper that conscientious parents should be suspicious and even unjust. There were probably people in the world as bad as her father supposed Morris to be, and if there were the slightest chance of Morris being one of these sinister persons, the Doctor was right in taking it into account. Of course he could not know what she knew, how the purest love and truth were seated in the young man's eyes; but Heaven, in its time, might appoint a way of bringing him to such knowledge. Catherine expected a good deal of Heaven, and referred to the skies the initiative, as the French say,* in dealing with her dilemma. She could not imagine herself imparting any kind of knowledge to her father, there was something superior even in his injustice and absolute in his mistakes. But she could at least be good, and if she were only good enough, Heaven would invent some way of reconciling all things—the dignity of her father's errors and the sweetness of her own confidence, the strict performance of her filial duties and the enjoyment of Morris Townsend's affection. Poor Catherine would have been glad to regard Mrs Penniman as an illuminating agent, a part which this lady herself indeed was but imperfectly prepared to play. Mrs Penniman took too much satisfaction in the sentimental shadows of this little drama to have, for the moment, any great interest in dissipating them. She wished the plot to thicken, and the advice that she gave her niece tended, in her own imagination, to produce this result. It was rather incoherent counsel, and from one day to another it contradicted itself; but it was pervaded by an earnest desire that Catherine should do something striking. 'You must *act*, my dear; in your situation the great thing is to act,' said Mrs Penniman, who found her niece altogether beneath her opportunities. Mrs Penniman's real hope was that the girl would make a secret marriage, at which she should officiate as brideswoman or duenna.* She had a vision of this ceremony being performed in some subterranean chapel—subterranean chapels in

New York were not frequent, but Mrs Penniman's imagination was not chilled by trifles—and of the guilty couple—she liked to think of poor Catherine and her suitor as the guilty couple—being shuffled away in a fastwhirling vehicle to some obscure lodging in the suburbs, where she would pay them (in a thick veil) clandestine visits, where they would endure a period of romantic privation, and where ultimately, after she should have been their earthly providence, their intercessor, their advocate, and their medium of communication with the world, they should be reconciled to her brother in an artistic tableau, in which she herself should be somehow the central figure. She hesitated as yet to recommend this course to Catherine, but she attempted to draw an attractive picture of it to Morris Townsend. She was in daily communication with the young man, whom she kept informed by letters of the state of affairs in Washington Square. As he had been banished, as she said, from the house, she no longer saw him; but she ended by writing to him that she longed for an interview. This interview could take place only on neutral ground, and she bethought herself greatly before selecting a place of meeting. She had an inclination for Greenwood Cemetery,* but she gave it up as too distant; she could not absent herself for so long, as she said, without exciting suspicion. Then she thought of the Battery, but that was rather cold and windy, besides one's being exposed to intrusion from the Irish emigrants who at this point alight, with large appetites, in the New World; and at last she fixed upon an oyster saloon in the Seventh Avenue,* kept by a negro—an establishment of which she knew nothing save that she had noticed it in passing. She made an appointment with Morris Townsend to meet him there, and she went to the tryst at dusk, enveloped in an impenetrable veil. He kept her waiting for half-an-hour—he had almost the whole width of the city to traverse—but she liked to wait, it seemed to intensify the situation. She ordered a cup of tea, which proved excessively bad, and this gave her a sense that she was suffering in a romantic cause. When Morris at last arrived, they sat together for half-an-hour in the duskiest corner of a back shop; and it is hardly too much to say that this was the happiest half-hour that Mrs Penniman had known for years. The situation was really thrilling, and it scarcely seemed to her a false note when her companion asked for an oyster-stew, and proceeded to consume it before her eyes. Morris, indeed, needed all the satisfaction that stewed oysters could give him, for it may be intimated to the reader that he regarded Mrs Penniman in the light of a fifth wheel to his coach. He was in a state of irritation natural to a gentleman of fine parts who had been snubbed in a benevolent attempt to confer a distinction upon a young woman of inferior characteristics, and the insinuating sympathy of this somewhat desiccated matron appeared to offer him no practical relief. He thought her a humbug, and he judged of humbugs with a good deal of confidence. He had listened and made himself agreeable to her at first, in order to get a footing in Washington Square; and at present he needed all his self-command to be decently civil. It would have gratified him to tell her that she was a fantastic old woman, and that he should like to put her into an omnibus and send her home. We know, however, that Morris possessed the virtue of self-control, and he had moreover the constant habit of seeking to be agreeable; so that, although Mrs Penniman's demeanour only exasperated his already unquiet nerves, he listened to her with a sombre deference in which she found much to admire.

XVI

THEY had of course immediately spoken of Catherine. 'Did she send me a message, or—or anything?' Morris asked. He appeared to think that she might have sent him a trinket or a lock of her hair.

Mrs Penniman was slightly embarrassed, for she had not told her niece of her intended expedition. 'Not exactly a message,' she said; 'I didn't ask her for one, because I was afraid to—to excite her.'

'I am afraid she is not very excitable!' And Morris gave a smile of some bitterness.

'She is better than that. She is steadfast—she is true!'

'Do you think she will hold fast then?'

'To the death!'

'Oh, I hope it won't come to that,' said Morris.

'We must be prepared for the worst, and that is what I wish to speak to you about.'

'What do you call the worst?'

'Well,' said Mrs Penniman, 'my brother's hard, intellectual nature.'

'Oh, the devil!'

'He is impervious to pity,' Mrs Penniman added, by way of explanation.

'Do you mean that he won't come round?'

'He will never be vanquished by argument. I have studied him. He will be vanquished only by the accomplished fact.'

'The accomplished fact?'

'He will come round afterwards,' said Mrs Penniman, with extreme significance. 'He cares for nothing but facts; he must be met by facts!'

'Well,' rejoined Morris, 'it is a fact that I wish to marry his daughter. I met him with that the other day, but he was not at all vanquished.'

Mrs Penniman was silent a little, and her smile beneath the shadow of her capacious bonnet, on the edge of which her black veil was arranged curtain-wise, fixed itself upon Morris's face with a still more tender brilliancy. 'Marry Catherine first, and meet him afterwards!' she exclaimed.

'Do you recommend that?' asked the young man, frowning heavily.

She was a little frightened, but she went on with considerable boldness. 'That is the way I see it: a private marriage—a private marriage.' She repeated the phrase because she liked it.

'Do you mean that I should carry Catherine off? What do they call it—elope with her?'

'It is not a crime when you are driven to it,' said Mrs Penniman. 'My husband, as I have told you, was a distinguished clergyman; one of the most eloquent men of his day. He once married a young couple that had fled from the house of the young lady's father. He was so interested in their story. He had no hesitation, and everything came out beautifully. The father was afterwards reconciled, and thought everything of the young man. Mr Penniman married them in the evening, about seven o'clock. The church was so dark, you could scarcely see; and Mr Penniman was intensely agitated; he was so sympathetic. I don't believe he could have done it again.'

'Unfortunately Catherine and I have not Mr Penniman to marry us,' said Morris.

'No, but you have me!' rejoined Mrs Penniman, expressively. 'I can't perform the ceremony, but I can help you. I can watch.'

'The woman's an idiot,' thought Morris; but he was obliged to say something different. It was not, however, materially more civil. 'Was it in order to tell me this that you requested I would meet you here?'

Mrs Penniman had been conscious of a certain vagueness in her errand, and of not being able to offer him any very tangible reward for his long walk. 'I thought perhaps you would like to see one who is so near to Catherine,' she observed with considerable majesty. 'And also,' she added, 'that you would value an opportunity of sending her something.'

Morris extended his empty hands with a melancholy smile. 'I am greatly obliged to you, but I have nothing to send.'

'Haven't you a *word*?' asked his companion, with her suggestive smile coming back.

Morris frowned again. 'Tell her to hold fast,' he said, rather curtly.

'That is a good word—a noble word. It will make her happy for many days. She is very touching, very brave,' Mrs Penniman went on, arranging her mantle and preparing to depart. While she was so engaged she had an inspiration. She found the phrase that she could boldly offer as a vindication of the step she had taken. 'If you marry Catherine at all risks,' she said, 'you will give my brother a proof of your being what he pretends to doubt.'

'What he pretends to doubt?'

'Don't you know what that is?' Mrs Penniman asked, almost playfully.

'It does not concern me to know,' said Morris, grandly.

'Of course it makes you angry.'

'I despise it,' Morris declared.

'Ah, you know what it is, then?' said Mrs Penniman, shaking her finger at him. 'He pretends that you like—you like the money.'

Morris hesitated a moment; and then, as if he spoke advisedly—'I *do* like the money!'

'Ah, but not—but not as he means it. You don't like it more than Catherine?'

He leaned his elbows on the table and buried his head in his hands, 'You torture me!' he murmured. And, indeed, this was almost the effect of the poor lady's too importunate interest in his situation.

But she insisted on making her point. 'If you marry her in spite of him, he will take for granted that you expect nothing of him, and are prepared to do without it. And so he will see that you are disinterested.'

Morris raised his head a little, following this argument. 'And what shall I gain by that?'

'Why, that he will see that he has been wrong in thinking that you wished to get his money.'

'And seeing that I wish he would go to the deuce with it, he will leave it to a hospital. Is that what you mean?' asked Morris.

'No, I don't mean that; though that would be very grand!' Mrs Penniman quickly added. 'I mean that having done you such an injustice, he will think it his duty, at the end, to make some amends.'

Morris shook his head, though it must be confessed he was a little struck with this idea. 'Do you think he is so sentimental?'

'He is not sentimental,' said Mrs Penniman; 'but, to be perfectly fair to him, I think he has, in his own narrow way, a certain sense of duty.'

There passed through Morris Townsend's mind a rapid wonder as to what he might, even under a remote contingency, be indebted to from the action of this principle in Dr Sloper's breast, and the inquiry exhausted itself in his sense of the ludicrous. 'Your brother has no duties to me,' he said presently, 'and I none to him.'

'Ah, but he has duties to Catherine.'

'Yes, but you see that on that principle Catherine has duties to him as well.'

Mrs Penniman got up, with a melancholy sigh, as if she thought him very unimaginative. 'She has always performed them faithfully; and now do you think she has no duties to *you*?' Mrs Penniman always, even in conversation, italicised her personal pronouns.

'It would sound harsh to say so! I am so grateful for her love,' Morris added.

'I will tell her you said that! And now, remember that if you need me, I am there.' And Mrs Penniman, who could think of nothing more to say, nodded vaguely in the direction of Washington Square.

Morris looked some moments at the sanded floor of the shop; he seemed to be disposed to linger a moment. At last, looking up with a certain abruptness, 'It is your belief that if she marries me he will cut her off?' he asked.

Mrs Penniman stared a little, and smiled. 'Why, I have explained to you what I think would happen—that in the end it would be the best thing to do.'

'You mean that, whatever she does, in the long run she will get the money?'

'It doesn't depend upon her, but upon you. Venture to appear as disinterested as you are!' said Mrs Penniman ingeniously. Morris dropped his eyes on the sanded floor again, pondering this; and she pursued. 'Mr Penniman and I had nothing, and we were very happy. Catherine, moreover, has her mother's fortune, which, at the time my sister-in-law married, was considered a very handsome one.'

'Oh, don't speak of that!' said Morris; and, indeed, it was quite superfluous, for he had contemplated the fact in all its lights.

'Austin married a wife with money—why shouldn't you?'

'Ah! but your brother was a doctor,' Morris objected.

'Well, all young men can't be doctors!'

'I should think it an extremely loathsome profession,' said Morris, with an air of intellectual independence. Then, in a moment, he went on rather inconsequently, 'Do you suppose there is a will already made in Catherine's favour?'

'I suppose so—even doctors must die; and perhaps a little in mine,' Mrs Penniman frankly added.

'And you believe he would certainly change it—as regards Catherine?'

'Yes; and then change it back again.'

'Ah, but one can't depend on that!' said Morris.

'Do you want to *depend* on it?' Mrs Penniman asked.

Morris blushed a little. 'Well, I am certainly afraid of being the cause of an injury to Catherine.'

'Ah! you must not be afraid. Be afraid of nothing, and everything will go well!'

And then Mrs Penniman paid for her cup of tea, and Morris paid for his oyster stew, and they went out together into the dimly-lighted wilderness of the Seventh Avenue. The dusk had closed in completely and the street lamps were separated by wide intervals of a pavement in which cavities and fissures played a disproportionate part. An omnibus, emblazoned with strange pictures, went tumbling over the dislocated cobble-stones.

'How will you go home?' Morris asked, following this vehicle with an interested eye. Mrs Penniman had taken his arm.

She hesitated a moment. 'I think this manner would be pleasant,' she said; and she continued to let him feel the value of his support.

So he walked with her through the devious ways of the west side of the town, and through the bustle of gathering nightfall in populous streets, to the quiet precinct of Washington Square. They lingered a moment at the foot of Dr Sloper's white marble steps, above which a spotless white door, adorned with a glittering silver plate, seemed to figure, for Morris, the closed portal of happiness; and then Mrs Penniman's companion rested a melancholy eye upon a lighted window in the upper part of the house.

'That is my room—my dear little room!' Mrs Penniman remarked.

Morris started. 'Then I needn't come walking round the square to gaze at it.'

'That's as you please. But Catherine's is behind; two noble windows on the second floor. I think you can see them from the other street.'

'I don't want to see them, ma'am!' And Morris turned his back to the house.

'I will tell her you have been *here*, at any rate,' said Mrs Penniman, pointing to the spot where they stood; 'and I will give her your message—that she is to hold fast!'

'Oh, yes! of course. You know I write her all that.'

'It seems to say more when it is spoken! And remember, if you need me, that I am *there*;' and Mrs Penniman glanced at the third floor.

On this they separated, and Morris, left to himself, stood looking at the house a moment; after which he turned away, and took a gloomy walk round the Square, on the opposite side, close to the wooden fence. Then he came back, and paused for a minute in front of Dr Sloper's dwelling. His eyes travelled over it; they even rested on the ruddy windows of Mrs Penniman's apartment. He thought it a devilish comfortable house.

XVII

Mrs Penniman told Catherine that evening—the two ladies were sitting in the back parlour—that she had had an interview with Morris Townsend; and on receiving this news the girl started with a sense of pain. She felt angry for the moment; it was almost the first time she had ever felt angry. It seemed to her that her aunt was meddlesome; and from this came a vague apprehension that she would spoil something.

'I don't see why you should have seen him. I don't think it was right,' Catherine said.

'I was so sorry for him—it seemed to me some one ought to see him.'

'No one but I,' said Catherine, who felt as if she were making the most presumptuous speech of her life, and yet at the same time had an instinct that she was right in doing so.

'But you wouldn't, my dear,' Aunt Lavinia rejoined; 'and I didn't know what might have become of him.'

'I have not seen him, because my father has forbidden it,' Catherine said, very simply.

There was a simplicity in this, indeed, which fairly vexed Mrs Penniman. 'If your father forbade you to go to sleep, I suppose you would keep awake!' she commented.

Catherine looked at her. 'I don't understand you. You seem to be very strange.'

'Well, my dear, you will understand me some day!' And Mrs Penniman, who was reading the evening paper, which she perused daily from the first line to the last, resumed her occupation. She wrapped herself in silence; she was determined.

Catherine should ask her for an account of her interview with Morris. But Catherine was silent for so long, that she almost lost patience; and she was on the point of remarking to her that she was very heartless, when the girl at last spoke.

'What did he say?' she asked.

'He said he is ready to marry you any day, in spite of everything.'

Catherine made no answer to this, and Mrs Penniman almost lost patience again; owing to which she at last volunteered the information that Morris looked very handsome, but terribly haggard.

'Did he seem sad?' asked her niece.

'He was dark under the eyes,' said Mrs Penniman. 'So different from when I first saw him; though I am not sure that if I had seen him in this condition the first time, I should not have been even more struck with him. There is something brilliant in his very misery.'

This was, to Catherine's sense, a vivid picture, and though she disapproved, she felt herself gazing at it. 'Where did you see him?' she asked presently.

'In—in the Bowery;* at a confectioner's,' said Mrs Penniman, who had a general idea that she ought to dissemble a little.

'Whereabouts is the place?' Catherine inquired, after another pause.

'Do you wish to go there, my dear?' said her aunt.

'Oh, no!' And Catherine got up from her seat and went to the fire, where she stood looking awhile at the glowing coals.

'Why are you so dry, Catherine?' Mrs Penniman said at last.

'So dry?'

'So cold—so irresponsive.'

The girl turned, very quickly. 'Did *he* say that?'

Mrs Penniman hesitated a moment. 'I will tell you what he said. He said he feared only one thing—that you would be afraid.'

'Afraid of what?'

'Afraid of your father.'

Catherine turned back to the fire again, and then, after a pause, she said—'I *am* afraid of my father.'

Mrs Penniman got quickly up from her chair and approached her niece. 'Do you mean to give him up, then?'

Catherine for some time never moved; she kept her eyes on the coals. At last she raised her head and looked at her aunt.

'Why do you push me so?' she asked.

'I don't push you. When have I spoken to you before?'

'It seems to me that you have spoken to me several times.'

'I am afraid it is necessary, then, Catherine,' said Mrs Penniman, with a good deal of solemnity. 'I am afraid you don't feel the importance—' She paused a little; Catherine was looking at her. 'The importance of not disappointing that gallant young heart!' And Mrs Penniman went back to her chair, by the lamp, and, with a little jerk, picked up the evening paper again.

Catherine stood there before the fire, with her hands behind her, looking at her aunt, to whom it seemed that the girl had never had just this dark fixedness in her gaze. 'I don't think you understand—or that you know me,' she said.

'If I don't, it is not wonderful; you trust me so little.'

Catherine made no attempt to deny this charge, and for sometime more nothing was said. But Mrs Penniman's imagination was restless, and the evening paper failed on this occasion to enchain it.

'If you succumb to the dread of your father's wrath,' she said, 'I don't know what will become of us.'

'Did *he* tell you to say these things to me?'

'He told me to use my influence.'

'You must be mistaken,' said Catherine. 'He trusts me.'

'I hope he may never repent of it!' And Mrs Penniman gave a little sharp slap to her newspaper. She knew not what to make of her niece, who had suddenly become stern and contradictious.

This tendency on Catherine's part was presently even more apparent. 'You had much better not make any more appointments with Mr Townsend,' she said. 'I don't think it is right.'

Mrs Penniman rose with considerable majesty. 'My poor child, are you jealous of me?' she inquired.

'Oh, Aunt Lavinia!' murmured Catherine blushing.

'I don't think it is your place to teach me what is right.'

On this point Catherine made no concession. 'It can't be right to deceive.'

'I certainly have not deceived *you*!'

'Yes; but I promised my father—'

'I have no doubt you promised your father. But I have promised him nothing!'

Catherine had to admit this, and she did so in silence. 'I don't believe Mr Townsend himself likes it,' she said at last.

'Doesn't like meeting me?'

'Not in secret.'

'It was not in secret; the place was full of people.'

'But it was a secret place—away off in the Bowery.'

Mrs Penniman flinched a little. 'Gentlemen enjoy such things,' she remarked, presently. 'I know what gentlemen like.'

'My father wouldn't like it, if he knew.'

'Pray, do you propose to inform him?' Mrs Penniman inquired.

'No, Aunt Lavinia. But please don't do it again.'

'If I do it again, you will inform him: is that what you mean? I do not share your dread of my brother; I have always known how to defend my own position. But I shall certainly never again take any step on your behalf; you are much too thankless. I knew you were not a spontaneous nature, but I believed you were firm, and I told your father that he would find you so. I am disappointed—but your father will not be!' And with this, Mrs Penniman offered her niece a brief good-night, and withdrew to her own apartment.

XVIII

CATHERINE sat alone by the parlour fire—sat there for more than an hour, lost in her meditations. Her aunt seemed to her aggressive and foolish, and to see it so clearly—to judge Mrs Penniman so positively—made her feel old and grave. She did not resent the imputation of weakness; it made no impression on her, for she had not the sense of weakness, and she was not hurt at not being appreciated. She had an immense respect for her father, and she felt that to displease him would be a misdemeanour analogous to an act of profanity in a great temple: but her purpose had slowly ripened, and she believed that her prayers had purified it of its violence. The evening advanced, and the lamp burned dim without her noticing it; her eyes were fixed upon her terrible plan. She knew her father was in his study—that he had been there all the evening; from time to time she expected to hear him move. She thought he would perhaps come, as he sometimes came, into the parlour. At last the clock struck eleven, and the house was wrapped in silence; the servants had gone to bed. Catherine got up and went slowly to the door of the library, where she waited a moment, motionless. Then she knocked, and then she waited again. Her father had answered her, but she had not the courage to turn the latch. What she had said to her aunt was true enough—she was afraid of him; and in saying that she had no sense of weakness she meant that she was not afraid of herself. She heard him move within, and he came and opened the door for her.

'What is the matter?' asked the Doctor. 'You are standing there like a ghost.'

She went into the room, but it was some time before she contrived to say what she had come to say. Her father, who was in his dressing-gown and slippers, had been busy at his writing-table, and after looking at her for some moments, and waiting for her to speak, he went and seated himself at his papers again. His back was turned to her—she began to hear the scratching of his pen. She remained near the door, with her heart thumping beneath her bodice; and she was very glad that his back was turned, for it seemed to her that she could more easily address herself to this portion of his person than to his face. At last she began, watching it while she spoke.

'You told me that if I should have anything more to say about Mr Townsend you would be glad to listen to it.'

'Exactly, my dear,' said the Doctor, not turning round, but stopping his pen.

Catherine wished it would go on, but she herself continued. 'I thought I would tell you that I have not seen him again, but that I should like to do so.'

'To bid him good-bye?' asked the Doctor.

The girl hesitated a moment. 'He is not going away.'

The Doctor wheeled slowly round in his chair, with a smile that seemed to accuse her of an epigram; but extremes meet, and Catherine had not intended one. 'It is not to bid him good-bye, then?' her father said.

'No, father, not that; at least, not for ever. I have not seen him again, but I should like to see him,' Catherine repeated.

The Doctor slowly rubbed his under lip with the feather of his quill. 'Have you written to him?'

'Yes, four times.'

'You have not dismissed him, then. Once would have done that.'

'No,' said Catherine; 'I have asked him—asked him to wait.'

Her father sat looking at her, and she was afraid he was going to break out into wrath; his eyes were so fine and cold.

'You are a dear, faithful child,' he said at last. 'Come here to your father.' And he got up, holding out his hands toward her.

The words were a surprise, and they gave her an exquisite joy. She went to him, and he put his arm round her tenderly, soothingly; and then he kissed her. After this he said—

'Do you wish to make me very happy?'

'I should like to—but I am afraid I can't,' Catherine answered.

'You can if you will. It all depends on your will.'

'Is it to give him up?' said Catherine.

'Yes, it is to give him up.'

And he held her still, with the same tenderness, looking into her face and resting his eyes on her averted eyes. There was a long silence; she wished he would release her.

'You are happier than I, father,' she said, at last.

'I have no doubt you are unhappy just now. But it is better to be unhappy for three months and get over it, than for many years and never get over it.'

'Yes, if that were so,' said Catherine.

'It would be so; I am sure of that.' She answered nothing, and he went on. 'Have you no faith in my wisdom, in my tenderness, in my solicitude for your future?'

'Oh, father!' murmured the girl.

'Don't you suppose that I know something of men: their vices, their follies, their falsities?'

She detached herself, and turned upon him. 'He is not vicious—he is not false!'

Her father kept looking at her with his sharp, pure eye. 'You make nothing of my judgment, then?'

'I can't believe that!'

'I don't ask you to believe it, but to take it on trust.'

Catherine was far from saying to herself that this was an ingenious sophism; but she met the appeal none the less squarely. 'What has he done—what do you know?'

'He has never done anything—he is a selfish idler.'

'Oh, father, don't abuse him!' she exclaimed, pleadingly.

'I don't mean to abuse him; it would be a great mistake. You may do as you choose,' he added, turning away.

'I may see him again?'

'Just as you choose.'

'Will you forgive me?'

'By no means.'

'It will only be for once.'

'I don't know what you mean by once. You must either give him up or continue the acquaintance.'

'I wish to explain—to tell him to wait.'

'To wait for what?'

'Till you know him better—till you consent.'

'Don't tell him any such nonsense as that. I know him well enough, and I shall never consent.'

'But we can wait a long time,' said poor Catherine, in a tone which was meant to express the humblest conciliation, but which had upon her father's nerves the effect of an iteration not characterized by tact.

The Doctor answered, however, quietly enough: 'Of course you can wait till I die, if you like.'

Catherine gave a cry of natural horror.

'Your engagement will have one delightful effect upon you; it will make you extremely impatient for that event.'

Catherine stood staring, and the Doctor enjoyed the point he had made. It came to Catherine with the force—or rather with the vague impressiveness—of a logical axiom which it was not in her province to controvert; and yet, though it was a scientific truth, she felt wholly unable to accept it.

'I would rather not marry, if that were true,' she said.

'Give me a proof of it, then; for it is beyond a question that by engaging yourself to Morris Townsend you simply wait for my death.'

She turned away, feeling sick and faint; and the Doctor went on. 'And if you wait for it with impatience, judge, if you please, what *his* eagerness will be!'

Catherine turned it over—her father's words had such an authority for her that her very thoughts were capable of obeying him. There was a dreadful ugliness in it, which seemed to glare at her through the interposing medium of her own feebler reason. Suddenly, however, she had an inspiration—she almost knew it to be an inspiration.

'If I don't marry before your death, I will not after,' she said.

To her father, it must be admitted, this seemed only another epigram; and as obstinacy, in unaccomplished minds, does not usually select such a mode of expression, he was the more surprised at this wanton play of a fixed idea.

'Do you mean that for an impertinence?' he inquired; an inquiry of which, as he made it, he quite perceived the grossness.

'An impertinence? Oh, father, what terrible things you say!'

'If you don't wait for my death, you might as well marry immediately; there is nothing else to wait for.'

For some time Catherine made no answer; but finally she said—

'I think Morris—little by little—might persuade you.'

'I shall never let him speak to me again. I dislike him too much.'

Catherine gave a long, low sigh; she tried to stifle it, for she had made up her mind that it was wrong to make a parade of her trouble, and to endeavour to act upon her father by the meretricious aid of emotion. Indeed, she even thought it wrong—in the sense of being inconsiderate—to attempt to act upon his feelings at all; her part was to effect some gentle, gradual change in his intellectual perception of poor Morris's character. But the means of effecting such a change were at present shrouded in mystery, and she felt miserably helpless and hopeless. She had exhausted all arguments, all replies. Her father might have pitied her, and in fact he did so; but he was sure he was right.

'There is one thing you can tell Mr Townsend, when you see him again,' he said: 'that if you marry without my consent, I don't leave you a farthing of money.* That will interest him more than anything else you can tell him.'

'That would be very right,' Catherine answered. 'I ought not in that case have a farthing of your money.'

'My dear child,' the Doctor observed, laughing, 'your simplicity is touching. Make that remark, in that tone, and with that expression of countenance, to Mr Townsend and take a note of his answer. It won't be polite—it will express irritation; and I shall be glad of that, as it will put me in the right; unless, indeed—which is perfectly possible—you should like him the better for being rude to you.'

'He will never be rude to me,' said Catherine, gently.

'Tell him what I say, all the same.'

She looked at her father, and her quiet eyes filled with tears.

'I think I will see him, then,' she murmured, in her timid voice.

'Exactly as you choose!' And he went to the door and opened it for her to go out. The movement gave her a terrible sense of his turning her off.

'It will be only once, for the present,' she added, lingering a moment.

'Exactly as you choose,' he repeated, standing there with his hand on the door. 'I have told you what I think. If you see him, you will be an ungrateful, cruel child; you will have given your old father the greatest pain of his life.'

This was more than the poor girl could bear; her tears overflowed, and she moved towards her grimly consistent parent with a pitiful cry. Her hands were raised in supplication, but he sternly evaded this appeal. Instead of letting her sob out her misery on his shoulder, he simply took her by the arm and directed her course across the threshold, closing the door gently but firmly behind her. After he had done so, he remained listening. For a long time there was no sound; he knew that she was standing outside. He was sorry for her, as I have said; but he was so sure he was right. At last he heard her move away, and then her footstep creaked faintly upon the stairs.

The Doctor took several turns round his study, with his hands in his pockets, and a thin sparkle, possibly of irritation, but partly also of something like humour, in his eye. 'By Jove,' he said to himself, 'I believe she will stick—I believe she will stick!' And this idea of Catherine 'sticking' appeared to have a comical side, and to offer a prospect of entertainment. He determined, as he said to himself, to see it out.

XIX

Iт was for reasons connected with this determination that on the morrow he sought a few words of private conversation with Mrs Penniman. He sent for her to the library, and he there informed her that he hoped very much that, as regarded this affair of Catherine's, she would mind her *p*'s and *q*'s.

'I don't know what you mean by such an expression,' said his sister. 'You speak as if I were learning the alphabet.'

'The alphabet of common sense is something you will never learn,' the Doctor permitted himself to respond.

'Have you called me here to insult me?' Mrs Penniman inquired.

'Not at all. Simply to advise you. You have taken up young Townsend; that's your own affair. I have nothing to do with your sentiments, your fancies, your affections, your delusions; but what I request of you is that you will keep these things to yourself. I have explained my views to Catherine; she understands them perfectly, and anything that she does further in the way of encouraging Mr Townsend's attentions will be in deliberate opposition to my wishes. Anything that you should do in the way of giving her aid and comfort will be—permit me the expression—distinctly treasonable. You know high treason is a capital offence; take care how you incur the penalty.'

Mrs Penniman threw back her head, with a certain expansion of the eye which she occasionally practised. 'It seems to me that you talk like a great autocrat.'

'I talk like my daughter's father.'

'Not like your sister's brother!' cried Lavinia.

'My dear Lavinia,' said the Doctor, 'I sometimes wonder whether I am your brother. We are so extremely different. In spite of differences, however, we can, at a pinch, understand each other; and that is the essential thing just now. Walk straight with regard to Mr Townsend; that's all I ask. It is highly probable you have been corresponding with him for the last three weeks—perhaps even seeing him. I don't ask you—you needn't tell me.' He had a moral conviction that she would contrive to tell a fib about the matter, which it would disgust him to listen to. 'Whatever you have done, stop doing it. That's all I wish.'

'Don't you wish also by chance to murder your child?' Mrs Penniman inquired.

'On the contrary, I wish to make her live and be happy.'

'You will kill her; she passed a dreadful night.'

'She won't die of one dreadful night, nor of a dozen. Remember that I am a distinguished physician.'

Mrs Penniman hesitated a moment. Then she risked her retort. 'Your being a distinguished physician has not prevented you from already losing *two members* of your family!'

She had risked it, but her brother gave her such a terribly incisive look—a look so like a surgeon's lancet—that she was frightened at her courage. And he answered her in words that corresponded to the look: 'It may not prevent me, either, from losing the society of still another.'

Mrs Penniman took herself off, with whatever air of depreciated merit was at her command, and repaired to Catherine's room, where the poor girl was closeted. She knew all about her dreadful night, for the two had met again, the evening before, after Catherine left her father. Mrs Penniman was on the landing of the second floor when her niece came upstairs. It was not remarkable that a person of so much subtlety should have discovered that Catherine had been shut up with the Doctor. It was still less remarkable that she should have felt an extreme curiosity to learn the result of this interview, and that this sentiment, combined with her great amiability and generosity, should have prompted her to regret the sharp words lately exchanged between her niece and herself. As the unhappy girl came into sight, in the dusky corridor, she made a lively demonstration of sympathy. Catherine's bursting heart was equally oblivious. She only knew that her aunt was taking her into her arms. Mrs Penniman drew her into Catherine's own room, and the two women sat there together, far into the small hours; the younger one with her head on the other's lap, sobbing and sobbing at first in a soundless, stifled manner, and then at last perfectly still. It gratified Mrs Penniman to be able to feel conscientiously that this scene virtually removed the interdict which Catherine had placed upon her further communion with Morris Townsend. She was not gratified, however, when, in coming back to her niece's room before breakfast, she found that Catherine had risen and was preparing herself for this meal.

'You should not go to breakfast,' she said; 'you are not well enough, after your fearful night.'

'Yes, I am very well, and I am only afraid of being late.'

'I can't understand you!' Mrs Penniman cried. 'You should stay in bed for three days.'

'Oh, I could never do that!' said Catherine, to whom this idea presented no attractions.

Mrs Penniman was in despair, and she noted, with extreme annoyance, that the trace of the night's tears had completely vanished from Catherine's eyes. She had a most impracticable *physique*. 'What effect do you expect to have upon your father,' her aunt demanded, 'if you come plumping down, without a vestige of any sort of feeling, as if nothing in the world had happened?'

'He would not like me to lie in bed,' said Catherine, simply.

'All the more reason for your doing it. How else do you expect to move him?'

Catherine thought a little. 'I don't know how; but not in that way. I wish to be just as usual.' And she finished dressing, and, according to her aunt's expression, went plumping down into the paternal presence. She was really too modest for consistent pathos.

And yet it was perfectly true that she had had a dreadful night. Even after Mrs Penniman left her she had had no sleep.

She lay staring at the uncomforting gloom, with her eyes and ears filled with the movement with which her father had turned her out of his room, and of the words in which he had told her that she was a heartless daughter. Her heart was breaking. She had heart enough for that. At moments it seemed to her that she believed him, and that to do what she was doing, a girl must indeed be bad. She *was* bad; but she couldn't help it. She would try to appear good, even if her heart were perverted; and from time to time she had a fancy that she might accomplish something by ingenious concessions to form, though she should persist in caring for Morris. Catherine's ingenuities were indefinite, and we are not called upon to expose their hollowness. The best of them perhaps showed itself in that freshness of aspect which was so discouraging to Mrs Penniman, who was amazed at the absence of haggardness in a young woman who for a whole night had lain quivering beneath a father's curse. Poor Catherine was conscious of her freshness; it gave her a feeling about the future which rather added to the weight upon her mind. It seemed a proof that she was strong and solid and dense, and would live to a great age—longer than might be generally convenient; and this idea was depressing, for it appeared to saddle her with a pretension the more, just when the cultivation of any pretension was inconsistent with her doing right. She wrote that day to Morris Townsend, requesting him to come and see her on the morrow; using very few words, and explaining nothing. She would explain everything face to face.

XX

ON the morrow, in the afternoon, she heard his voice at the door, and his step in the hall. She received him in the big, bright front-parlour, and she instructed the servant that if any one should call she was particularly engaged. She was not afraid of her father's coming in, for at that hour he was always driving about town. When Morris stood there before her, the first thing that she was conscious of was that he was even more beautiful to look at than fond recollection had painted him; the next was that he had pressed her in his arms. When she was free again it appeared to her that she had now indeed thrown herself into the gulf of defiance, and even, for an instant, that she had been married to him.

He told her that she had been very cruel, and had made him very unhappy; and Catherine felt acutely the difficulty of her destiny, which forced her to give pain in such opposite quarters. But she wished that, instead of reproaches, however tender, he would give her help; he was certainly wise enough, and clever enough, to invent some issue from their troubles. She expressed this belief, and Morris received the assurance as if he thought it natural; but he interrogated, at first—as was natural too—rather than committed himself to marking out a course.

'You should not have made me wait so long,' he said. 'I don't know how I have been living; every hour seemed like years. You should have decided sooner.'

'Decided?' Catherine asked.

'Decided whether you would keep me or give me up.'

'Oh, Morris,' she cried, with a long tender murmur, 'I never thought of giving you up!'

'What, then, were you waiting for?' The young man was ardently logical.

'I thought my father might—might—' and she hesitated.

'Might see how unhappy you were?'

'Oh, no! But that he might look at it differently.'

'And now you have sent for me to tell me that at last he does so. Is that it?'

This hypothetical optimism gave the poor girl a pang. 'No, Morris,' she said solemnly, 'he looks at it still in the same way.'

'Then why have you sent for me?'

'Because I wanted to see you!' cried Catherine, piteously.

'That's an excellent reason, surely. But did you want to look at me only? Have you nothing to tell me?'

His beautiful persuasive eyes were fixed upon her face, and she wondered what answer would be noble enough to make to such a gaze as that. For a moment her own eyes took it in, and then—'I *did* want to look at you!' she said, gently. But after this speech, most inconsistently, she hid her face.

Morris watched her for a moment, attentively. 'Will you marry me to-morrow?' he asked suddenly.

'To-morrow?'

'Next week, then. Any time within a month.'

'Isn't it better to wait?' said Catherine.

'To wait for what?'

She hardly knew for what; but this tremendous leap alarmed her. 'Till we have thought about it a little more.'

He shook his head, sadly and reproachfully. 'I thought you had been thinking about it these three weeks. Do you want to turn it over in your mind for five years? You have given me more than time enough. My poor girl,' he added in a moment, 'you are not sincere!'

Catherine coloured from brow to chin, and her eyes filled with tears. 'Oh, how can you say that?' she murmured.

'Why, you must take me or leave me,' said Morris, very reasonably. 'You can't please your father and me both; you must choose between us.'

'I have chosen you!' she said, passionately.

'Then marry me next week.'

She stood gazing at him. 'Isn't there any other way?'

'None that I know of for arriving at the same result. If there is, I should be happy to hear of it.'

Catherine could think of nothing of the kind, and Morris's luminosity seemed almost pitiless. The only thing she could think of was that her father might after all come round, and she articulated, with an awkward sense of her helplessness in doing so, a wish that this miracle might happen.

'Do you think it is in the least degree likely?' Morris asked.

'It would be, if he could only know you?'

'He can know me if he will. What is to prevent it?'

'His ideas, his reasons,' said Catherine. 'They are so—so terribly strong.' She trembled with the recollection of them yet.

'Strong?' cried Morris. 'I would rather you should think them weak.'

'Oh, nothing about my father is weak!' said the girl.

Morris turned away, walking to the window, where he stood looking out. 'You are terribly afraid of him!' he remarked at last.

She felt no impulse to deny it, because she had no shame in it; for if it was no honour to herself, at least it was an honour to him. 'I suppose I must be,' she said, simply.

'Then you don't love me—not as I love you. If you fear your father more than you love me, then your love is not what I hoped it was.'

'Ah, my friend!' she said, going to him.

'Do *I* fear anything?' he demanded, turning round on her. 'For your sake what am I not ready to face?'

'You are noble—you are brave!' she answered, stopping short at a distance that was almost respectful.

'Small good it does me, if you are so timid.'

'I don't think that I am—*really*,' said Catherine.

'I don't know what you mean by "really". It is really enough to make us miserable.'

'I should be strong enough to wait—to wait a long time.'

'And suppose after a long time your father should hate me worse than ever?'

'He wouldn't—he couldn't!'

'He would be touched by my fidelity? Is that what you mean? If he is so easily touched, then why should you be afraid of him?'

This was much to the point, and Catherine was struck by it. 'I will try not to be,' she said. And she stood there, submissively, the image, in advance, of a dutiful and responsible wife. This image could not fail to recommend itself to Morris Townsend, and he continued to give proof of the high estimation in which he held her. It could only have been at the prompting of such a sentiment that he presently mentioned to her that the course recommended by Mrs Penniman was an immediate union, regardless of consequences.

'Yes, Aunt Penniman would like that,' Catherine said, simply—and yet with a certain shrewdness. It must, however, have been in pure simplicity, and from motives quite untouched by sarcasm, that, a few moments after, she went on to say to Morris that her father had given her a message for him. It was quite on her conscience to deliver this message, and had the mission been ten times more painful she would have as scrupulously performed it. 'He told me to tell you—to tell you very distinctly, and directly from himself, that if I marry without his consent, I shall not inherit a penny of his fortune. He made a great point of this. He seemed to think—he seemed to think—'

Morris flushed, as any young man of spirit might have flushed at an imputation of baseness.

'What did he seem to think?'

'That it would make a difference.'

'It *will* make a difference—in many things. We shall be by many thousands of dollars the poorer; and that is a great difference. But it will make none in my affection.'

'We shall not want the money,' said Catherine; 'for you know I have a good deal myself.'

'Yes, my dear girl, I know you have something. And he can't touch that!'

'He would never,' said Catherine. 'My mother left it to me.'

Morris was silent awhile. 'He was very positive about this, was he?' he asked at last. 'He thought such a message would annoy me terribly, and make me throw off the mask, eh?'

'I don't know what he thought,' said Catherine, wearily.

'Please tell him that I care for his message as much as for that!' And Morris snapped his fingers sonorously.

'I don't think I could tell him that.'

'Do you know you sometimes disappoint me?' said Morris.

'I should think I might. I disappoint every one—father and Aunt Penniman.'

'Well, it doesn't matter with me, because I am fonder of you than they are.'

'Yes, Morris,' said the girl, with her imagination—what there was of it—swimming in this happy truth, which seemed, after all, invidious to no one.

'Is it your belief that he will stick to it—stick to it for ever, to this idea of disinheriting you?—that your goodness and patience will never wear out his cruelty?'

'The trouble is that if I marry you, he will think I am not good. He will think that a proof.'

'Ah, then, he will never forgive you!'

This idea, sharply expressed by Morris's handsome lips, renewed for a moment, to the poor girl's temporarily pacified conscience, all its dreadful vividness. 'Oh, you must love me very much!' she cried.

'There is no doubt of that, my dear!' her lover rejoined. 'You don't like that word "disinherited",' he added in a moment.

'It isn't the money; it is that he should—that he should feel so.'

'I suppose it seems to you a kind of curse,' said Morris. 'It must be very dismal. But don't you think,' he went on presently, 'that if you were to try to be very clever, and to set rightly about it, you might in the end conjure it away? Don't you think,' he continued further, in a tone of sympathetic speculation, 'that a really clever woman, in your place, might bring him round at last? Don't you think—'

Here, suddenly, Morris was interrupted; these ingenious inquiries had not reached Catherine's ears. The terrible word 'disinheritance', with all its impressive moral reprobation, was still ringing there; seemed indeed to gather force as it lingered. The mortal chill of her situation struck more deeply into her child-like heart, and she was overwhelmed by a feeling of loneliness and danger. But her refuge was there, close to her, and she put out her hands to grasp it. 'Ah, Morris,' she said, with a shudder, 'I will marry you as soon as you please!' And she surrendered herself, leaning her head on his shoulder.

'My dear good girl!' he exclaimed, looking down at his prize. And then he looked up again, rather vaguely, with parted lips and lifted eyebrows.

XXI

Dr Sloper very soon imparted his conviction to Mrs Almond, in the same terms in which he had announced it to himself. 'She's going to stick, by Jove! she's going to stick.'

'Do you mean that she is going to marry him?' Mrs Almond inquired.

'I don't know that; but she is not going to break down. She is going to drag out the engagement, in the hope of making me relent.'

'And shall you not relent?'

'Shall a geometrical proposition relent? I am not so superficial.'

'Doesn't geometry treat of surfaces?' asked Mrs Almond, who, as we know, was clever, smiling.

'Yes; but it treats of them profoundly. Catherine and her young man are my surfaces; I have taken their measure.'

'You speak as if it surprised you.'

'It is immense; there will be a great deal to observe.'

'You are shockingly cold-blooded!' said Mrs Almond.

'I need to be, with all this hot blood about me. Young Townsend indeed is cool; I must allow him that merit.'

'I can't judge him,' Mrs Almond answered; 'but I am not at all surprised at Catherine.'

'I confess I am a little; she must have been so deucedly divided and bothered.'

'Say it amuses you outright! I don't see why it should be such a joke that your daughter adores you.'

'It is the point where the adoration stops that I find it interesting to fix.'

'It stops where the other sentiment begins.'

'Not at all—that would be simple enough. The two things are extremely mixed up, and the mixture is extremely odd. It will produce some third element, and that's what I am waiting to see. I wait with suspense—with positive excitement; and that is a sort of emotion that I didn't suppose Catherine would ever provide for me. I am really very much obliged to her.'

'She will cling,' said Mrs Almond; 'she will certainly cling.'

'Yes; as I say, she will stick.'

'Cling is prettier. That's what those very simple natures always do, and nothing could be simpler than Catherine. She doesn't take many impressions; but when she takes one she keeps it. She is like a copper kettle that receives a dent; you may polish up the kettle, but you can't efface the mark.'

'We must try and polish up Catherine,' said the Doctor. 'I will take her to Europe.'

'She won't forget him in Europe.'

'He will forget her, then.'

Mrs Almond looked grave. 'Should you really like that?'

'Extremely!' said the Doctor.

Mrs Penniman, meanwhile, lost little time in putting herself again in communication with Morris Townsend. She requested him to favour her with another interview, but she did not on this occasion select an oyster-saloon as the scene of their meeting. She proposed that he should join her at the door of a certain church, after service on Sunday afternoon, and she was careful not to appoint the place of worship which she usually visited, and where, as she said, the congregation would have spied upon her. She picked out a less elegant resort, and on issuing from its portal at the hour she had fixed she saw the young man standing apart. She offered him no recognition till she had crossed the street and he had followed her to some distance. Here, with a smile—'Excuse my apparent want of cordiality,' she said. 'You know what to believe about that. Prudence before everything.' And on his asking her in what direction they should walk, 'Where we shall be least observed,' she murmured.

Morris was not in high good-humour, and his response to this speech was not particularly gallant. 'I don't flatter myself we shall be much observed anywhere.' Then he turned recklessly toward the centre of the town. 'I hope you have come to tell me that he has knocked under,' he went on.

'I am afraid I am not altogether a harbinger of good; and yet, too, I am to a certain extent a messenger of peace. I have been thinking a great deal, Mr Townsend,' said Mrs Penniman.

'You think too much.'

'I suppose I do; but I can't help it, my mind is so terribly active. When I give myself, I give myself. I pay the penalty in my headaches, my famous headaches—a perfect circlet of pain! But I carry it as a queen carries her crown. Would you believe that I have one now?

I wouldn't, however, have missed our rendezvous for anything. I have something very important to tell you.'

'Well let's have it,' said Morris.

'I was perhaps a little headlong the other day in advising you to marry immediately. I have been thinking it over, and now I see it just a little differently.'

'You seem to have a great many different ways of seeing the same object.'

'Their number is infinite!' said Mrs Penniman, in a tone which seemed to suggest that this convenient faculty was one of her brightest attributes.

'I recommend you to take one way and stick to it,' Morris replied.

'Ah! but it isn't easy to choose. My imagination is never quiet, never satisfied. It makes me a bad adviser, perhaps; but it makes me a capital friend!'

'A capital friend who gives bad advice!' said Morris.

'Not intentionally—and who hurries off, at every risk, to make the most humble excuses!'

'Well, what do you advise me now?'

'To be very patient; to watch and wait.'

'And is that bad advice or good?'

'That is not for me to say,' Mrs Penniman rejoined, with some dignity. 'I only pretend it's sincere.'

'And will you come to me next week and recommend something different and equally sincere?'

'I may come to you next week and tell you that I am in the streets!'

'In the streets?'

'I have had a terrible scene with my brother, and he threatens, if anything happens, to turn me out of the house. You know I am a poor woman.'

Morris had a speculative idea that she had a little property; but he naturally did not press this.

'I should be very sorry to see you suffer martyrdom for me,' he said. 'But you make your brother out a regular Turk.'

Mrs Penniman hesitated a little.

'I certainly do not regard Austin as a satisfactory Christian.'

'And am I to wait till he is converted?'

'Wait at any rate till he is less violent. Bide your time, Mr Townsend; remember the prize is great!'

Morris walked along some time in silence, tapping the railings and gateposts very sharply with his stick.

'You certainly are devilish inconsistent!' he broke out at last. 'I have already got Catherine to consent to a private marriage.'

Mrs Penniman was indeed inconsistent, for at this news she gave a little jump of gratification.

'Oh! when and where?' she cried. And then she stopped short.

Morris was a little vague about this.

'That isn't fixed; but she consents. It's deuced awkward, now, to back out.'

Mrs Penniman, as I say, had stopped short; and she stood there with her eyes fixed, brilliantly, on her companion.

'Mr Townsend,' she proceeded, 'shall I tell you something? Catherine loves you so much that you may do anything.'

This declaration was slightly ambiguous, and Morris opened his eyes.

'I am happy to hear it! But what do you mean by "anything"?'

'You may postpone—you may change about; she won't think the worse of you.'

Morris stood there still, with his raised eyebrows; then he said simply and rather dryly—'Ah!' After this he remarked to Mrs Penniman that if she walked so slowly she would attract notice, and he succeeded, after a fashion, in hurrying her back to the domicile of which her tenure had become so insecure.

XXII

HE had slightly misrepresented the matter in saying that Catherine had consented to take the great step. We left her just now declaring that she would burn her ships behind her; but Morris, after having elicited this declaration, had become conscious of good reasons for not taking it up. He avoided, gracefully enough, fixing a day, though he left her under the impression that he had his eye on one. Catherine may have had her difficulties; but those of her circumspect suitor are also worthy of consideration. The prize was certainly great; but it was only to be won by striking the happy mean between precipitancy and caution. It would be all very well to take one's jump and trust to Providence; Providence was more especially on the side of clever people, and clever people were known by an indisposition to risk their bones. The ultimate reward of a union with a young woman who was both unattractive and impoverished ought to be connected with immediate disadvantages by some very palpable chain. Between the fear of losing Catherine and her possible fortune altogether, and the fear of taking her too soon and finding this possible fortune as void of actuality as a collection of emptied bottles, it was not comfortable for Morris Townsend to choose; a fact that should be remembered by readers disposed to judge harshly of a young man who may have struck them as making but an indifferently successful use of fine natural parts. He had not forgotten that in any event Catherine had her own ten thousand a year; he had devoted an abundance of meditation to this circumstance. But with his fine parts he rated himself high, and he had a perfectly definite appreciation of his value, which seemed to him inadequately represented by the sum I have mentioned. At the same time he reminded himself that this sum was considerable, that everything is relative, and that if a modest income is less desirable than a large one, the complete absence of revenue is nowhere accounted an advantage. These reflections gave him plenty of occupation, and made it necessary that he should trim his sail. Dr Sloper's opposition was the unknown quantity in the problem he had to work out. The natural way to work it out was by marrying Catherine; but in mathematics there are many short cuts, and Morris was not without a hope that he should yet discover one.

When Catherine took him at his word and consented to renounce the attempt to mollify her father, he drew back skilfully enough, as I have said, and kept the wedding-day still an open question. Her faith in his sincerity was so complete that she was incapable of suspecting that he was playing with her; her trouble just now was of another kind. The poor girl had an admirable sense of honour; and from the moment she had brought herself to the point of violating her father's wish, it seemed to her that she had no right to enjoy his protection. It was on her conscience that she ought to live under his roof only so long as she conformed to his wisdom. There was a great deal of glory in such a position, but poor Catherine felt that she had forfeited her claim to it. She had cast her lot with a young man against whom he had solemnly warned her, and broken the contract under which he provided her with a happy home. She could not give up the young man, so she must leave the home; and the sooner the object of her preference offered her another, the sooner her situation would lose its awkward twist. This was close reasoning; but it was commingled with an infinite amount of merely instinctive penitence. Catherine's days, at this time, were dismal, and the weight of some of her hours was almost more than she could bear. Her father never looked at her, never spoke to her. He knew perfectly what he was about, and this was part of a plan. She looked at him as much as she dared (for she was afraid of seeming to offer herself to his observation), and she pitied him for the sorrow she had brought upon him. She held up her head and busied her hands, and went about her daily occupations; and when the state of things in Washington Square seemed intolerable she closed her eyes and indulged herself with an intellectual vision of the man for whose sake she had broken a sacred law. Mrs Penniman, of the three persons in Washington Square, had much the most of the manner that belongs to a great crisis. If Catherine was quiet, she was quietly quiet, as I may say, and her pathetic effects, which there was no one to notice, were entirely unstudied and unintended. If the Doctor was stiff and dry and absolutely indifferent to the presence of his companions, it was so lightly, neatly, easily done, that you would have had to know him well to discover that on the whole he rather enjoyed having to be so disagreeable. But Mrs Penniman was elaborately reserved and significantly silent; there was a richer rustle in the very deliberate movements to which she confined herself, and when she occasionally spoke, in connection with some very trivial event, she had the air of meaning something deeper than what she said. Between Catherine and her father nothing had passed since the evening she went to speak to him in his study. She had something to say to him—it seemed to her she ought to say it; but she kept it back, for fear of irritating him. He also had something to say to her; but he was determined not to speak first. He was interested, as we know, in seeing how, if she were left to herself, she would 'stick'. At last she told him she had seen Morris Townsend again, and that their relations remained quite the same.

'I think we shall marry—before very long. And probably, meanwhile, I shall see him rather often; about once a week, not more.'

The Doctor looked at her coldly from head to foot, as if she had been a stranger. It was the first time his eyes had rested on her for a week, which was fortunate, if that was to be their expression. 'Why not three times a day?' he asked. 'What prevents your meeting as often as you choose?'

She turned away a moment; there were tears in her eyes. Then she said, 'It is better once a week.'

'I don't see how it is better. It is as bad as it can be. If you flatter yourself that I care for little modifications of that sort, you are very much mistaken. It is as wrong of you to see him once a week as it would be to see him all day long. Not that it matters to me, however.'

Catherine tried to follow these words, but they seemed to lead towards a vague horror from which she recoiled. 'I think we shall marry pretty soon,' she repeated at last.

Her father gave her his dreadful look again, as if she were some one else. 'Why do you tell me that? It's no concern of mine.'

'Oh, father!' she broke out, 'don't you care, even if you do feel so?'

'Not a button. Once you marry, it's quite the same to me when or where or why you do it; and if you think to compound for your folly by hoisting your flag* in this way, you may spare yourself the trouble.'

With this he turned away. But the next day he spoke to her of his own accord, and his manner was somewhat changed. 'Shall you be married within the next four or five months?' he asked.

'I don't know, father,' said Catherine. 'It is not very easy for us to make up our minds.'

'Put it off, then, for six months, and in the meantime I will take you to Europe. I should like you very much to go.'

It gave her such delight, after his words of the day before, to hear that he should 'like' her to do something, and that he still had in his heart any of the tenderness of preference, that she gave a little exclamation of joy. But then she became conscious that Morris was not included in this proposal, and that—as regards really going—she would greatly prefer to remain at home with him. But she blushed, none the less, more comfortably than she had done of late. 'It would be delightful to go to Europe,' she remarked, with a sense that the idea was not original, and that her tone was not all it might be.

'Very well, then, we will go. Pack up your clothes.'

'I had better tell Mr Townsend,' said Catherine.

Her father fixed his cold eyes upon her. 'If you mean that you had better ask his leave, all that remains to me is to hope he will give it.'

The girl was sharply touched by the pathetic ring of the words; it was the most calculated, the most dramatic little speech the Doctor had ever uttered. She felt that it was a great thing for her, under the circumstances, to have this fine opportunity of showing him her respect; and yet there was something else that she felt as well, and that she presently expressed. 'I sometimes think that if I do what you dislike so much, I ought not to stay with you.'

'To stay with me?'

'If I live with you, I ought to obey you.'

'If that's your theory, it's certainly mine,' said the Doctor, with a dry laugh.

'But if I don't obey you, I ought not to live with you—to enjoy your kindness and protection.'

This striking argument gave the Doctor a sudden sense of having underestimated his daughter; it seemed even more than worthy of a young woman who had revealed the quality of unaggressive obstinacy. But it displeased him—displeased him deeply, and he signified as much. 'That idea is in very bad taste,' he said. 'Did you get it from Mr Townsend?'

'Oh no; it's my own!' said Catherine eagerly.

'Keep it to yourself, then,' her father answered, more than ever determined she should go to Europe.

XXIII

IF Morris Townsend was not to be included in this journey, no more was Mrs Penniman, who would have been thankful for an invitation, but who (to do her justice) bore her disappointment in a perfectly lady-like manner. 'I should enjoy seeing the works of Raphael and the ruins—the ruins of the Pantheon,* she said to Mrs Almond; 'but on the other hand, I shall not be sorry to be alone and at peace for the next few months in Washington Square. I want rest; I have been through so much in the last four months.' Mrs Almond thought it rather cruel that her brother should not take poor Lavinia abroad; but she easily understood that, if the purpose of his expedition was to make Catherine forget her lover, it was not in his interest to give his daughter this young man's best friend as a companion. 'If Lavinia had not been so foolish, she might visit the ruins of the Pantheon,' she said to herself; and she continued to regret her sister's folly, even though the latter assured her that she had often heard the relics in question most satisfactorily described by Mr Penniman. Mrs Penniman was perfectly aware that her brother's motive in undertaking a foreign tour was to lay a trap for Catherine's constancy; and she imparted this conviction very frankly to her niece.

'He thinks it will make you forget Morris,' she said (she always called the young man 'Morris' now); 'out of sight, out of mind, you know. He thinks that all the things you will see over there will drive him out of your thoughts.'

Catherine looked greatly alarmed. 'If he thinks that, I ought to tell him beforehand.'

Mrs Penniman shook her head. 'Tell him afterwards my dear! After he has had all the trouble and the expense! That's the way to serve him.' And she added, in a softer key, that it must be delightful to think of those who love us among the ruins of the Pantheon.

Her father's displeasure had cost the girl, as we know, a great deal of deep-welling sorrow—sorrow of the purest and most generous kind, without a touch of resentment or rancour; but for the first time, after he had dismissed with such contemptuous brevity her apology for being a charge upon him, there was a spark of anger in her grief. She had felt his contempt; it had scorched her; that speech about her bad taste made her ears burn for three days. During this period she was less considerate; she had an idea—a rather vague one, but it was agreeable to her sense of injury—that now she was absolved from penance, and might do what she chose. She chose to write to Morris Townsend to meet her in the Square and take her to walk about the town. If she were going to Europe out of respect to her father, she might at least give herself this satisfaction. She felt in every way at present more free and more resolute; there was a force that urged her. Now at last, completely and unreservedly, her passion possessed her.

Morris met her at last, and they took a long walk. She told him immediately what had happened—that her father wished to take her away. It would be for six months, to Europe; she would do absolutely what Morris should think best. She hoped inexpressibly that he would think it best she should stay at home. It was some time before he said what he thought: he asked, as they walked along, a great many questions. There was one that especially struck her; it seemed so incongruous.

'Should you like to see all those celebrated things over there?'

'Oh, no, Morris!' said Catherine quite deprecatingly.

'Gracious Heaven, what a dull woman!' Morris exclaimed to himself.

'He thinks I will forget you,' said Catherine; 'that all these things will drive you out of my mind.'

'Well, my dear, perhaps they will!'

'Please don't say that,' Catherine answered gently, as they walked along. 'Poor father will be disappointed.'

Morris gave a little laugh. 'Yes, I verily believe that your poor father will be disappointed! But you will have seen Europe,' he added humorously. 'What a take-in!'

'I don't care for seeing Europe,' Catherine said.

'You ought to care, my dear. And it may mollify your father.'

Catherine, conscious of her obstinacy, expected little of this, and could not rid herself of the idea that in going abroad and yet remaining firm, she should play her father a trick. 'Don't you think it would be a kind of deception?' she asked.

'Doesn't he want to deceive you?' cried Morris. 'It will serve him right! I really think you had better go.'

'And not be married for so long?'

'Be married when you come back. You can buy your wedding-clothes in Paris.' And then Morris, with great kindness of tone, explained his view of the matter. It would be a good thing that she should go; it would put them completely in the right. It would show they were reasonable and willing to wait. Once they were so sure of each other, they could afford to wait—what had they to fear? If there was a particle of chance that her father would be favourably affected by her going, that ought to settle it; for, after all, Morris was very unwilling to be the cause of her being disinherited. It was not for himself, it was for her and for her children. He was willing to wait for her; it would be hard, but he could do it. And over there, among beautiful scenes and noble monuments, perhaps the old gentleman would be softened; such things were supposed to exert a humanis-ing influence. He might be touched by her gentleness, her patience, her willingness to make any sacrifice but *that* one; and if she should appeal to him some day, in some celebrated spot—in Italy, say, in the evening; in Venice, in a gondola, by moonlight—if she should be a little clever about it and touch the right chord, perhaps he would fold her in his arms and tell her that he forgave her. Catherine was immensely struck with this conception of the affair, which seemed eminently worthy of her lover's brilliant intellect; though she viewed it askance in so far as it depended upon her own powers of execution. The idea of being 'clever' in a gondola by moonlight appeared to her to involve elements of which her grasp was not active.

But it was settled between them that she should tell her father that she was ready to follow him obediently anywhere, making the mental reservation that she loved Morris Townsend more than ever.

She informed the Doctor she was ready to embark, and he made rapid arrangements for this event. Catherine had many farewells to make, but with only two of them are we actively concerned. Mrs Penniman took a discriminating view of her niece's journey; it seemed to her very proper that Mr Townsend's destined bride should wish to embellish her mind by a foreign tour.

'You leave him in good hands,' she said, pressing her lips to Catherine's forehead. (She was very fond of kissing people's fore-heads; it was an involuntary expression of sympathy with the intel-lectual part.) 'I shall see him often; I shall feel like one of the vestals of old, tending the sacred flame.'*

'You behave beautifully about not going with us,' Catherine answered, not presuming to examine this analogy.

'It is my pride that keeps me up,' said Mrs Penniman, tapping the body of her dress, which always gave forth a sort of metallic ring.

Catherine's parting with her lover was short, and few words were exchanged.

'Shall I find you just the same when I come back?' she asked; though the question was not the fruit of scepticism.

'The same—only more so!' said Morris, smiling.

It does not enter into our scheme to narrate in detail Dr Sloper's proceedings in the Eastern hemisphere. He made the grand tour of Europe, travelled in considerable splendour, and (as was to have been expected in a man of his high cultivation) found so much in art and antiquity to interest him, that he remained abroad, not for six months, but for twelve. Mrs Penniman, in Washington Square, accommodated herself to his absence. She enjoyed her uncontested dominion in the empty house, and flattered herself that she made it more attractive to their friends than when her brother was at home. To Morris Townsend, at least, it would have appeared that she made it singularly attractive. He was altogether her most frequent visitor, and Mrs Penniman was very fond of asking him to tea. He had his chair—a very easy one—at the fireside in the back-parlour (when the great mahogany sliding-doors, with silver knobs and hinges, which divided this apartment from its more formal neighbour, were closed), and he used to smoke cigars in the Doctor's study, where he often spent an hour in turning over the curious collections of its absent proprietor. He thought Mrs Penniman a goose, as we know; but he was no goose himself, and, as a young man of luxurious tastes and scanty resources, he found the house a perfect castle of indolence.* It became for him a club with a single member. Mrs Penniman saw much less of her sister than while the Doctor was at home; for Mrs Almond had felt moved to tell her that she disapproved of her relations with Mr Townsend. She had no business to be so friendly to a young man of whom their brother thought so meanly, and Mrs Almond was surprised at her levity in foisting a most deplorable engagement upon Catherine.

'Deplorable?' cried Lavinia. 'He will make her a lovely husband!'

'I don't believe in lovely husbands,' said Mrs Almond; 'I only believe in good ones. If he marries her, and she comes into Austin's money, they may get on. He will be an idle, amiable, selfish, and doubtless tolerably good-natured fellow. But if she doesn't get the money and he finds himself tied to her, Heaven have mercy on her! He will have none. He will hate her for his disappointment, and take his revenge; he will be pitiless and cruel. Woe betide poor Catherine! I recommend you to talk a little with his sister; it's a pity Catherine can't marry *her*!'

Mrs Penniman had no appetite whatever for conversation with Mrs Montgomery, whose acquaintance she made no trouble to cultivate; and the effect of this alarming forecast of her niece's destiny was to make her think it indeed a thousand pities that Mr Townsend's generous nature should be embittered. Bright enjoyment was his natural element, and how could he be comfortable if there should prove to be nothing to enjoy? It became a fixed idea with Mrs Penniman that he should yet enjoy her brother's fortune, on which she had acuteness enough to perceive that her own claim was small.

'If he doesn't leave it to Catherine, it certainly won't be to leave it to me,' she said.

XXIV

THE Doctor, during the first six months he was abroad, never spoke to his daughter of their little difference; partly on system, and partly because he had a great many other things to think about. It was idle to attempt to ascertain the state of her affections without direct inquiry, because, if she had not had an expressive manner among the familiar influences of home, she failed to gather animation from the mountains of Switzerland or the monuments of Italy. She was always her father's docile and reasonable associate—going through their sight-seeing in deferential silence, never complaining of fatigue, always ready to start at the hour he had appointed over-night, making no foolish criticisms and indulging in no refinements of appreciation. 'She is about as intelligent as the bundle of shawls,' the Doctor said; her main superiority being that while the bundle of shawls sometimes got lost, or tumbled out of the carriage, Catherine was always at her post, and had a firm and ample seat. But her father had expected this, and he was not constrained to set down her intellectual limitations as a tourist to sentimental depression; she had completely divested herself of the characteristics of a victim, and during the whole time that they were abroad she never uttered an audible sigh. He supposed she was in correspondence with Morris Townsend; but he held his peace about it, for he never saw the young man's letters, and Catherine's own missives were always given to the courier to post. She heard from her lover with considerable regularity, but his letters came enclosed in Mrs Penniman's; so that whenever the Doctor handed her a packet addressed in his sister's hand, he was an involuntary instrument of the passion he condemned.

Catherine made this reflection, and six months earlier she would have felt bound to give him warning; but now she deemed herself absolved. There was a sore spot in her heart that his own words had made when once she spoke to him as she thought honour prompted; she would try and please him as far as she could, but she would never speak that way again. She read her lover's letters in secret.

One day, at the end of the summer, the two travellers found themselves in a lonely valley of the Alps. They were crossing one of the passes, and on the long ascent they had got out of the carriage and had wandered much in advance. After a while the Doctor descried a footpath which, leading through a transverse valley, would bring them out, as he justly supposed, at a much higher point of the ascent. They followed this devious way and finally lost the path; the valley proved very wild and rough, and their walk became rather a scramble. They were good walkers, however, and they took their adventure easily; from time to time they stopped, that Catherine might rest; and then she sat upon a stone and looked about her at the hard-featured rocks and the glowing sky. It was late in the afternoon, in the last of August; night was coming on, and, as they had reached a great elevation, the air was cold and sharp. In the west there was a great suffusion of cold, red light, which made the sides of the little valley look only the more rugged and dusky. During one of their pauses, her father left her and wandered away to some high place, at a distance, to get a view. He was out of sight; she sat there alone, in the stillness, which was just touched by the vague murmur, somewhere, of a mountain brook. She thought of Morris Townsend, and the place was so desolate and lonely that he seemed very far away. Her father remained absent a long time; she began to wonder what had become of him. But at last he reappeared, coming towards her in the clear twilight, and she got up, to go on. He made no motion to proceed, however, but came close to her, as if he had something to say. He stopped in front of her and stood looking at her, with eyes that had kept the light of the flushing snow-summits on which they had just been fixed.

Then, abruptly, in a low tone, he asked her an unexpected question—

'Have you given him up?'

The question was unexpected, but Catherine was only superficially unprepared.

'No, father!' she answered.

He looked at her again, for some moments, without speaking.

'Does he write to you?' he asked.

'Yes—about twice a month.'

The Doctor looked up and down the valley, swinging his stick; then he said to her, in the same low tone—

'I am very angry.'

She wondered what he meant—whether he wished to frighten her. If he did, the place was well chosen; this hard, melancholy dell, abandoned by the summer light, made her feel her loneliness. She looked around her, and her heart grew cold; for a moment her fear was great. But she could think of nothing to say, save to murmur gently, 'I am sorry.'

'You try my patience,' her father went on, 'and you ought to know what I am, I am not a very good man. Though I am very smooth externally, at bottom I am very passionate; and I assure you I can be very hard.'

She could not think why he told her these things. Had he brought her there on purpose, and was it part of a plan? What was the plan? Catherine asked herself. Was it to startle her suddenly into a retraction—to take an advantage of her by dread? Dread of what? The place was ugly and lonely, but the place could do her no harm. There was a kind of still intensity about her father which made him dangerous, but Catherine hardly went so far as to say to herself that it might be part of his plan to fasten his hand—the neat, fine, supple hand of a distinguished physician—in her throat. Nevertheless, she receded a step. 'I am sure you can be anything you please,' she said. And it was her simple belief.

'I am very angry,' he replied, more sharply.

'Why has it taken you so suddenly?'

'It has not taken me suddenly. I have been raging inwardly for the last six months. But just now this seemed a good place to flare out. It's so quiet, and we are alone.'

'Yes, it's very quiet,' said Catherine vaguely, looking about her. 'Won't you come back to the carriage?'

'In a moment. Do you mean that in all this time you have not yielded an inch?'

'I would if I could, father; but I can't.'

The Doctor looked round him too. 'Should you like to be left in such a place as this, to starve?'

'What do you mean?' cried the girl.

'That will be your fate—that's how he will leave you.'

He would not touch her, but he had touched Morris. The warmth came back to her heart. 'That is not true, father,' she broke out, 'and you ought not to say it! It is not right, and it's not true!'

He shook his head slowly. 'No, it's not right, because you won't believe it. But it *is* true. Come back to the carriage.'

He turned away, and she followed him; he went faster, and was presently much in advance. But from time to time he stopped, without turning round, to let her keep up with him, and she made her way forward with difficulty, her heart beating with the excitement of having for the first time spoken to him in violence. By this time it had grown almost dark, and she ended by losing sight of him. But she kept her course, and after a little, the valley making a sudden turn, she gained the road, where the carriage stood waiting. In it sat her father, rigid and silent; in silence, too, she took her place beside him.

It seemed to her, later, in looking back upon all this, that for days afterwards not a word had been exchanged between them. The scene had been a strange one, but it had not permanently affected her feeling towards her father, for it was natural, after all, that he should occasionally make a scene of some kind, and he had let her alone for six months. The strangest part of it was that he had said he was not a good man; Catherine wondered a great deal what he had meant by that. The statement failed to appeal to her credence, and it was not grateful to any resentment that she entertained. Even in the utmost bitterness that she might feel, it would give her no satisfaction to think him less complete. Such a saying as that was a part of his great subtlety—men so clever as he might say anything and mean anything. And as to his being hard, that surely, in a man, was a virtue.

He let her alone for six months more—six months during which she accommodated herself without a protest to the extension of their tour. But he spoke again at the end of this time; it was at the very last, the night before they embarked for New York, in the hotel at Liverpool. They had been dining together in a great dim, musty sitting-room; and then the cloth had been removed, and the Doctor walked slowly up and down. Catherine at last took her candle to go to bed, but her father motioned her to stay.

'What do you mean to do when you get home?' he asked, while she stood there with her candle in her hand.

'Do you mean about Mr Townsend?'

'About Mr Townsend.'

'We shall probably marry.'

The Doctor took several turns again while she waited. 'Do you hear from him as much as ever?'

'Yes; twice a month,' said Catherine, promptly.

'And does he always talk about marriage?'

'Oh, yes! That is, he talks about other things too, but he always says something about that.'

'I am glad to hear he varies his subjects; his letters might otherwise be monotonous.'

'He writes beautifully,' said Catherine, who was very glad of a chance to say it.

'They always write beautifully. However, in a given case that doesn't diminish the merit. So, as soon as you arrive, you are going off with him?'

This seemed a rather gross way of putting it, and something that there was of dignity in Catherine resented it. 'I cannot tell you till we arrive,' she said.

'That's reasonable enough,' her father answered. 'That's all I ask of you—that you *do* tell me, that you give me definite notice. When a poor man is to lose his only child, he likes to have an inkling of it beforehand.'

'Oh, father, you will not lose me!' Catherine said, spilling her candle-wax.

'Three days before will do,' he went on, 'if you are in a position to be positive then. He ought to be very thankful to me, do you know. I have done a mighty good thing for him in taking you abroad; your value is twice as great, with all the knowledge and taste that you have acquired. A year ago, you were perhaps a little limited—a little rustic; but now you have seen everything, and appreciated everything, and you will be a most entertaining companion. We have fattened the sheep for him before he kills it!' Catherine turned away, and stood staring at the blank door. 'Go to bed,' said her father; 'and, as we don't go aboard till noon, you may sleep late. We shall probably have a most uncomfortable voyage.'

XXV

THE voyage was indeed uncomfortable, and Catherine, on arriving in New York, had not the compensation of 'going off', in her father's phrase, with Morris Townsend. She saw him, however, the day after she landed; and, in the meantime, he formed a natural subject of conversation between our heroine and her Aunt Lavinia, with whom, the night she disembarked, the girl was closeted for a long time before either lady retired to rest.

'I have seen a great deal of him,' said Mrs Penniman. 'He is not very easy to know. I suppose you think you know him; but you don't, my dear. You will some day; but it will only be after you have lived with him. I may almost say *I* have lived with him,' Mrs Penniman proceeded, while Catherine stared. 'I think I know him now; I have had such remarkable opportunities. You will have the same—or rather, you will have better!' and Aunt Lavinia smiled. 'Then you will see what I mean. It's a wonderful character, full of passion and energy, and just as true!'

Catherine listened with a mixture of interest and apprehension. Aunt Lavinia was intensely sympathetic, and Catherine, for the past year, while she wandered through foreign galleries and churches, and rolled over the smoothness of posting roads,* nursing the thoughts that never passed her lips, had often longed for the company of some intelligent person of her own sex. To tell her story to some kind woman—at moments it seemed to her that this would give her comfort, and she had more than once been on the point of taking the landlady, or the nice young person from the dressmaker's, into her confidence. If a woman had been near her she would on certain occasions have treated such a companion to a fit of weeping; and she had an apprehension that, on her return, this would form her response to Aunt Lavinia's first embrace. In fact, however, the two ladies had met, in Washington Square, without tears, and when they found themselves alone together a certain dryness fell upon the girl's emotion. It came over her with a greater force that Mrs Penniman had enjoyed a whole year of her lover's society, and it was not a pleasure to her to hear her aunt explain and interpret the young man, speaking of him as if her own knowledge of him were supreme. It was not that Catherine was jealous; but her sense of Mrs Penniman's innocent falsity, which had lain dormant, began to haunt her again, and she was glad that she was safely at home. With this, however, it was a blessing to be able to talk of Morris, to sound his name, to be with a person who was not unjust to him.

'You have been very kind to him,' said Catherine. 'He has written me that, often. I shall never forget that, Aunt Lavinia.'

'I have done what I could; it has been very little. To let him come and talk to me, and give him his cup of tea—that was all. Your Aunt Almond thought it was too much, and used to scold me terribly; but she promised me, at least, not to betray me.'

'To betray you?'

'Not to tell your father. He used to sit in your father's study!' said Mrs Penniman, with a little laugh.

Catherine was silent a moment. This idea was disagreeable to her, and she was reminded again, with pain, of her aunt's secretive habits. Morris, the reader may be informed, had had the tact not to tell her that he sat in her father's study. He had known her but for a few months, and her aunt had known her for fifteen years; and yet he would not have made the mistake of thinking that Catherine would see the joke of the thing. 'I am sorry you made him go into father's room,' she said, after a while.

'I didn't make him go; he went himself. He liked to look at the books, and at all those things in the glass cases. He knows all about them; he knows all about everything.'

Catherine was silent again; then, 'I wish he had found some employment,' she said.

'He has found some employment! It's beautiful news, and he told me to tell you as soon as you arrived. He has gone into partnership with a commission-merchant.* It was all settled, quite suddenly, a week ago.'

This seemed to Catherine indeed beautiful news; it had a fine prosperous air. 'Oh, I'm so glad!' she said; and now, for a moment, she was disposed to throw herself on Aunt Lavinia's neck.

'It's much better than being under some one; and he has never been used to that,' Mrs Penniman went on. 'He is just as good as his partner—they are perfectly equal! You see how right he was to wait. I should like to know what your father can say now! They have got an office in Duane Street,* and little printed cards; he brought me one to show me. I have got it in my room, and you shall see it to-morrow. That's what he said to me the last time he was here—"You see how right I was to wait!" He has got other people under him, instead of being a subordinate. He could never be a subordinate; I have often told him I could never think of him in that way.'

Catherine assented to this proposition, and was very happy to know that Morris was his own master; but she was deprived of the satisfaction of thinking that she might communicate this news in triumph to her father. Her father would care equally little whether Morris were established in business or transported for life. Her trunks had been brought into her room, and further reference to her lover was for a short time suspended, while she opened them and displayed to her aunt some of the spoils of foreign travel. These were rich and abundant; and Catherine had brought home a present to every one—to every one save Morris, to whom she had brought simply her undiverted heart. To Mrs Penniman she had been lavishly generous, and Aunt Lavinia spent half-an-hour in unfolding and folding again, with little ejaculations of gratitude and taste. She marched about for some time in a splendid cashmere shawl,* which Catherine had begged her to accept, settling it on her shoulders, and twisting down her head to see how low the point descended behind.

'I shall regard it only as a loan,' she said. 'I will leave it to you again when I die; or rather,' she added, kissing her niece again, 'I will leave it to your first-born little girl!' And draped in her shawl, she stood there smiling.

'You had better wait till she comes,' said Catherine.

'I don't like the way you say that,' Mrs Penniman rejoined, in a moment. 'Catherine, are you changed?'

'No; I am the same.'

'You have not swerved a line?'

'I am exactly the same,' Catherine repeated, wishing her aunt were a little less sympathetic.

'Well, I am glad!' and Mrs Penniman surveyed her cashmere in the glass. Then, 'How is your father?' she asked in a moment, with her eyes on her niece. 'Your letters were so meagre—I could never tell!'

'Father is very well.'

'Ah, you know what I mean,' said Mrs Penniman, with a dignity to which the cashmere gave a richer effect. 'Is he still implacable!'

'Oh, yes!'

'Quite unchanged?'

'He is, if possible, more firm.'

Mrs Penniman took off her great shawl, and slowly folded it up. 'That is very bad. You had no success with your little project?'

'What little project?'

'Morris told me all about it. The idea of turning the tables on him, in Europe; of watching him, when he was agreeably impressed by some celebrated sight—he pretends to be so artistic, you know—and then just pleading with him and bringing him round.'

'I never tried it. It was Morris's idea; but if he had been with us, in Europe, he would have seen that father was never impressed in that way. He *is* artistic—tremendously artistic; but the more celebrated places we visited, and the more he admired them, the less use it would have been to plead with him. They seemed only to make him more determined—more terrible,' said poor Catherine. 'I shall never bring him round, and I expect nothing now.'

'Well, I must say,' Mrs Penniman answered, 'I never supposed you were going to give it up.'

'I have given it up. I don't care now.'

'You have grown very brave,' said Mrs Penniman, with a short laugh. 'I didn't advise you to sacrifice your property.'

'Yes, I am braver than I was. You asked me if I had changed; I have changed in that way. Oh,' the girl went on, 'I have changed very much. And it isn't my property. If *he* doesn't care for it, why should I?'

Mrs Penniman hesitated. 'Perhaps he does care for it.'

'He cares for it for my sake, because he doesn't want to injure me. But he will know—he knows already—how little he need be afraid about that. Besides,' said Catherine, 'I have got plenty of money of my own. We shall be very well off; and now hasn't he got his business? I am delighted about that business.' She went on talking, showing a good deal of excitement as she proceeded. Her aunt had never seen her with just this manner, and Mrs Penniman, observing her, set it down to foreign travel, which had made her more positive, more mature. She thought also that Catherine had improved in appearance; she looked rather handsome. Mrs Penniman wondered whether Morris Townsend would be struck with that. While she was engaged in this speculation, Catherine broke out, with a certain sharpness, 'Why are you so contradictory, Aunt Penniman? You seem to think one thing at one time, and another at another. A year ago, before I went away, you wished me not to mind about displeasing father; and now you seem to recommend me to take another line. You change about so.'

This attack was unexpected, for Mrs Penniman was not used, in any discussion, to seeing the war carried into her own country—possibly because the enemy generally had doubts of finding subsistence there. To her own consciousness, the flowery fields of her reason had rarely been ravaged by a hostile force. It was perhaps on this account that in defending them she was majestic rather than agile.

'I don't know what you accuse me of, save of being too deeply interested in your happiness. It is the first time I have been told I am capricious. That fault is not what I am usually reproached with.'

'You were angry last year that I wouldn't marry immediately, and now you talk about my winning my father over. You told me it would serve him right if he should take me to Europe for nothing. Well, he has taken me for nothing, and you ought to be satisfied. Nothing is changed—nothing but my feeling about father. I don't mind nearly so much now. I have been as good as I could, but he doesn't care. Now I don't care either. I don't know whether I have grown bad; perhaps I have. But I don't care for that. I have come home to be married—that's all I know. That ought to please you, unless you have taken up some new idea; you are so strange. You may do as you please; but you must never speak to me again about pleading with father. I shall never plead with him for anything; that is all over. He has put me off. I am come home to be married.'

This was a more authoritative speech than she had ever heard on her niece's lips, and Mrs Penniman was proportionately startled. She was indeed a little awe-struck, and the force of the girl's emotion and resolution left her nothing to reply. She was easily frightened, and she always carried off her discomfiture by a concession; a concession which was often accompanied, as in the present case, by a little nervous laugh.

XXVI

IF she had disturbed her niece's temper—she began from this moment forward to talk a good deal about Catherine's temper, an article which up to that time had never been mentioned in connection with our heroine—Catherine had opportunity, on the morrow, to recover her serenity. Mrs Penniman had given her a message from Morris Townsend, to the effect that he would come and welcome her home on the day after her arrival. He came in the afternoon; but, as may be imagined, he was not on this occasion made free of Dr Sloper's study. He had been coming and going, for the past year, so comfortably and irresponsibly, that he had a certain sense of being wronged by finding himself reminded that he must now limit his horizon to the front-parlour, which was Catherine's particular province.

'I am very glad you have come back,' he said; 'it makes me very happy to see you again. And he looked at her, smiling, from head to foot; though it did not appear, afterwards, that he agreed with Mrs Penniman (who, womanlike, went more into details) in thinking her embellished.

To Catherine he appeared resplendent; it was some time before she could believe again that this beautiful young man was her own exclusive property. They had a great deal of characteristic lovers' talk—a soft exchange of inquiries and assurances. In these matters Morris had an excellent grace, which flung a picturesque interest even over the account of his debut in the commission-business—a subject as to which his companion earnestly questioned him. From time to time he got up from the sofa where they sat together, and walked about the room; after which he came back, smiling and passing his hand through his hair. He was unquiet, as was natural in a young man who has just been re-united to a long-absent mistress, and Catherine made the reflection that she had never seen him so excited. It gave her pleasure, somehow, to note this fact. He asked her questions about her travels, to some of which she was unable to reply, for she had forgotten the names of places and the order of her father's journey. But for the moment she was so happy, so lifted up by the belief that her troubles at last were over, that she forgot to be ashamed of her meagre answers. It seemed to her now that she could marry him without the remnant of a scruple or a single tremor save those that belonged to joy. Without waiting for him to ask, she told him that her father had come back in exactly the same state of mind—that he had not yielded an inch.

'We must not expect it now,' she said, 'and we must do without it.'

Morris sat looking and smiling. 'My poor dear girl!' he exclaimed.

'You mustn't pity me,' said Catherine; 'I don't mind it now—I am used to it.'

Morris continued to smile, and then he got up and walked about again. 'You had better let me try him!'

'Try to bring him over? You would only make him worse,' Catherine answered, resolutely.

'You say that because I managed it so badly before. But I should manage it differently now. I am much wiser; I have had a year to think of it. I have more tact.'

'Is that what you have been thinking of for a year?'

'Much of the time. You see, the idea sticks in my crop.* I don't like to be beaten.'

'How are you beaten if we marry?'

'Of course, I am not beaten on the main issue; but I am, don't you see, on all the rest of it—on the question of my reputation, of my relations with your father, of my relations with my own children, if we should have any.'

'We shall have enough for our children—we shall have enough for everything. Don't you expect to succeed in business?'

'Brilliantly, and we shall certainly be very comfortable. But it isn't of the mere material comfort I speak; it is of the moral comfort,' said Morris—'of the intellectual satisfaction!'

'I have great moral comfort now,' Catherine declared, very simply.

'Of course you have. But with me it is different. I have staked my pride on proving to your father that he is wrong; and now that I am at the head of a flourishing business, I can deal with him as an equal. I have a capital plan—do let me go at him!'

He stood before her with his bright face, his jaunty air, his hands in his pockets; and she got up, with her eyes resting on his own. 'Please don't, Morris; please don't,' she said; and there was a certain mild, sad firmness in her tone which he heard for the first time. 'We must ask no favours of him—we must ask nothing more. He won't relent, and nothing good will come of it. I know it now—I have a very good reason.'

'And pray what is your reason?'

She hesitated to bring it out, but at last it came. 'He is not very fond of me!'

'Oh, bother!' cried Morris, angrily.

'I wouldn't say such a thing without being sure. I saw it, I felt it, in England, just before he came away. He talked to me one night—the last night; and then it came over me. You can tell when a person feels that way. I wouldn't accuse him if he hadn't made me feel that way. I don't accuse him; I just tell you that that's how it is. He can't help it; we can't govern our affections. Do I govern mine? mightn't he say that to me? It's because he is so fond of my mother, whom we lost so long ago. She was beautiful, and very, very brilliant; he is always thinking of her. I am not at all like her; Aunt Penniman has told me that. Of course it isn't my fault; but neither is it his fault. All I mean is, it's true; and it's a stronger reason for his never being reconciled than simply his dislike for you.'

'"Simply?"' cried Morris, with a laugh, 'I am much obliged for that!'

'I don't mind about his disliking you now; I mind everything less. I feel differently; I feel separated from my father.'

'Upon my word,' said Morris, 'you are a queer family!'

'Don't say that—don't say anything unkind,' the girl entreated. 'You must be very kind to me now, because, Morris—because,' and she hesitated a moment—'because I have done a great deal for you.'

'Oh, I know that, my dear!'

She had spoken up to this moment without vehemence or outward sign of emotion, gently, reasoningly, only trying to explain. But her emotion had been ineffectually smothered, and it betrayed itself at last in the trembling of her voice. 'It is a great thing to be separated like that from your father, when you have worshipped him before. It has made me very unhappy; or it would have made me so if I didn't love you. You can tell when a person speaks to you as if—as if—'

'As if what?'

'As if they despised you!' said Catherine, passionately. 'He spoke that way the night before we sailed. It wasn't much, but it was enough, and I thought of it on the voyage, all the time. Then I made up my mind. I will never ask him for anything again, or expect anything from him.

It would not be natural now. We must be very happy together, and we must not seem to depend upon his forgiveness. And Morris, Morris, you must never despise me!'

This was an easy promise to make, and Morris made it with fine effect. But for the moment he undertook nothing more onerous.

XXVII

THE Doctor, of course, on his return, had a good deal of talk with his sisters. He was at no great pains to narrate his travels or to communicate his impressions of distant lands to Mrs Penniman, upon whom he contented himself with bestowing a memento of his enviable experience, in the shape of a velvet gown. But he conversed with her at some length about matters nearer home, and lost no time in assuring her that he was still an inflexible father.

'I have no doubt you have seen a great deal of Mr Townsend, and done your best to console him for Catherine's absence,' he said. 'I don't ask you, and you needn't deny it. I wouldn't put the question to you for the world, and expose you to the inconvenience of having to—a—excogitate an answer. No one has betrayed you, and there has been no spy upon your proceedings. Elizabeth has told no tales, and has never mentioned you except to praise your good looks and good spirits. The thing is simply an inference of my own—an induction, as the philosophers say. It seems to me likely that you would have offered an asylum to an interesting sufferer. Mr Townsend has been a good deal in the house; there is something in the house that tells me so. We doctors, you know, end by acquiring fine perceptions, and it is impressed upon my sensorium* that he has sat in these chairs, in a very easy attitude, and warmed himself at that fire. I don't grudge him the comfort of it; it is the only one he will ever enjoy at my expense. It seems likely, indeed, that I shall be able to economize at his own. I don't know what you may have said to him, or what you may say hereafter; but I should like you to know that if you have encouraged him to believe that he will gain anything by hanging on, or that I have budged a hair's breadth from the position I took up a year ago, you have played him a trick for which he may exact reparation. I'm not sure that he may not bring a suit against you. Of course you have done it conscientiously; you have made yourself believe that I can be tired out. This is the most baseless hallucination that ever visited the brain of a genial optimist. I am not in the least tired; I am as fresh as when I started; I am good for fifty years yet. Catherine appears not to have budged an inch either; she is equally fresh; so we are about where we were before. This, however, you know as well as I.

What I wish is simply to give you notice of my own state of mind! Take it to heart, dear Lavinia. Beware of the just resentment of a deluded fortune-hunter!'

'I can't say I expected it,' said Mrs Penniman. 'And I had a sort of foolish hope that you would come home without that odious ironical tone with which you treat the most sacred subjects.'

'Don't undervalue irony, it is often of great use. It is not, however, always necessary, and I will show you how gracefully I can lay it aside. I should like to know whether you think Morris Townsend will hang on.'

'I will answer you with your own weapons,' said Mrs Penniman. 'You had better wait and see!'

'Do you call such a speech as that one of my own weapons? I never said anything so rough.'

'He will hang on long enough to make you very uncomfortable, then.'

'My dear Lavinia,' exclaimed the Doctor, 'do you call that irony? I call it pugilism.'

Mrs Penniman, however, in spite of her pugilism, was a good deal frightened, and she took counsel of her fears. Her brother meanwhile took counsel, with many reservations, of Mrs Almond, to whom he was no less generous than to Lavinia, and a good deal more communicative.

'I suppose she has had him there all the while,' he said. 'I must look into the state of my wine! You needn't mind telling me now; I have already said all I mean to say to her on the subject.'

'I believe he was in the house a good deal,' Mrs Almond answered. 'But you must admit that your leaving Lavinia quite alone was a great change for her, and that it was natural she should want some society.'

'I do admit that, and that is why I shall make no row about the wine; I shall set it down as compensation to Lavinia. She is capable of telling me that she drank it all herself. Think of the inconceivable bad taste, in the circumstances, of that fellow making free with the house—or coming there at all! If that doesn't describe him, he is indescribable.'

'His plan is to get what he can. Lavinia will have supported him for a year,' said Mrs Almond. 'It's so much gained.'

'She will have to support him for the rest of his life, then!' cried the Doctor. 'But without wine, as they say at the *tables d'hôte.*'*

'Catherine tells me he has set up a business, and is making a great deal of money.'

The Doctor stared. 'She has not told me that—and Lavinia didn't deign. Ah!' he cried, 'Catherine has given me up. Not that it matters, for all that the business amounts to.'

'She has not given up Mr Townsend,' said Mrs Almond. 'I saw that in the first half-minute. She has come home exactly the same.'

'Exactly the same; not a grain more intelligent. She didn't notice a stick or a stone all the while we were away—not a picture nor a view, not a statue nor a cathedral.'

'How could she notice? She had other things to think of; they are never for an instant out of her mind. She touches me very much.'

'She would touch me if she didn't irritate me. That's the effect she has upon me now. I have tried everything upon her; I really have been quite merciless. But it is of no use whatever; she is absolutely *glued*. I have passed, in consequence, into the exasperated stage. At first I had a good deal of a certain genial curiosity about it; I wanted to see if she really would stick. But, good Lord, one's curiosity is satisfied! I see she is capable of it, and now she can let go.'

'She will never let go,' said Mrs Almond.

'Take care, or you will exasperate me too. If she doesn't let go, she will be shaken off—sent tumbling into the dust! That's a nice position for my daughter. She can't see that if you are going to be pushed you had better jump. And then she will complain of her bruises.'

'She will never complain,' said Mrs Almond.

'That I shall object to even more. But the deuce will be that I can't prevent anything.'

'If she is to have a fall,' said Mrs Almond, with a gentle laugh, 'we must spread as many carpets as we can.' And she carried out this idea by showing a great deal of motherly kindness to the girl.

Mrs Penniman immediately wrote to Morris Townsend. The intimacy between these two was by this time consummate, but I must content myself with noting but a few of its features. Mrs Penniman's own share in it was a singular sentiment, which might have been misinterpreted, but which in itself was not discreditable to the poor lady. It was a romantic interest in this attractive and unfortunate young man, and yet it was not such an interest as Catherine might have been jealous of. Mrs Penniman had not a particle of jealousy of her niece. For herself, she felt as if she were Morris's mother or sister—a mother or sister of an emotional temperament—and she had an absorbing desire to make him comfortable and happy. She had striven to do so during the year that her brother left her an open field, and her efforts had been attended with the success that has been pointed out. She had never had a child of her own, and Catherine, whom she had done her best to invest with the importance that would naturally belong to a youthful Penniman, had only partly rewarded her zeal. Catherine, as an object of affection and solicitude, had never had that picturesque charm which (as it seemed to her) would have been a natural attribute of her own progeny. Even the maternal passion in Mrs Penniman would have been romantic and factitious, and Catherine was not constituted to inspire a romantic passion. Mrs Penniman was as fond of her as ever, but she had grown to feel that with Catherine she lacked opportunity. Sentimentally speaking, therefore, she had (though she had not disinherited her niece) adopted Morris Townsend, who gave her opportunity in abundance. She would have been very happy to have a handsome and tyrannical son, and would have taken an extreme interest in his love affairs. This was the light in which she had come to regard Morris, who had conciliated her at first, and made his impression by his delicate and calculated deference—a sort of exhibition to which Mrs Penniman was particularly sensitive. He had largely abated his deference afterwards, for he economized his resources, but the impression was made, and the young man's very brutality came to have a sort of filial value. If Mrs Penniman had had a son, she would probably have been afraid of him, and at this stage of our narrative she was certainly afraid of Morris Townsend. This was one of the results of his domestication in Washington Square. He took his ease with her—as, for that matter, he would certainly have done with his own mother.

XXVIII

THE letter was a word of warning; it informed him that the Doctor had come home more impracticable than ever. She might have reflected that Catherine would supply him with all the information he needed on this point; but we know that Mrs Penniman's reflections were rarely just; and, moreover, she felt that it was not for her to depend on what Catherine might do. She was to do her duty, quite irrespective of Catherine. I have said that her young friend took his ease with her, and it is an illustration of the fact that he made no answer to her letter. He took note of it, amply; but he lighted his cigar with it, and he waited, in tranquil confidence that he should receive another. 'His state of mind really freezes my blood,' Mrs Penniman had written, alluding to her brother; and it would have seemed that upon this statement she could hardly improve. Nevertheless, she wrote again, expressing herself with the aid of a different figure. 'His hatred of you burns with a lurid flame—the flame that never dies,' she wrote. 'But it doesn't light up the darkness of your future. If my affection could do so, all the years of your life would be an eternal sunshine. I can extract nothing from C.; she is so terribly secretive, like her father. She seems to expect to be married very soon, and has evidently made preparations in Europe—quantities of clothing, ten pairs of shoes, etc. My dear friend, you cannot set up in married life simply with a few pairs of shoes, can you? Tell me what you think of this. I am intensely anxious to see you; I have so much to say. I miss you dreadfully; the house seems so empty without you. What is the news down town? Is the business extending? That dear little business—I think it's so brave of you! Couldn't I come to your office?—just for three minutes? I might pass for a customer—is that what you call them? I might come in to buy something—some shares or some railroad things. *Tell me what you think of this plan.* I would carry a little reticule,* like a woman of the people.'

In spite of the suggestion about the reticule, Morris appeared to think poorly of the plan, for he gave Mrs Penniman no encouragement whatever to visit his office, which he had already represented to her as a place peculiarly and unnaturally difficult to find. But as she persisted in desiring an interview—up to the last, after months of

intimate colloquy, she called these meetings 'interviews'—he agreed
that they should take a walk together, and was even kind enough to
leave his office for this purpose, during the hours at which business
might have been supposed to be liveliest. It was no surprise to him,
when they met at a street-corner, in a region of empty lots and undeveloped pavements (Mrs Penniman being attired as much as possible
like a 'woman of the people'), to find that, in spite of her urgency, what
she chiefly had to convey to him was the assurance of her sympathy.
Of such assurances, however, he had already a voluminous collection,
and it would not have been worth his while to forsake a fruitful avoca-
tion merely to hear Mrs Penniman say, for the thousandth time, that
she had made his cause her own. Morris had something of his own to
say. It was not an easy thing to bring out,* and while he turned it over
the difficulty made him acrimonious.

'Oh yes, I know perfectly that he combines the properties of a lump
of ice and a red-hot coal,' he observed. 'Catherine has made it thoroughly clear, and you have told me so till I am sick of it. You needn't
tell me again; I am perfectly satisfied. He will never give us a penny;
I regard that as mathematically proved.'

Mrs Penniman at this point had an inspiration.

'Couldn't you bring a lawsuit against him?' She wondered that this
simple expedient had never occurred to her before.

'I will bring a lawsuit against *you*,' said Morris, 'if you ask me any
more such aggravating questions. A man should know when he is
beaten,' he added, in a moment. 'I must give her up!'

Mrs Penniman received this declaration in silence, though it made
her heart beat a little. It found her by no means unprepared, for she
had accustomed herself to the thought that, if Morris should decidedly not be able to get her brother's money, it would not do for him
to marry Catherine without it. 'It would not do' was a vague way of
putting the thing; but Mrs Penniman's natural affection completed
the idea, which, though it had not as yet been so crudely expressed
between them as in the form that Morris had just given it, had nevertheless been implied so often, in certain easy intervals of talk, as he
sat stretching his legs in the Doctor's well-stuffed arm-chairs, that
she had grown first to regard it with an emotion which she flattered
herself was philosophic, and then to have a secret tenderness for
it. The fact that she kept her tenderness secret proves, of course,
that she was ashamed of it; but she managed to blink her shame by

reminding herself that she was, after all, the official protector of her niece's marriage. Her logic would scarcely have passed muster with the Doctor. In the first place, Morris *must* get the money, and she would help him to it. In the second, it was plain it would never come to him, and it would be a grievous pity he should marry without it—a young man who might so easily find something better. After her brother had delivered himself, on his return from Europe, of that incisive little address that has been quoted, Morris's cause seemed so hopeless that Mrs Penniman fixed her attention exclusively upon the latter branch of her argument. If Morris had been her son, she would certainly have sacrificed Catherine to a superior conception of his future; and to be ready to do so as the case stood was therefore even a finer degree of devotion. Nevertheless, it checked her breath a little to have the sacrificial knife, as it were, suddenly thrust into her hand.

Morris walked along a moment, and then he repeated, harshly—

'I must give her up!'

'I think I understand you,' said Mrs Penniman, gently.

'I certainly say it distinctly enough—brutally and vulgarly enough.'

He was ashamed of himself, and his shame was uncomfortable; and as he was extremely intolerant of discomfort, he felt vicious and cruel. He wanted to abuse somebody, and he began, cautiously—for he was always cautious—with himself.

'Couldn't you take her down a little?' he asked.

'Take her down?'

'Prepare her—try and ease me off.'

Mrs Penniman stopped, looking at him very solemnly.

'My poor Morris, do you know how much she loves you?'

'No, I don't. I don't want to know. I have always tried to keep from knowing. It would be too painful.'

'She will suffer much,' said Mrs Penniman.

'You must console her. If you are as good a friend to me as you pretend to be, you will manage it.'

Mrs Penniman shook her head, sadly.

'You talk of my "pretending" to like you; but I can't pretend to hate you. I can only tell her I think very highly of you; and how will that console her for losing you?'

'The Doctor will help you. He will be delighted at the thing being broken off, and, as he is a knowing fellow, he will invent something to comfort her.'

'He will invent a new torture!' cried Mrs Penniman. 'Heaven deliver her from her father's comfort. It will consist of his crowing over her and saying, "I always told you so!"'

Morris coloured a most uncomfortable red.

'If you don't console her any better than you console me, you certainly won't be of much use! It's a damned disagreeable necessity; I feel it extremely, and you ought to make it easy for me.'

'I will be your friend for life!' Mrs Penniman declared.

'Be my friend *now*!' And Morris walked on.

She went with him; she was almost trembling.

'Should you like me to tell her?' she asked.

'You mustn't tell her, but you can—you can—'. And he hesitated, trying to think what Mrs Penniman could do. 'You can explain to her why it is. It's because I can't bring myself to step in between her and her father—to give him the pretext he grasps at so eagerly (it's a hideous sight) for depriving her of her rights.'

Mrs Penniman felt with remarkable promptitude the charm of this formula.

'That's so like you,' she said; 'it's so finely felt.'

Morris gave his stick an angry swing.

'Oh botheration!' he exclaimed perversely.

Mrs Penniman, however, was not discouraged.

'It may turn out better than you think. Catherine is, after all, so very peculiar.' And she thought she might take it upon herself to assure him that, whatever happened, the girl would be very quiet— she wouldn't make a noise. They extended their walk, and, while they proceeded, Mrs Penniman took upon herself other things besides, and ended by having assumed a considerable burden; Morris being ready enough, as may be imagined, to put everything off upon her. But he was not for a single instant the dupe of her blundering alacrity; he knew that of what she promised she was competent to perform but an insignificant fraction, and the more she professed her willingness to serve him, the greater fool he thought her.

'What will you do if you don't marry her?' she ventured to inquire in the course of this conversation.

'Something brilliant,' said Morris. 'Shouldn't you like me to do something brilliant?'

The idea gave Mrs Penniman exceeding pleasure.

'I shall feel sadly taken in if you don't.'

'I shall have to, to make up for this. This isn't at all brilliant, you know.'

Mrs Penniman mused a little, as if there might be some way of making out that it was; but she had to give up the attempt, and, to carry off the awkwardness of failure, she risked a new inquiry.

'Do you mean—do you mean another marriage?'

Morris greeted this question with a reflection which was hardly the less impudent from being inaudible. 'Surely, women are more crude than men!' And then he answered audibly—

'Never in the world!'

Mrs Penniman felt disappointed and snubbed, and she relieved herself in a little vaguely sarcastic cry. He was certainly perverse.

'I give her up not for another woman, but for a wider career!' Morris announced.

This was very grand; but still Mrs Penniman, who felt that she had exposed herself, was faintly rancorous.

'Do you mean never to come to see her again?' she asked, with some sharpness.

'Oh no, I shall come again; but what is the use of dragging it out? I have been four times since she came back, and it's terribly awkward work. I can't keep it up indefinitely; she oughtn't to expect that, you know. A woman should never keep a man dangling!' he added, finely.

'Ah, but you must have your last parting!' urged his companion, in whose imagination the idea of last partings occupied a place inferior in dignity only to that of first meetings.

XXIX

HE came again, without managing the last parting; and again and again, without finding that Mrs Penniman had as yet done much to pave the path of retreat with flowers. It was devilish awkward, as he said, and he felt a lively animosity for Catherine's aunt, who, as he had now quite formed the habit of saying to himself, had dragged him into the mess and was bound in common charity to get him out of it. Mrs Penniman, to tell the truth, had, in the seclusion of her own apartment—and, I may add, amid the suggestiveness of Catherine's, which wore in those days the appearance of that of a young lady laying out her *trousseau*—Mrs Penniman had measured her responsibilities, and taken fright at their magnitude. The task of preparing Catherine and easing off Morris presented difficulties which increased in the execution, and even led the impulsive Lavinia to ask herself whether the modification of the young man's original project had been conceived in a happy spirit. A brilliant future, a wider career, a conscience exempt from the reproach of interference between a young lady and her natural rights—these excellent things might be too troublesomely purchased. From Catherine herself Mrs Penniman received no assistance whatever; the poor girl was apparently without suspicion of her danger. She looked at her lover with eyes of undiminished trust, and though she had less confidence in her aunt than in a young man with whom she had exchanged so many tender vows, she gave her no handle for explaining or confessing. Mrs Penniman, faltering and wavering, declared Catherine was very stupid, put off the great scene, as she would have called it, from day to day, and wandered about very uncomfortably, primed, to repletion, with her apology, but unable to bring it to the light. Morris's own scenes were very small ones just now; but even these were beyond his strength. He made his visits as brief as possible, and, while he sat with his mistress, found terribly little to talk about. She was waiting for him, in vulgar parlance, to name the day; and so long as he was unprepared to be explicit on this point, it seemed a mockery to pretend to talk about matters more abstract. She had no airs and no arts; she never attempted to disguise her expectancy. She was waiting on his good pleasure, and would wait modestly and patiently; his hanging back at this supreme time might appear strange, but of course he must have a good reason for it. Catherine would have made a wife of the gentle old-fashioned pattern—regarding reasons as favours and windfalls, but no more expecting one every day than she would have expected a bouquet of camellias. During the period of her engagement, however, a young lady even of the most slender pretensions counts upon more bouquets than at other times; and there was a want of perfume in the air at this moment which at last excited the girl's alarm.

'Are you sick?' she asked of Morris. 'You seem so restless, and you look pale.'

'I am not at all well,' said Morris; and it occurred to him that, if he could only make her pity him enough, he might get off.

'I am afraid you are overworked; you oughtn't to work so much.'

'I must do that.' And then he added, with a sort of calculated brutality, 'I don't want to owe you everything!'

'Ah, how can you say that?'

'I am too proud,' said Morris.

'Yes—you are too proud!'

'Well, you must take me as I am,' he went on. 'You can never change me.'

'I don't want to change you,' she said, gently. 'I will take you as you are!' And she stood looking at him.

'You know people talk tremendously about a man's marrying a rich girl,' Morris remarked. 'It's excessively disagreeable.'

'But I am not rich?' said Catherine.

'You are rich enough to make me talked about!'

'Of course you are talked about. It's an honour!'

'It's an honour I could easily dispense with.'

She was on the point of asking him whether it were not a compensation for this annoyance that the poor girl who had the misfortune to bring it upon him loved him so dearly and believed in him so truly; but she hesitated, thinking that this would perhaps seem an exacting speech, and while she hesitated, he suddenly left her.

The next time he came, however, she brought it out, and she told him again that he was too proud. He repeated that he couldn't change, and this time she felt the impulse to say that with a little effort he might change.

Sometimes he thought that if he could only make a quarrel with her it might help him; but the question was how to quarrel with a young woman who had such treasures of concession. 'I suppose you think the effort is all on your side!' he was reduced to exclaiming. 'Don't you believe that I have my own effort to make?'

'It's all yours now,' she said. 'My effort is finished and done with!'

'Well, mine is not.'

'We must bear things together,' said Catherine. 'That's what we ought to do.'

Morris attempted a natural smile. 'There are some things which we can't very well bear together—for instance, separation.'

'Why do you speak of separation?'

'Ah! you don't like it; I knew you wouldn't!'

'Where are you going, Morris?' she suddenly asked.

He fixed his eye on her a moment, and for a part of that moment she was afraid of it. 'Will you promise not to make a scene?'

'A scene!—do I make scenes?'

'All women do!' said Morris, with the tone of large experience.

'I don't. Where are you going?'

'If I should say I was going away on business, should you think it very strange?'

She wondered a moment, gazing at him. 'Yes—no. Not if you will take me with you.'

'Take you with me—on business?'

'What is your business? Your business is to be with me.'

'I don't earn my living with you,' said Morris, 'Or rather,' he cried with a sudden inspiration, 'that's just what I do—or what the world says I do?'

This ought perhaps to have been a great stroke, but it miscarried. 'Where are you going?' Catherine simply repeated.

'To New Orleans. About buying some cotton.'

'I am perfectly willing to go to New Orleans,' Catherine said.

'Do you suppose I would take you to a nest of yellow fever?'* cried Morris. 'Do you suppose I would expose you at such a time as this?'

'If there is yellow fever, why should you go? Morris, you must not go!'

'It is to make six thousand dollars,' said Morris. 'Do you grudge me that satisfaction?'

'We have no need of six thousand dollars. You think too much about money!'

'You can afford to say that? This is a great chance; we heard of it last night.' And he explained to her in what the chance consisted; and told her a long story, going over more than once several of the details, about the remarkable stroke of business which he and his partner had planned between them.

But Catherine's imagination, for reasons best known to herself, absolutely refused to be fired. 'If you can go to New Orleans, I can go,' she said. 'Why shouldn't you catch yellow fever quite as easily as I? I am every bit as strong as you, and not in the least afraid of any fever. When we were in Europe, we were in very unhealthy places; my father used to make me take some pills. I never caught anything, and I never was nervous. What will be the use of six thousand dollars if you die of a fever? When persons are going to be married, they oughtn't to think so much about business. You shouldn't think about cotton, you should think about me. You can go to New Orleans some other time—there will always be plenty of cotton. It isn't the moment to choose—we have waited too long already.' She spoke more forcibly and volubly than he had ever heard her, and she held his arm in her two hands.

'You said you wouldn't make a scene!' cried Morris. 'I call this a scene.'

'It's you that are making it! I have never asked you anything before. We have waited too long already.' And it was a comfort to her to think that she had hitherto asked so little; it seemed to make her right to insist the greater now.

Morris bethought himself a little. 'Very well, then; we won't talk about it any more. I will transact my business by letter.' And he began to smooth his hat, as if to take leave.

'You won't go?' And she stood looking up at him.

He could not give up his idea of provoking a quarrel; it was so much the simplest way! He bent his eyes on her upturned face, with the darkest frown he could achieve. 'You are not discreet. You mustn't bully me!'

But, as usual, she conceded everything. 'No, I am not discreet; I know I am too pressing. But isn't it natural? It is only for a moment.'

'In a moment you may do a great deal of harm. Try and be calmer the next time I come.'

'When will you come?'

'Do you want to make conditions?' Morris asked. 'I will come next Saturday.'

'Come to-morrow,' Catherine begged; 'I want you to come to-morrow. I will be very quiet,' she added; and her agitation had by this time become so great that the assurance was not unbecoming. A sudden fear had come over her; it was like the solid conjunction of a dozen disembodied doubts, and her imagination, at a single bound, had traversed an enormous distance. All her being, for the moment, centred in the wish to keep him in the room.

Morris bent his head and kissed her forehead. 'When you are quiet, you are perfection,' he said; 'but when you are violent, you are not in character.'

It was Catherine's wish that there should be no violence about her save the beating of her heart, which she could not help; and she went on, as gently as possible, 'Will you promise to come tomorrow?'

'I said Saturday!' Morris answered smiling. He tried a frown at one moment, a smile at another; he was at his wit's end.

'Yes, Saturday too,' she answered, trying to smile. 'But tomorrow first.' He was going to the door, and she went with him, quickly. She leaned her shoulder against it; it seemed to her that she would do anything to keep him.

'If I am prevented from coming to-morrow, you will say I have deceived you!' he said.

'How can you be prevented? You can come if you will.'

'I am a busy man—I am not a dangler!'* cried Morris, sternly.

His voice was so hard and unnatural that, with a helpless look at him, she turned away; and then he quickly laid his hand on the door-knob. He felt as if he were absolutely running away from her. But in an instant she was close to him again, and murmuring in a tone none the less penetrating for being low, 'Morris, you are going to leave me.'

'Yes, for a little while.'

'For how long?'

'Till you are reasonable again.'

'I shall never be reasonable in that way!' And she tried to keep him longer; it was almost a struggle. 'Think of what I have done!' she broke out. 'Morris, I have given up everything!'

'You shall have everything back!'

'You wouldn't say that if you didn't mean something. What is it?—what has happened?—what have I done?—what has changed you?'

'I will write to you—that is better,' Morris stammered.

'Ah, you won't come back!' she cried, bursting into tears.

'Dear Catherine,' he said, 'don't believe that! I promise you that you shall see me again!' And he managed to get away and to close the door behind him.

XXX

IT was almost her last outbreak of passive grief; at least, she never indulged in another that the world knew anything about. But this one was long and terrible; she flung herself on the sofa and gave herself up to her misery. She hardly knew what had happened; ostensibly she had only had a difference with her lover, as other girls had had before, and the thing was not only not a rupture, but she was under no obligation to regard it even as a menace. Nevertheless, she felt a wound, even if he had not dealt it; it seemed to her that a mask had suddenly fallen from his face. He had wished to get away from her; he had been angry and cruel, and said strange things, with strange looks. She was smothered and stunned; she buried her head in the cushions, sobbing and talking to herself. But at last she raised herself, with the fear that either her father or Mrs Penniman would come in; and then she sat there, staring before her, while the room grew darker. She said to herself that perhaps he would come back to tell her he had not meant what he said; and she listened for his ring at the door, trying to believe that this was probable. A long time passed, but Morris remained absent; the shadows gathered; the evening settled down on the meagre elegance of the light, clear-coloured room; the fire went out. When it had grown dark, Catherine went to the window and looked out; she stood there for half an hour, on the mere chance that he would come up the steps. At last she turned away, for she saw her father come in. He had seen her at the window looking out, and he stopped a moment at the bottom of the white steps, and gravely, with an air of exaggerated courtesy, lifted his hat to her. The gesture was so incongruous to the condition she was in, this stately tribute of respect to a poor girl despised and forsaken was so out of place, that the thing gave her a kind of horror, and she hurried away to her room. It seemed to her that she had given Morris up.

She had to show herself half an hour later, and she was sustained at table by the immensity of her desire that her father should not perceive that anything had happened. This was a great help to her afterwards, and it served her (though never as much as she supposed) from the first. On this occasion Dr Sloper was rather talkative. He told a great many stories about a wonderful poodle that he had seen at the house of an old lady whom he visited professionally. Catherine not only tried to appear to listen to the anecdotes of the poodle, but she endeavoured to interest herself in them, so as not to think of her scene with Morris. That perhaps was an hallucination; he was mistaken, she was jealous; people didn't change like that from one day to another. Then she knew that she had had doubts before—strange suspicions, that were at once vague and acute—and that he had been different ever since her return from Europe: whereupon she tried again to listen to her father, who told a story so remarkably well. Afterwards she went straight to her own room; it was beyond her strength to undertake to spend the evening with her aunt. All the evening, alone, she questioned herself. Her trouble was terrible; but was it a thing of her imagination, engendered by an extravagant sensibility, or did it represent a clear-cut reality, and had the worst that was possible actually come to pass? Mrs Penniman, with a degree of tact that was as unusual as it was commendable, took the line of leaving her alone. The truth is, that her suspicions having been aroused, she indulged a desire, natural to a timid person, that the explosion should be localized. So long as the air still vibrated she kept out of the way.

She passed and repassed Catherine's door several times in the course of the evening, as if she expected to hear a plaintive moan behind it. But the room remained perfectly still; and accordingly, the last thing before retiring to her own couch, she applied for admittance. Catherine was sitting up, and had a book that she pretended to be reading. She had no wish to go to bed, for she had no expectation of sleeping. After Mrs Penniman had left her she sat up half the night, and she offered her visitor no inducement to remain. Her aunt came stealing in very gently, and approached her with great solemnity.

'I am afraid you are in trouble, my dear. Can I do anything to help you?'

'I am not in any trouble whatever, and do not need any help,' said Catherine, fibbing roundly, and proving thereby that not only our faults, but our most involuntary misfortunes, tend to corrupt our morals.

'Has nothing happened to you?'

'Nothing whatever.'

'Are you very sure, dear?'

'Perfectly sure.'

'And can I really do nothing for you?'

'Nothing, aunt, but kindly leave me alone,' said Catherine.

Mrs Penniman, though she had been afraid of too warm a welcome before, was now disappointed at so cold a one; and in relating afterwards, as she did to many persons, and with considerable variations of detail, the history of the termination of her niece's engagement, she was usually careful to mention that the young lady, on a certain occasion, had 'hustled' her out of the room. It was characteristic of Mrs Penniman that she related this fact, not in the least out of malignity to Catherine, whom she very sufficiently pitied, but simply from a natural disposition to embellish any subject that she touched.

Catherine, as I have said, sat up half the night, as if she still expected to hear Morris Townsend ring at the door. On the morrow this expectation was less unreasonable; but it was not gratified by the reappearance of the young man. Neither had he written; there was not a word of explanation or reassurance. Fortunately for Catherine she could take refuge from her excitement, which had now become intense, in her determination that her father should see nothing of it. How well she deceived her father we shall have occasion to learn; but her innocent arts were of little avail before a person of the rare perspicacity of Mrs Penniman. This lady easily saw that she was agitated, and if there was any agitation going forward, Mrs Penniman was not a person to forfeit her natural share in it. She returned to the charge the next evening, and requested her niece to lean upon her—to unburden her heart. Perhaps she should be able to explain certain things that now seemed dark, and that she knew more about than Catherine supposed. If Catherine had been frigid the night before, to-day she was haughty.

'You are completely mistaken, and I have not the least idea what you mean. I don't know what you are trying to fasten on me, and I have never had less need of any one's explanations in my life.'

In this way the girl delivered herself, and from hour to hour kept her aunt at bay. From hour to hour Mrs Penniman's curiosity grew. She would have given her little finger to know what Morris had said and done, what tone he had taken, what pretext he had found. She wrote to him, naturally, to request an interview; but she received, as naturally, no answer to her petition. Morris was not in a writing mood; for Catherine had addressed him two short notes which met with no acknowledgment. These notes were so brief that I may give them entire. 'Won't you give me some sign that you didn't mean to be so cruel as you seemed on Tuesday?'—that was the first; the other was a little longer. 'If I was unreasonable or suspicious, on Tuesday—if I annoyed you or troubled you in any way—I beg your forgiveness, and I promise never again to be so foolish. I am punished enough, and I don't understand. Dear Morris, you are killing me!' These notes were despatched on the Friday and Saturday; but Saturday and Sunday passed without bringing the poor girl the satisfaction she desired. Her punishment accumulated; she continued to bear it, however, with a good deal of superficial fortitude. On Saturday morning, the Doctor, who had been watching in silence, spoke to his sister Lavinia.

'The thing has happened—the scoundrel has backed out!'

'Never!' cried Mrs Penniman, who had bethought herself what she should say to Catherine, but was not provided with a line of defence against her brother, so that indignant negation was the only weapon in her hands.

'He has begged for a reprieve, then, if you like that better!'

'It seems to make you very happy that your daughter's affections have been trifled with.'

'It does,' said the Doctor; 'for I had foretold it! It's a great pleasure to be in the right.'

'Your pleasures make one shudder!' his sister exclaimed.

Catherine went rigidly through her usual occupations; that is, up to the point of going with her aunt to church on Sunday morning. She generally went to afternoon service as well; but on this occasion her courage faltered, and she begged of Mrs Penniman to go without her

'I am sure you have a secret,' said Mrs Penniman, with great significance, looking at her rather grimly.

'If I have, I shall keep it!' Catherine answered, turning away.

Mrs Penniman started for church; but before she had arrived, she stopped and turned back, and before twenty minutes had elapsed she re-entered the house, looked into the empty parlours, and then went upstairs and knocked at Catherine's door. She got no answer; Catherine was not in her room, and Mrs Penniman presently ascertained that she was not in the house. 'She has gone to him, she has fled!' Lavinia cried, clasping her hands with admiration and envy. But she soon perceived that Catherine had taken nothing with her—all her personal property in her room was intact—and then she jumped at the hypothesis that the girl had gone forth, not in tenderness,

but in resentment. 'She has followed him to his own door—she has
burst upon him in his own apartment!' It was in these terms that
Mrs Penniman depicted to herself her niece's errand, which, viewed
in this light, gratified her sense of the picturesque only a shade less
strongly than the idea of a clandestine marriage. To visit one's lover,
with tears and reproaches, at his own residence, was an image so
agreeable to Mrs Penniman's mind that she felt a sort of aesthetic
disappointment at its lacking, in this case, the harmonious accompaniments of darkness and storm. A quiet Sunday afternoon appeared
an inadequate setting for it; and, indeed, Mrs Penniman was quite
out of humour with the conditions of the time, which passed very
slowly as she sat in the front-parlour, in her bonnet and her cashmere
shawl, awaiting Catherine's return.

This event at last took place. She saw her—at the window—mount
the steps, and she went to await her in the hall, where she pounced
upon her as soon as she had entered the house, and drew her into the
parlour, closing the door with solemnity. Catherine was flushed, and
her eye was bright. Mrs Penniman hardly knew what to think.

'May I venture to ask where you have been?' she demanded.

'I have been to take a walk,' said Catherine. 'I thought you had
gone to church.'

'I did go to church; but the service was shorter than usual. And
pray where did you walk?'

'I don't know!' said Catherine.

'Your ignorance is most extraordinary! Dear Catherine, you can
trust me.'

'What am I to trust you with?'

'With your secret—your sorrow.'

'I have no sorrow!' said Catherine fiercely.

'My poor child,' Mrs Penniman insisted, 'you can't deceive me.
I know everything. I have been requested to—a—to converse with
you.'

'I don't want to converse!'

'It will relieve you. Don't you know Shakespeare's lines?—"the
grief that does not speak!"* My dear girl, it is better as it is.'

'What is better?' Catherine asked.

She was really too perverse. A certain amount of perversity was to
be allowed for in a young lady whose lover had thrown her over; but
not such an amount as would prove inconvenient to his apologists.

'That you should be reasonable,' said Mrs Penniman, with some stern-ness. 'That you should take counsel of worldly prudence, and submit to practical considerations. That you should agree to—a—separate.'

Catherine had been ice up to this moment, but at this word she flamed up. 'Separate? What do you know about our separating?'

Mrs Penniman shook her head with a sadness in which there was almost a sense of injury. 'Your pride is my pride, and your suscep-tibilities are mine. I see your side perfectly, but I also'—and she smiled with melancholy suggestiveness—'I also see the situation as a whole!'

This suggestiveness was lost upon Catherine, who repeated her violent inquiry. 'Why do you talk about separation; what do you know about it?'

'We must study resignation,' said Mrs Penniman, hesitating, but sententious at a venture.

'Resignation to what?'

'To a change of—of our plans.'

'My plans have not changed!' said Catherine, with a little laugh.

'Ah, but Mr Townsend's have,' her aunt answered very gently.

'What do you mean?'

There was an imperious brevity in the tone of this inquiry, against which Mrs Penniman felt bound to protest; the information with which she had undertaken to supply her niece was after all a favour. She had tried sharpness, and she had tried sternness; but neither would do; she was shocked at the girl's obstinacy. 'Ah, well,' she said, 'if he hasn't told you! . . .' and she turned away.

Catherine watched her a moment in silence; then she hurried after her, stopping her before she reached the door. 'Told me what? What do you mean? What are you hinting at and threatening me with?'

'Isn't it broken off?' asked Mrs Penniman.

'My engagement? Not in the least!'

'I beg your pardon in that case. I have spoken too soon!'

'Too soon! Soon or late,' Catherine broke out, 'you speak foolishly and cruelly!'

'What has happened between you then?' asked her aunt struck by the sincerity of this cry. 'For something certainly has happened.'

'Nothing has happened but that I love him more and more!'

Mrs Penniman was silent an instant. 'I suppose that's the reason you went to see him this afternoon.'

Catherine flushed as if she had been struck. 'Yes, I did go to see him! But that's my own business.'

'Very well, then; we won't talk about it.' And Mrs Penniman moved towards the door again. But she was stopped by a sudden imploring cry from the girl.

'Aunt Lavinia, *where* has he gone?'

'Ah, you admit then that he has gone away? Didn't they know at his house?'

'They said he had left town. I asked no more questions; I was ashamed,' said Catherine simply enough.

'You needn't have taken so compromising a step if you had had a little more confidence in me,' Mrs Penniman observed, with a good deal of grandeur.

'Is it to New Orleans!' Catherine went on, irrelevantly.

It was the first time Mrs Penniman had heard of New Orleans in this connection; but she was averse to letting Catherine know that she was in the dark. She attempted to strike an illumination from the instructions she had received from Morris. 'My dear Catherine,' she said, 'when a separation has been agreed upon, the farther he goes away the better.'

'Agreed upon? Has he agreed upon it with you?' A consummate sense of her aunt's meddlesome folly had come over her during the last five minutes, and she was sickened at the thought that Mrs Penniman had been let loose, as it were, upon her happiness.

'He certainly has sometimes advised with me,' said Mrs Penniman.

'Is it you then that have changed him and made him so unnatural?' Catherine cried. 'Is it you that have worked on him and taken him from me! He doesn't belong to you, and I don't see how you have anything to do with what is between us! Is it you that have made this plot and told him to leave me? How could you be so wicked, so cruel? What have I ever done to you; why can't you leave me alone? I was afraid you would spoil everything; for you *do* spoil everything you touch! I was afraid of you all the time we were abroad; I had no rest when I thought that you were always talking to him.' Catherine went on with growing vehemence, pouring out in her bitterness and in the clairvoyance of her passion (which suddenly, jumping all processes, made her judge her aunt finally and without appeal), the uneasiness which had lain for so many months upon her heart.

Mrs Penniman was scared and bewildered; she saw no prospect of introducing her little account of the purity of Morris's motives. 'You are a most ungrateful girl!' she cried. 'Do you scold me for talking with him! I am sure we never talked of anything but you!'

'Yes; and that was the way you worried him; you made him tired of my very name! I wish you had never spoken of me to him; I never asked your help!'

'I am sure if it hadn't been for me he would never have come to the house, and you would never have known what he thought of you,' Mrs Penniman rejoined with a good deal of justice.

'I wish he never had come to the house, and that I never had known it! That's better than this,' said poor Catherine.

'You are a very ungrateful girl,' Aunt Lavinia repeated.

Catherine's outbreak of anger and the sense of wrong gave her, while they lasted, the satisfaction that comes from all assertion of force; they hurried her along, and there is always a sort of pleasure in cleaving the air. But at the bottom she hated to be violent, and she was conscious of no aptitude for organized resentment. She calmed herself with a great effort, but with great rapidity, and walked about the room a few moments, trying to say to herself that her aunt had meant everything for the best. She did not succeed in saying it with much conviction, but after a little she was able to speak quietly enough.

'I am not ungrateful, but I am very unhappy. It's hard to be grateful for that,' she said. 'Will you please tell me where he is?'

'I haven't the least idea; I am not in secret correspondence with him!' And Mrs Penniman wished indeed that she were, so that she might let him know how Catherine abused her, after all she had done.

'Was it a plan of his, then, to break off——?' By this time Catherine had become completely quiet.

Mrs Penniman began again to have a glimpse of her chance for explaining. 'He shrank—he shrank,' she said. 'He lacked courage, but it was the courage to injure you! He couldn't bear to bring down on you your father's curse.'

Catherine listened to this with her eyes fixed upon her aunt, and continued to gaze at her for some time afterwards. 'Did he tell you to say that?'

'He told me to say many things—all so delicate, so discriminating. And he told me to tell you he hoped you wouldn't despise him.'

'I don't,' said Catherine. And then she added: 'And will he stay away for ever?'

'Oh, for ever is a long time. Your father, perhaps, won't live for ever.'

'Perhaps not.'

'I am sure you appreciate—you understand—even though your heart bleeds,' said Mrs Penniman. 'You doubtless think him too scrupulous. So do I, but I respect his scruples. What he asks of you is that you should do the same.'

Catherine was still gazing at her aunt, but she spoke, at last, as if she had not heard or not understood her. 'It has been a regular plan, then. He has broken it off deliberately; he has given me up.'

'For the present, dear Catherine. He has put it off, only.'

'He has left me alone,' Catherine went on.

'Haven't you *me*?' asked Mrs Penniman, with much expression.

Catherine shook her head slowly. 'I don't believe it!' and she left the room.

XXXI

THOUGH she had forced herself to be calm, she preferred practising this virtue in private, and she forbore to show herself at tea—a repast which, on Sundays, at six o'clock, took the place of dinner. Dr Sloper and his sister sat face to face, but Mrs Penniman never met her brother's eye. Late in the evening she went with him, but without Catherine, to their sister Almond's, where, between the two ladies, Catherine's unhappy situation was discussed with a frankness that was conditioned by a good deal of mysterious reticence on Mrs Penniman's part.

'I am delighted he is not to marry her,' said Mrs Almond, 'but he ought to be horsewhipped all the same.'

Mrs Penniman, who was shocked at her sister's coarseness, replied that he had been actuated by the noblest of motives—the desire not to impoverish Catherine.

'I am very happy that Catherine is not to be impoverished—but I hope he may never have a penny too much! And what does the poor girl say to *you*?' Mrs Almond asked.

'She says I have a genius for consolation,' said Mrs Penniman.

This was the account of the matter that she gave to her sister, and it was perhaps with the consciousness of genius that, on her return that evening to Washington Square, she again presented herself for admittance at Catherine's door. Catherine came and opened it; she was apparently very quiet.

'I only want to give you a little word of advice,' she said. 'If your father asks you, say that everything is going on.'

Catherine stood there, with her hand on the knob, looking at her aunt, but not asking her to come in. 'Do you think he will ask me?'

'I am sure he will. He asked me just now, on our way home from your Aunt Elizabeth's. I explained the whole thing to your Aunt Elizabeth. I said to your father I know nothing about it.'

'Do you think he will ask me, when he sees—when he sees—?' But here Catherine stopped.

'The more he sees, the more disagreeable he will be,' said her aunt.

'He shall see as little as possible!' Catherine declared.

'Tell him you are to be married.'

'So I am,' said Catherine, softly; and she closed the door upon her aunt.

She could not have said this two days later—for instance, on Tuesday, when she at last received a letter from Morris Townsend. It was an epistle of considerable length, measuring five large square pages, and written at Philadelphia. It was an explanatory document, and it explained a great many things, chief among which were the considerations that had led the writer to take advantage of an urgent 'professional' absence to try and banish from his mind the image of one whose path he had crossed only to scatter it with ruins. He ventured to expect but partial success in this attempt, but he could promise her that, whatever his failure, he would never again interpose between her generous heart and her brilliant prospects and filial duties. He closed with an intimation that his professional pursuits might compel him to travel for some months, and with the hope that when they should each have accommodated themselves to what was sternly involved in their respective positions—even should this result not be reached for years—they should meet as friends, as fellow-sufferers, as innocent but philosophic victims of a great social law. That her life should be peaceful and happy was the dearest wish of him who ventured still to subscribe himself her most obedient servant. The letter was beautifully written, and Catherine who kept it for many years after this, was able, when her sense of the bitterness of its meaning and the hollowness of its tone had grown less acute, to admire its grace of expression. At present, for a long time after she received it, all she had to help her was the determination, daily more rigid, to make no appeal to the compassion of her father.

He suffered a week to elapse, and then one day, in the morning, at an hour at which she rarely saw him, he strolled into the back-parlour. He had watched his time, and he found her alone. She was sitting with some work, and he came and stood in front of her. He was going out, he had on his hat and was drawing on his gloves.

'It doesn't seem to me that you are treating me just now with all the consideration I deserve,' he said in a moment.

'I don't know what I have done,' Catherine answered, with her eyes on her work.

'You have apparently quite banished from your mind the request I made you at Liverpool, before we sailed; the request that you would notify me in advance before leaving my house.'

'I have not left your house!' said Catherine.

'But you intend to leave it, and by what you gave me to understand, your departure must be impending. In fact, though you are still here in body, you are already absent in spirit. Your mind has taken up its residence with your prospective husband, and you might quite as well be lodged under the conjugal roof, for all the benefit we get from your society.'

'I will try and be more cheerful!' said Catherine.

'You certainly ought to be cheerful, you ask a great deal if you are not. To the pleasure of marrying a brilliant young man, you add that of having your own way; you strike me as a very lucky young lady!'

Catherine got up; she was suffocating. But she folded her work, deliberately and correctly, bending her burning face upon it. Her father stood where he had planted himself; she hoped he would go, but he smoothed and buttoned his gloves, and then he rested his hands upon his hips.

'It would be a convenience to me to know when I may expect to have an empty house,' he went on. 'When you go, your aunt marches.'

She looked at him at last, with a long silent gaze, which, in spite of her pride and her resolution, uttered part of the appeal she had tried not to make. Her father's cold gray eye sounded her own, and he insisted on his point.

'Is it to-morrow? Is it next week, or the week after?'

'I shall not go away!' said Catherine.

The Doctor raised his eyebrows. 'Has he backed out?'

'I have broken off my engagement.'

'Broken it off?'

'I have asked him to leave New York, and he has gone away for a long time.'

The Doctor was both puzzled and disappointed, but he solved his perplexity by saying to himself that his daughter simply misrepresented—justifiably, if one would, but nevertheless, misrepresented—the facts; and he eased off his disappointment, which was that of a man losing a chance for a little triumph that he had rather counted on, by a few words that he uttered aloud.

'How does he take his dismissal?'

'I don't know!' said Catherine, less ingeniously than she had hitherto spoken.

'You mean you don't care? You are rather cruel, after encouraging him and playing with him for so long!'

The Doctor had his revenge after all.

XXXII

OUR story has hitherto moved with very short steps, but as it approaches its termination it must take a long stride. As time went on, it might have appeared to the Doctor that his daughter's account of her rupture with Morris Townsend, mere bravado as he had deemed it, was in some degree justified by the sequel. Morris remained as rigidly and unremittingly absent as if he had died of a broken heart, and Catherine had apparently buried the memory of this fruitless episode as deep as if it had terminated by her own choice. We know that she had been deeply and incurably wounded, but the Doctor had no means of knowing it. He was certainly curious about it, and would have given a good deal to discover the exact truth; but it was his punishment that he never knew—his punishment, I mean, for the abuse of sarcasm in his relations with his daughter. There was a good deal of effective sarcasm in her keeping him in the dark, and the rest of the world conspired with her, in this sense, to be sarcastic. Mrs Penniman told him nothing, partly because he never questioned her—he made too light of Mrs Penniman for that—and partly because she flattered herself that a tormenting reserve, and a serene profession of ignorance, would avenge her for his theory that she had meddled in the matter. He went two or three times to see Mrs Montgomery, but Mrs Montgomery had nothing to impart. She simply knew that her brother's engagement was broken off, and now that Miss Sloper was out of danger, she preferred not to bear witness in any way against Morris. She had done so before—however unwillingly—because she was sorry for Miss Sloper; but she was not sorry for Miss Sloper now—not at all sorry. Morris had told her nothing about his relations with Miss Sloper at the time, and he had told her nothing since. He was always away, and he very seldom wrote to her; she believed he had gone to California. Mrs Almond had, in her sister's phrase, 'taken up' Catherine violently since the recent catastrophe; but though the girl was very grateful to her for her kindness, she revealed no secrets, and the good lady could give the Doctor no satisfaction. Even, however, had she been able to narrate to him the private history of his daughter's unhappy love-affair, it would have given her a certain comfort to leave him in ignorance; for Mrs Almond was at this time not altogether in sympathy with her brother. She had guessed for her-self that Catherine had been cruelly jilted—she knew nothing from Mrs Penniman, for Mrs Penniman had not ventured to lay the famous explanation of Morris's motives before Mrs Almond, though she had thought it good enough for Catherine—and she pronounced her brother too consistently indifferent to what the poor creature must have suffered and must still be suffering. Dr Sloper had his theory, and he rarely altered his theories. The marriage would have been an abominable one, and the girl had had a blessed escape. She was not to be pitied for that, and to pretend to condole with her would have been to make concessions to the idea that she had ever had a right to think of Morris.

'I put my foot on this idea from the first, and I keep it there now,' said the Doctor. 'I don't see anything cruel in that; one can't keep it there too long.' To this Mrs Almond more than once replied that if Catherine had got rid of her incongruous lover, she deserved the credit of it, and that to bring herself to her father's enlightened view of the matter must have cost her an effort that he was bound to appreciate.

'I am by no means sure she has got rid of him,' the Doctor said. 'There is not the smallest probability that, after having been as ob-stinate as a mule for two years, she suddenly became amenable to reason. It is infinitely more probable that he got rid of her.'

'All the more reason you should be gentle with her.'

'I *am* gentle with her. But I can't do the pathetic; I can't pump up tears, to look graceful, over the most fortunate thing that ever happened to her.'

'You have no sympathy,' said Mrs Almond; 'that was never your strong point. You have only to look at her to see that, right or wrong, and whether the rupture came from herself or from him, her poor little heart is grievously bruised.'

'Handling bruises—and even dropping tears on them—doesn't make them any better! My business is to see she gets no more knocks, and that I shall carefully attend to. But I don't at all recognize your description of Catherine. She doesn't strike me in the least as a young woman going about in search of a moral poultice. In fact, she seems to me much better than while the fellow was hanging about. She is perfectly comfortable and blooming; she eats and sleeps, takes her usual exercise, and overloads herself, as usual, with finery. She is always knitting some purse or embroidering some handkerchief, and it seems to me she turns these articles out about as fast as ever. She hasn't much to say; but when had she anything to say? She had her little dance, and now she is sitting down to rest. I suspect that, on the whole, she enjoys it.'

'She enjoys it as people enjoy getting rid of a leg that has been crushed. The state of mind after amputation is doubtless one of comparative repose.'

'If your leg is a metaphor for young Townsend, I can assure you he has never been crushed. Crushed? Not he! He is alive and perfectly intact, and that's why I am not satisfied.'

'Should you have liked to kill him?' asked Mrs Almond.

'Yes, very much. I think it is quite possible that it is all a blind.'

'A blind?'

'An arrangement between them. *Il fait le mort*,* as they say in France; but he is looking out of the corner of his eye. You can depend upon it he has not burned his ships; he has kept one to come back in. When I am dead, he will set sail again, and then she will marry him.'

'It is interesting to know that you accuse your only daughter of being the vilest of hypocrites,' said Mrs Almond.

'I don't see what difference her being my only daughter makes. It is better to accuse one than a dozen. But I don't accuse any one. There is not the smallest hypocrisy about Catherine, and I deny that she even pretends to be miserable.'

The Doctor's idea that the thing was a 'blind' had its intermissions and revivals; but it may be said on the whole to have increased as he grew older; together with his impression of Catherine's blooming and comfortable condition. Naturally, if he had not found grounds for viewing her as a lovelorn maiden during the year or two that followed her great trouble, he found none at a time when she had completely recovered her self-possession. He was obliged to recognize the fact that if the two young people were waiting for him to get out of the way, they were at least waiting very patiently. He had heard from time to time that Morris was in New York; but he never remained there long, and, to the best of the Doctor's belief, had no communication with Catherine. He was sure they never met, and he had reason to suspect that Morris never wrote to her. After the letter that has been mentioned, she heard from him twice again, at considerable intervals; but on none of these occasions did she write herself. On the other hand, as the Doctor observed, she averted herself rigidly from the idea of marrying other people. Her opportunities for doing so were not numerous, but they occurred often enough to test her disposition. She refused a widower, a man with a genial temperament, a handsome fortune, and three little girls (he had heard that she was very fond of children, and he pointed to his own with some confidence); and she turned a deaf ear to the solicitations of a clever young lawyer, who, with the prospect of a great practice, and the reputation of a most agreeable man, had had the shrewdness, when he came to look about him for a wife, to believe that she would suit him better than several younger and prettier girls. Mr Macalister, the widower, had desired to make a marriage of reason, and had chosen Catherine for what he supposed to be her latent matronly qualities; but John Ludlow, who was a year the girl's junior, and spoken of always as a young man who might have his 'pick', was seriously in love with her. Catherine, however, would never look at him; she made it plain to him that she thought he came to see her too often. He afterwards consoled himself, and married a very different person, little Miss Sturtevant, whose attractions were obvious to the dullest comprehension. Catherine, at the time of these events, had left her thirtieth year well behind her, and had quite taken her place as an old maid. Her father would have preferred she should marry, and he once told her that he hoped she would not be too fastidious. 'I should like to see you an honest man's wife before I die,' he said. This was after John Ludlow had been compelled to give it up, though the Doctor had advised him to persevere. The Doctor exercised no further pressure, and had the credit of not 'worrying' at all over his daughter's singleness. In fact he worried rather more than appeared, and there were considerable periods during which he felt sure that Morris Townsend was hidden behind some door. 'If he is not, why doesn't she marry?' he asked himself. 'Limited as her intelligence may be, she must understand perfectly well that she is made to do the usual thing.' Catherine, however, became an admirable old maid. She formed habits, regulated her days upon a system of her own, interested herself in charitable institutions, asylums, hospitals, and aid-societies,* and went generally, with an even and noiseless step,* about the rigid business of her life. This life had, however, a secret history as well as a public one—if I may talk of the public history of a mature and diffident spinster for whom publicity had always a combination of terrors. From her own point of view the great facts of her career were that Morris Townsend had trifled with her affection, and that her father had broken its spring. Nothing could ever alter these facts; they were always there, like her name, her age, her plain face. Nothing could ever undo the wrong or cure the pain that Morris had inflicted on her, and nothing could ever make her feel towards her father as she felt in her younger years. There was something dead in her life, and her duty was to try and fill the void. Catherine recognized this duty to the utmost; she had a great disapproval of brooding and moping. She had of course no faculty for quenching memory in dissipation; but she mingled freely in the usual gaieties of the town, and she became at last an inevitable figure at all respectable entertainments. She was greatly liked, and as time went on she grew to be a sort of kindly maiden-aunt to the younger portion of society. Young girls were apt to confide to her their love-affairs (which they never did to Mrs Penniman), and young men to be fond of her without knowing why. She developed a few harmless eccentricities; her habits, once formed, were rather stiffly maintained; her opinions, on all moral and social matters, were extremely conservative; and before she was forty she was regarded as an old-fashioned person, and an authority on customs that had passed away. Mrs Penniman, in comparison, was quite a girlish figure; she grew younger as she advanced in life. She lost none of her relish for beauty and mystery, but she had little opportunity to exercise it. With Catherine's later wooers she failed to establish relations as intimate as those which had given her so many interesting hours in the society of Morris Townsend. These gentlemen had an indefinable mistrust of her good offices, and they never talked to her about Catherine's charms. Her ringlets, her buckles and bangles glistened more brightly with each succeeding year, and she remained quite the same officious and imaginative Mrs Penniman, and the odd mixture of impetuosity and circumspection, that we have hitherto known. As regards one point, however, her circumspection prevailed, and she must be given due credit for it. For upwards of seventeen years she never mentioned Morris Townsend's name to her niece. Catherine was grateful to her, but this consistent silence, so little in accord with her aunt's character, gave her a certain alarm, and she could never wholly rid herself of a suspicion that Mrs Penniman sometimes had news of him.

XXXIII

LITTLE by little Dr Sloper had retired from his profession; he visited only those patients in whose symptoms he recognized a certain originality. He went again to Europe, and remained two years; Catherine went with him, and on this occasion Mrs Penniman was of the party. Europe apparently had few surprises for Mrs Penniman, who frequently remarked, in the most romantic sites—'You know I am very familiar with all this.' It should be added that such remarks were usually not addressed to her brother, or yet to her niece, but to fellow-tourists who happened to be at hand, or even to the cicerone* or the goat-herd in the foreground.

One day, after his return from Europe, the Doctor said something to his daughter that made her start—it seemed to come from so far out of the past.

'I should like you to promise me something before I die.'

'Why do you talk about your dying?' she asked.

'Because I am sixty-eight years old.'

'I hope you will live a long time,' said Catherine.

'I hope I shall! But some day I shall take a bad cold, and then it will not matter much what any one hopes. That will be the manner of my exit, and when it takes place, remember I told you so. Promise me not to marry Morris Townsend after I am gone.'

This was what made Catherine start, as I have said; but her start was a silent one, and for some moments she said nothing. 'Why do you speak of him?' she asked at last.

'You challenge everything I say. I speak of him because he's a topic, like any other. He's to be seen, like any one else, and he is still looking for a wife—having had one and got rid of her, I don't know by what means. He has lately been in New York, and at your cousin Marian's house; your Aunt Elizabeth saw him there.'

'They neither of them told me,' said Catherine.

'That's their merit; it's not yours. He has grown fat and bald, and he has not made his fortune. But I can't trust those facts alone to steel your heart against him, and that's why I ask you to promise.'

'Fat and bald': these words presented a strange image to Catherine's mind, out of which the memory of the most beautiful young man in the world had never faded. 'I don't think you understand,' she said. 'I very seldom think of Mr Townsend.'

'It will be very easy for you to go on, then. Promise me, after my death, to do the same.'

Again, for some moments, Catherine was silent; her father's request deeply amazed her; it opened an old wound and made it ache afresh. 'I don't think I can promise that,' she answered.

'It would be a great satisfaction,' said her father.

'You don't understand. I can't promise that.'

The Doctor was silent a minute. 'I ask you for a particular reason. I am altering my will.'

This reason failed to strike Catherine; and indeed she scarcely understood it. All her feelings were merged in the sense that he was trying to treat her as he had treated her years before. She had suffered from it then; and now all her experience, all her acquired tranquillity and rigidity, protested. She had been so humble in her youth that she could now afford to have a little pride, and there was something in this request, and in her father's thinking himself so free to make it, that seemed an injury to her dignity. Poor Catherine's dignity was not aggressive; it never sat in state; but if you pushed far enough you could find it. Her father had pushed very far.

'I can't promise,' she simply repeated.

'You are very obstinate,' said the Doctor.

'I don't think you understand.'

'Please explain, then.'

'I can't explain,' said Catherine. 'And I can't promise.'

'Upon my word,' her father exclaimed, 'I had no idea how obstinate you are!'

She knew herself that she was obstinate, and it gave her a certain joy. She was now a middle-aged woman.

About a year after this, the accident that the Doctor had spoken of occurred; he took a violent cold. Driving out to Bloomingdale* one April day to see a patient of unsound mind, who was confined in a private asylum for the insane, and whose family greatly desired a medical opinion from an eminent source, he was caught in a spring shower, and being in a buggy* without a hood, he found himself soaked to the skin. He came home with an ominous chill, and on the morrow he was seriously ill. 'It is congestion of the lungs,' he said to Catherine; 'I shall need very good nursing. It will make no difference, for I shall not recover; but I wish everything to be done, to the smallest detail, as if I should. I hate an ill-conducted sick-room; and you will be so good as to nurse me on the hypothesis that I shall get well.' He told her which of his fellow-physicians to send for, and gave her a multitude of minute directions; it was quite on the optimistic hypothesis that she nursed him. But he had never been wrong in his life, and he was not wrong now. He was touching his seventieth year, and though he had a very well-tempered constitution, his hold upon life had lost its firmness. He died after three weeks' illness, during which Mrs Penniman, as well as his daughter, had been assiduous at his bedside.

On his will being opened after a decent interval, it was found to consist of two portions. The first of these dated from ten years back, and consisted of a series of dispositions by which he left the great mass of property to his daughter, with becoming legacies to his two sisters. The second was a codicil, of recent origin, maintaining the annuities to Mrs Penniman and Mrs Almond, but reducing Catherine's share to a fifth of what he had first bequeathed her. 'She is amply provided for from her mother's side,' the document ran, 'never having spent more than a fraction of her income from this source; so that her fortune is already more than sufficient to attract those unscrupulous adventurers whom she has given me reason to believe that she persists in regarding as an interesting class.' The large remainder of his property, therefore, Dr Sloper had divided into seven unequal parts, which he left, as endowments, to as many different hospitals and schools of medicine, in various cities of the Union.

To Mrs Penniman it seemed monstrous that a man should play such tricks with other people's money; for after his death, of course, as she said, it was other people's. 'Of course you will dispute the will,' she remarked, fatuously, to Catherine.

'Oh no,' Catherine answered, 'I like it very much. Only I wish it had been expressed a little differently!'

XXXIV

It was her habit to remain in town very late in the summer; she preferred the house in Washington Square to any other habitation whatever, and it was under protest that she used to go to the seaside for the month of August. At the sea she spent her month at an hotel. The year that her father died she intermitted this custom altogether, not thinking it consistent with deep mourning; and the year after that she put off her departure till so late that the middle of August found her still in the heated solitude of Washington Square. Mrs Penniman, who was fond of a change, was usually eager for a visit to the country; but this year she appeared quite content with such rural impressions as she could gather, at the parlour window, from the ailantus-trees behind the wooden paling. The peculiar fragrance of this vegetation used to diffuse itself in the evening air, and Mrs Penniman, on the warm nights of July, often sat at the open window and inhaled it. This was a happy moment for Mrs Penniman; after the death of her brother she felt more free to obey her impulses. A vague oppression had disappeared from her life, and she enjoyed a sense of freedom of which she had not been conscious since the memorable time, so long ago, when the Doctor went abroad with Catherine and left her at home to entertain Morris Townsend. The year that had elapsed since her brother's death reminded her of that happy time, because, although Catherine, in growing older, had become a person to be reckoned with, yet her society was a very different thing, as Mrs Penniman said, from that of a tank of cold water. The elder lady hardly knew what use to make of this larger margin of her life; she sat and looked at it very much as she had often sat, with her poised needle in her hand, before her tapestry-frame. She had a confident hope, however, that her rich impulses, her talent for embroidery, would still find their application, and this confidence was justified before many months had elapsed.

Catherine continued to live in her father's house in spite of its being represented to her that a maiden-lady of quiet habits might find a more convenient abode in one of the smaller dwellings, with brown stone fronts,* which had at this time begun to adorn the transverse thoroughfares in the upper part of the town. She liked the earlier structure—it had begun by this time to be called an 'old' house—and proposed to herself to end her days in it. If it was too large for a pair of unpretending gentlewomen, this was better than the opposite fault; for Catherine had no desire to find herself in closer quarters with her aunt. She expected to spend the rest of her life in Washington Square, and to enjoy Mrs Penniman's society for the whole of this period; as she had a conviction that, long as she might live, her aunt would live at least as long, and always retain her brilliancy and activity. Mrs Penniman suggested to her the idea of a rich vitality.

On one of those warm evenings in July of which mention has been made, the two ladies sat together at an open window, looking out on the quiet Square. It was too hot for lighted lamps, for reading, or for work; it might have appeared too hot even for conversation, Mrs Penniman having long been speechless. She sat forward in the window, half on the balcony, humming a little song. Catherine was within the room, in a low rocking-chair, dressed in white, and slowly using a large palmetto fan.* It was in this way, at this season, that the aunt and niece, after they had had tea, habitually spent their evenings.

'Catherine,' said Mrs Penniman at last, 'I am going to say something that will surprise you.'

'Pray do,' Catherine answered; 'I like surprises. And it is so quiet now.'

'Well, then, I have seen Morris Townsend.'

If Catherine was surprised, she checked the expression of it; she gave neither a start nor an exclamation. She remained, indeed, for some moments intensely still, and this may very well have been a symptom of emotion. 'I hope he was well,' she said at last.

'I don't know; he is a great deal changed. He would like very much to see you.'

'I would rather not see him,' said Catherine, quickly.

'I was afraid you would say that. But you don't seem surprised!'

'I am—very much.'

'I met him at Marian's,' said Mrs Penniman. 'He goes to Marian's, and they are so afraid you will meet him there. It's my belief that that's why he goes. He wants so much to see you.' Catherine made no response to this, and Mrs Penniman went on. 'I didn't know him at first; he is so remarkably changed. But he knew me in a minute. He says I am not in the least changed. You know how polite he always was. He was coming away when I came, and we walked a little distance together. He is still very handsome, only, of course, he looks older, and he is not so—so animated as he used to be. There was a touch of sadness about him; but there was a touch of sadness about him before—especially when he went away. I am afraid he has not been very successful—that he has never got thoroughly established. I don't suppose he is sufficiently plodding, and that, after all, is what succeeds in this world.' Mrs Penniman had not mentioned Morris Townsend's name to her niece for upwards of the fifth of a century; but now that she had broken the spell, she seemed to wish to make up for lost time, as if there had been a sort of exhilaration in hearing herself talk of him. She proceeded, however, with considerable caution, pausing occasionally to let Catherine give some sign. Catherine gave no other sign than to stop the rocking of her chair and the swaying of her fan; she sat motionless and silent. 'It was on Tuesday last,' said Mrs Penniman, 'and I have been hesitating ever since about telling you. I didn't know how you might like it. At last I thought that it was so long ago that you would probably not have any particular feeling. I saw him again, after meeting him at Marian's. I met him in the street, and he went a few steps with me. The first thing he said was about you; he asked ever so many questions. Marian didn't want me to speak to you; she didn't want you to know that they receive him. I told him I was sure that after all these years you couldn't have any feeling about that; you couldn't grudge him the hospitality of his own cousin's house. I said you would be bitter indeed if you did that. Marian has the most extraordinary ideas about what happened between you; she seems to think he behaved in some very unusual manner. I took the liberty of reminding her of the real facts, and placing the story in its true light. *He* has no bitterness, Catherine, I can assure you; and he might be excused for it, for things have not gone well with him. He has been all over the world, and tried to establish himself everywhere; but his evil star was against him. It is most interesting to hear him talk of his evil star. Everything failed; everything but his—you know, you remember—his proud, high spirit. I believe he married some lady somewhere in Europe. You know they marry in such a peculiar matter-of-course way in Europe; a marriage of reason they call it. She died soon afterwards; as he said to me, she only flitted across his life. He has not been in New York for ten years; he came back a few days ago. The first thing he did was to ask me about you. He had heard you had never married; he seemed very much interested about that. He said you had been the real romance of his life.'

Catherine had suffered her companion to proceed from point to point, and pause to pause, without interrupting her; she fixed her eyes on the ground and listened. But the last phrase I have quoted was followed by a pause of peculiar significance, and then, at last, Catherine spoke. It will be observed that before doing so she had received a good deal of information about Morris Townsend. 'Please say no more; please don't follow up that subject.'

'Doesn't it interest you?' asked Mrs Penniman, with a certain timorous archness.

'It pains me,' said Catherine.

'I was afraid you would say that. But don't you think you could get used to it? He wants so much to see you.'

'Please don't, Aunt Lavinia,' said Catherine, getting up from her seat. She moved quickly away, and went to the other window, which stood open to the balcony; and here, in the embrasure, concealed from her aunt by the white curtains, she remained a long time, looking out into the warm darkness. She had had a great shock; it was as if the gulf of the past had suddenly opened, and a spectral figure had risen out of it. There were some things she believed she had got over, some feelings that she had thought of as dead; but apparently there was a certain vitality in them still. Mrs Penniman had made them stir themselves. It was but a momentary agitation, Catherine said to herself; it would presently pass away. She was trembling, and her heart was beating so that she could feel it; but this also would subside. Then, suddenly, while she waited for a return of her calmness, she burst into tears. But her tears flowed very silently, so that Mrs Penniman had no observation of them. It was perhaps, however, because Mrs Penniman suspected them that she said no more that evening about Morris Townsend.

XXXV

Her refreshed attention to this gentleman had not those limits of which Catherine desired, for herself, to be conscious; it lasted long enough to enable her to wait another week before speaking of him again. It was under the same circumstances that she once more attacked the subject. She had been sitting with her niece in the evening; only on this occasion, as the night was not so warm, the lamp had been lighted, and Catherine had placed herself near it with a morsel of fancy-work.* Mrs Penniman went and sat alone for half an hour on the balcony; then she came in, moving vaguely about the room. At last she sank into a seat near Catherine, with clasped hands, and a little look of excitement.

'Shall you be angry if I speak to you again about *him*?' she asked.

Catherine looked up at her quietly. 'Who is *he*?'

'He whom you once loved.'

'I shall not be angry, but I shall not like it.'

'He sent you a message,' said Mrs Penniman. 'I promised him to deliver it, and I must keep my promise.'

In all these years Catherine had had time to forget how little she had to thank her aunt for in the season of her misery; she had long ago forgiven Mrs Penniman for taking too much upon herself. But for a moment this attitude of interposition and disinterestedness, this carrying of messages and redeeming of promises, brought back the sense that her companion was a dangerous woman. She had said she would not be angry; but for an instant she felt sore. 'I don't care what you do with your promise!' she answered.

Mrs Penniman, however, with her high conception of the sanctity of pledges, carried her point. 'I have gone too far to retreat,' she said, though precisely what this meant she was not at pains to explain. 'Mr Townsend wishes most particularly to see you, Catherine; he believes that if you knew how much, and why, he wishes it, you would consent to do so.'

'There can be no reason,' said Catherine; 'no good reason.'

'His happiness depends upon it. Is not that a good reason?' asked Mrs Penniman, impressively.

'Not for me. My happiness does not.'

'I think you will be happier after you have seen him. He is going away again—going to resume his wanderings. It is a very lonely, restless, joyless life. Before he goes, he wishes to speak to you; it is a fixed idea with him—he is always thinking of it. He has something very important to say to you. He believes that you never understood him—that you never judged him rightly, and the belief has always weighed upon him terribly. He wishes to justify himself; he believes that in a very few words he could do so. He wishes to meet you as a friend.'

Catherine listened to this wonderful speech, without pausing in her work; she had now had several days to accustom herself to think of Morris Townsend again as an actuality. When it was over she said simply, 'Please say to Mr Townsend that I wish he would leave me alone.'

She had hardly spoken when a sharp, firm ring at the door vibrated through the summer night. Catherine looked up at the clock; it marked a quarter-past nine—a very late hour for visitors, especially in the empty condition of the town. Mrs Penniman at the same moment gave a little start, and then Catherine's eyes turned quickly to her aunt. They met Mrs Penniman's and sounded them for a moment, sharply. Mrs Penniman was blushing; her look was a conscious one; it seemed to confess something. Catherine guessed its meaning, and rose quickly from her chair.

'Aunt Penniman,' she said, in a tone that scared her companion, 'have you taken *the liberty* . . . ?'

'My dearest Catherine,' stammered Mrs Penniman, 'just wait till you see him!'

Catherine had frightened her aunt, but she was also frightened herself; she was on the point of rushing to give orders to the servant, who was passing to the door, to admit no one; but the fear of meeting her visitor checked her.

'Mr Morris Townsend.'

This was what she heard, vaguely but recognizably articulated by the domestic, while she hesitated. She had her back turned to the door of the parlour, and for some moments she kept it turned, feeling that he had come in. He had not spoken, however, and at last she faced about. Then she saw a gentleman standing in the middle of the room, from which her aunt had discreetly retired.

She would never have known him. He was forty-five years old, and his figure was not that of the straight, slim young man she remembered.

But it was a very fine person, and a fair and lustrous beard, spreading itself upon a well-presented chest, contributed to its effect. After a moment Catherine recognized the upper half of the face, which, though her visitor's clustering locks had grown thin, was still remarkably handsome. He stood in a deeply deferential attitude, with his eyes on her face. 'I have ventured—I have ventured,' he said; and then he paused, looking about him, as if he expected her to ask him to sit down. It was the old voice; but it had not the old charm. Catherine, for a minute, was conscious of a distinct determination not to invite him to take a seat. Why had he come? It was wrong for him to come. Morris was embarrassed, but Catherine gave him no help. It was not that she was glad of his embarrassment; on the contrary, it excited all her own liabilities of this kind, and gave her great pain. But how could she welcome him when she felt so vividly that he ought not to have come? 'I wanted so much—I was determined,' Morris went on. But he stopped again; it was not easy. Catherine still said nothing, and he may well have recalled with apprehension her ancient faculty of silence. She continued to look at him, however, and as she did so she made the strangest observation. It seemed to be he, and yet not he; it was the man who had been everything, and yet this person was nothing. How long ago it was—how old she had grown—how much she had lived! She had lived on something that was connected with *him*, and she had consumed it in doing so. This person did not look unhappy. He was fair and well-preserved, perfectly dressed, mature and complete. As Catherine looked at him, the story of his life defined itself in his eyes: he had made himself comfortable, and he had never been caught. But even while her perception opened itself to this, she had no desire to catch him; his presence was painful to her, and she only wished he would go.

'Will you not sit down?' he asked.

'I think we had better not,' said Catherine.

'I offend you by coming?' He was very grave; he spoke in a tone of the richest respect.

'I don't think you ought to have come.'

'Did not Mrs Penniman tell you—did she not give you my message?'

'She told me something, but I did not understand.'

'I wish you would let *me* tell you—let me speak for myself.'

'I don't think it is necessary,' said Catherine.

'Not for you, perhaps, but for me. It would be a great satisfaction—and I have not many.' He seemed to be coming nearer; Catherine turned away. 'Can we not be friends again?' he asked.

'We are not enemies,' said Catherine. 'I have none but friendly feelings to you.'

'Ah, I wonder whether you know the happiness it gives me to hear you say that!' Catherine uttered no intimation that she measured the influence of her words; and he presently went on, 'You have not changed—the years have passed happily for you.'

'They have passed very quietly,' said Catherine.

'They have left no marks; you are admirably young.' This time he succeeded in coming nearer—he was close to her; she saw his glossy perfumed beard, and his eyes above it looking strange and hard. It was very different from his old—from his young—face. If she had first seen him this way she would not have liked him. It seemed to her that he was smiling, or trying to smile. 'Catherine,' he said, lowering his voice, 'I have never ceased to think of you.'

'Please don't say those things,' she answered.

'Do you hate me?'

'Oh no,' said Catherine.

Something in her tone discouraged him, but in a moment he recovered himself. 'Have you still some kindness for me, then?'

'I don't know why you have come here to ask me such things!' Catherine exclaimed.

'Because for many years it has been the desire of my life that we should be friends again.'

'That is impossible.'

'Why so? Not if you will allow it.'

'I will not allow it!' said Catherine.

He looked at her again in silence. 'I see; my presence troubles you and pains you. I will go away; but you must give me leave to come again.'

'Please don't come again,' she said.

'Never?—never?'

She made a great effort; she wished to say something that would make it impossible he should ever again cross her threshold. 'It is wrong of you. There is no propriety in it—no reason for it.'

'Ah, dearest lady, you do me injustice!' cried Morris Townsend. 'We have only waited, and now we are free.'

'You treated me badly,' said Catherine.

'Not if you think of it rightly. You had your quiet life with your father—which was just what I could not make up my mind to rob you of.'

'Yes; I had that.'

Morris felt it to be a considerable damage to his cause that he could not add that she had had something more besides; for it is needless to say that he had learnt the contents of Doctor Sloper's will. He was nevertheless not at a loss. 'There are worse fates than that!' he exclaimed with expression; and he might have been supposed to refer to his own unprotected situation. Then he added, with a deeper tenderness, 'Catherine, have you never forgiven me?'

'I forgave you years ago, but it is useless for us to attempt to be friends.'

'Not if we forget the past. We have still a future, thank God!'

'I can't forget—I don't forget,' said Catherine. 'You treated me too badly. I felt it very much; I felt it for years.' And then she went on, with her wish to show him that he must not come to her this way, 'I can't begin again—I can't take it up. Everything is dead and buried. It was too serious; it made a great change in my life. I never expected to see you here.'

'Ah, you are angry!' cried Morris, who wished immensely that he could extort some flash of passion from her mildness. In that case he might hope.

'No, I am not angry. Anger does not last, that way, for years. But there are other things. Impressions last, when they have been strong.—But I can't talk.'

Morris stood stroking his beard, with a clouded eye. 'Why have you never married?' he asked abruptly. 'You have had opportunities.'

'I didn't wish to marry.'

'Yes, you are rich, you are free; you had nothing to gain.'

'I had nothing to gain,' said Catherine.

Morris looked vaguely round him, and gave a deep sigh.

'Well, I was in hopes that we might still have been friends.'

'I meant to tell you, by my aunt, in answer to your message—if you had waited for an answer—that it was unnecessary for you to come in that hope.'

'Good-bye, then,' said Morris. 'Excuse my indiscretion.'

He bowed, and she turned away—standing there, averted, with her eyes on the ground, for some moments after she had heard him close the door of the room.

In the hall he found Mrs Penniman, fluttered and eager; she appeared to have been hovering there under the irreconcilable promptings of her curiosity and her dignity.

'That was a precious plan of yours!' said Morris, clapping on his hat.

'Is she so hard!' asked Mrs Penniman.

'She doesn't care a button for me—with her confounded little dry manner.'

'Was it very dry?' pursued Mrs Penniman, with solicitude.

Morris took no notice of her question; he stood musing an instant, with his hat on. 'But why the deuce, then, would she never marry?'

'Yes—why indeed?' sighed Mrs Penniman. And then, as if from a sense of the inadequacy of this explanation, 'But you will not despair—you will come back?'

'Come back? Damnation!' And Morris Townsend strode out of the house, leaving Mrs Penniman staring.

Catherine, meanwhile, in the parlour, picking up her morsel of fancy-work, had seated herself with it again—for life, as it were.

APPENDIX 1

EXTRACT FROM JAMES'S JOURNAL

Extract from Henry James's Journal, 7 November 1878–11 March 1888. 'Correspondence and Journals of Henry James Jr.' (MS Am 1094, Volume 1), Houghton Library, Harvard University. By permission of the Houghton Library, Harvard University.

February 21ˢᵗ [1879]. Mrs Kemble told me last evening the history of her brother H.'s engagement to Miss T.[1] H.K. was a young ensign in a marching regiment, very handsome ('beautiful') said Mrs K., but very luxurious and selfish, and without a penny to his name. Miss T. was a dull, plain, common-place girl, only daughter of the Master of King's Coll., Cambridge, who had a handsome private fortune (£4000 a year). She was very much in love with H.K., and was of that slow, sober, dutiful nature that an impression once made upon her, was made for ever. Her father disapproved strongly (and justly) of the engagement and informed her that if she married young K. he would not leave her a penny of his money. It was only in her money that H. was interested; he wanted a rich wife who would enable him to live at his ease and pursue his pleasures. Miss T. was in much tribulation and she asked Mrs K. what she would advise her to do—Henry K. having taken the ground that if she would hold on and marry him the old Doctor would after a while relent and they should get the money. (It was in this belief that he was holding on to her.) Mrs K. advised the young girl by *no means* to marry her brother. 'If your father does relent and you are well off, he will make you a kindly enough husband, so long as all goes well. But if he should not, and you were to be poor, your lot would be miserable. *Then* my brother would be a very

---

[1] 'Brother H.' was Henry Kemble (1812–57), 'Miss T.' Mary Anne Thackeray, daughter of George Thackeray, of King's College, Cambridge, and 'Mrs S.' Mrs Edward Sartoris, née Adelaide Kemble (?1814–79). George Thackeray (1777–1850) was in fact not Master but Provost of King's, 1814–50, 'book-collector and chaplain to George III and his successors', so the *Dictionary of National Biography* informs us. Though Edel and Powers in their edition of the *Notebooks* (see Select Bibliography) deny any connection with William Makepeace Thackeray, the *DNB* tells us that George Thackeray and his elder brother, Frederick Rennell Thackeray (1775–1860), a distinguished military man and eventually a general (who cannot have approved of Henry Kemble), were indeed cousins of the writer.

uncomfortable companion—*then* he would visit upon you his disappointment and discontent.' Miss T. reflected awhile; but[2] then, as she was much in love with [him], she determined to disobey her father and take the consequences. Meanwhile H.K., however, had come to the conclusion that the father's forgiveness was not to be counted upon—that his attitude was very firm, and that if they should marry, he would never see the money. *Then* all his effort was to disentangle himself. He went off, shook himself free of the engagement, let the girl go. She was deeply wounded—they separated. Some few years elapsed—her father died and she came into his fortune. She never received the addresses of another man—she always cared in secret for Henry K.—but she was determined to remain unmarried. K. lived about the world in different military stations, and at last, at the end of 10 years (or more), came back to England—still a handsome, selfish, impecunious soldier. One of his other sisters (Mrs S.) then attempted to bring on the engagement again—knowing that Miss T. still cared for him. She tried to make Mrs K. join her in this undertaking, but the latter refused, saying that it was an ignoble speculation and that her brother had forfeited every claim to being thought well of by Miss T. But K. again, on his own responsibility, paid his addresses to Miss T. She refused him—it was too late. And yet, said Mrs K., she cared for him—and she would have married no other man. But H.K.'s selfishness had over-reached itself and this was the retribution[3] of time.

---

[2] In their edition Edel and Powers read 'and'. James's handwriting is difficult, but the final letter here is formed very differently from the 'd's at the end of other 'and's in this passage, so I read the no less plausible 'but'.

[3] James first wrote 'revenge'; this is cancelled by two lines and 'retribution' inserted instead.

APPENDIX 2

STAGE AND FILM VERSIONS

JAMES'S novels have inspired a substantial number of films, stage-plays, and operas, and the results have proved a subject of considerable interest in their own right. Michael Halliwell tells us that there have been three operas based on *Washington Square*, by J. H. Damase (1974), Thomas Pasatieri (1976), and Donald Hollier (1988) ('Henry James and Opera', *Henry James Review*, 19.3 (1998), 307–16).

Better known are the stage-play entitled *The Heiress* (1947), by Ruth and Augustus Goetz; the film of the same name (Paramount, 1949), based on the Goetzes' stage-play, directed by William Wyler, starring Olivia de Havilland, Ralph Richardson, Montgomery Clift, and Miriam Hopkins; and the film *Washington Square* (Hollywood Pictures/Caravan Pictures, 1997), directed by Agnieszka Holland with screenplay by Carol Doyle, starring Jennifer Jason Leigh, Ben Chaplin, Albert Finney, and Maggie Smith. For critical reflections on these works and their dealings with James's novel, see the items in the Select Bibliography by Chandler, Rivkin, Rowe, and Swaab.

The Goetzes' 1947 play was a success in both New York and London, and it continues to receive more revivals (including one at London's Royal National Theatre in 2000) than any of James's own plays; but this is faint praise. Though the subsequent film was not a runaway success at the box office, it enjoyed a notable *succès d'estime*, winning four Academy Awards, for best actress, art direction (black and white), costume design (black and white), and original music score. The reception for Holland's 1997 film was more mixed, though a good case can be made for its intelligent re-conception of the novel and the strength of its central performances (see Rivkin in particular; also Robin Wood, considering it alongside two other films from the same decade based on James novels (*The Wings of the Dove: Henry James in the 1990s* (London, 1999), 11–13).

Critical debate about all three versions focuses on the way they meet the challenge of translating James's novel into the terms of a different medium and the different socio-cultural context inhabited by later audiences. Attention is bound to be attracted by the differences that theatre and film choose to make over time and place, sound and look, by the physicalization of faces and movements, by the vocalization of speech. So, for example, the stage-play confines its entire action to the Slopers' front-parlour, the 1949 film restricts its European interlude to a Parisian café, the 1997 film opens by showing us the death of Catherine's mother in childbirth; all three reduce the amount of time that elapses after Dr Sloper's death before Morris's reappearance; every time Catherine and Morris are together their body language requires interpretation; the Goetzes have Dr Sloper explicitly voice the thought that 'She killed her mother in getting born', and Carol Doyle makes him tell Catherine to her face on the Alpine heights forgone by Wyler: 'How obscene that your mother gave her life that you might walk the earth'. In both films the music—by Aaron Copland and Jan Kaczmarek respectively—has a decisive influence on the mood and interpretation of crucial scenes, and hence the work overall.

The most significant issues however surround the portrayal of James's shy, comparatively inarticulate heroine and her development. Closely related to this is the disappearance of the narrator and the greater liberty (and responsibility) of characters who must speak for themselves, not only in words. The two films make very different choices over the use of this freedom, especially for Catherine. In neither case are we left with the image of her sitting down with her morsel of fancy-work for life, as it were. In Wyler's film she turns into a revenge-heroine who owes much of her icy violence to the conventions of *film noir* in the late 1940s. This Catherine does not nurse her dying father but sits stony-faced in the park across the street, and when Morris returns she lures him into thinking that she is ready (again) to elope, only to leave him hammering on the locked and bolted front door. One line may serve to mark her difference from James's Catherine. Aunt Penniman asks: 'Can you be so cruel?' and the younger woman retorts, 'Yes, I can be very cruel. I have been taught by masters.' Both Dr Sloper and Morris are likely to win some sympathy from audiences, especially the former, who does *not* in this version disinherit his daughter. The very final moments show Catherine ascending the stairs of her mansion in triumph and something like rapture.

The later film takes a completely different route towards the more muted satisfaction of its ending. Seizing on the hint in James's novel that Catherine has some aptitude for music, Holland makes this the symbol of a real emotional bond with Morris, who becomes a more plausible lover and potential husband than in any of the previous versions. Though the relationship fails, Catherine gains a renewed sense of her own 'inner child', and ends her story surrounded by literal children and characterized, in the final fading image, by a faint but distinct smile. So this is not the death of the heart, as Wyler's film has it, but a kind of healing, which for some viewers opens the ending to the charge of sentimentality. Reflecting on the challenge and opportunity to make Catherine more communicative than she is in the novel, Rivkin concludes that 'By making Catherine demonstrative, either in revenge or in love, the two films offer a kind of implicit tribute to the power of James's silent figure' (p. 168). Both films certainly accentuate the passion, violence, and pain that James's text deftly restrains.

EXPLANATORY NOTES

IF not provided here, full details of works referred to can be found in the Select Bibliography. These notes owe a debt to previous editions of the novel by Mark Le Fanu (Oxford World's Classics, 1982), Brian Lee (Penguin Classics, 1984), and Martha Banta (Penguin Classics, 2007).

3 *the first half of the present century . . . the latter part of it*: the main action of the novel appears to take place in the 1840s; for more precise dates see note to p. 4.

Dr Sloper: William Veeder (acknowledging a debt to U. C. Knoepflmacher) points out that this name forms the third term in a sequence starting with the 'inadequate physician' in Laurence Sterne's *Tristram Shandy* (1759–67), and continuing through the 'clever cleric' in Anthony Trollope's *Barchester Towers* (1857)—'Slop', 'Slope', 'Sloper' (*Henry James*, pp. 187, 270, n. 3). One might add that Dr Sloper's first name, 'Austin', connects him to the realm of another literary antecedent closer to the style and manner of this novel than Sterne's or Trollope's.

4 *in 1820*: after the vagueness of the novel's opening lines, this is teasingly precise. If Austin Sloper marries at the age of 27, and 1820 is the year of his marriage to Catherine Harrington, then he will have been born in 1793, and if he is 'some fifty years of age' at the time at which we are chiefly concerned with him, this puts the events of the novel firmly in the 1840s. Their marriage lasts 'for about five years', the son dying at the age of 3, and the mother two years later, so Catherine would have been born in 1825. Mrs Penniman comes to live with the Slopers when Catherine was 'about ten years old': *c.*1835. The reference to Catherine's 'eighteenth year' (p. 10) would make it 1842–3 (her author was born on 15 April 1843), and she would be 'twenty years old' (p. 12) in 1845. She is in 'her twenty-first year' (p. 12) at the time of the Almond engagement party, but by the start of Ch. VII she has gained a year and become 22 (p. 32). Dr Sloper moves uptown to Washington Square '[s]ome three or four years' before the Almonds' party (p. 12). The chronology so far established would place this change of residence in 1841–2, but then James deranges it by appearing to date the move some six years earlier in 1835 (p. 13). At various points he speaks of 'thirty years ago' (p. 36), 'forty years ago' (p. 13), and 'the fashion of fifty years ago' (p. 46).

the small but promising capital . . . the Battery . . . the Bay . . . Canal Street: New York City served briefly as the young republic's legislative capital from 1785 to 1790 before ceding that role to Philadelphia and then (in 1800) to Washington, DC. James's novel catches the city midway in its massive development as the nation's economic and commercial centre. A population of 60,000 in 1800 had grown to nearly one million by 1860, almost half of whom were foreign-born, and by 1900, it was over three million, two-thirds of whom were foreign-born (Paul S. Boyer, *Oxford Companion to United States History* (Oxford, 2001), entry on New York, p. 553). In the 1840s the great majority of immigrants were from Ireland, as James's own grandfather, William James of Albany, had been in the late 1700s. In choosing the venue for her tryst with Morris Mrs Penniman avoids rubbing shoulders with them as they alight at the Battery (p. 73). Both film versions by Wyler and Holland (see Appendix 2) provide the Slopers with Irish maid-servants, noticeably sympathetic to the cause of romance between Morris and Catherine. 'The Battery', so named for its original military purposes, is at the southern tip of Manhattan; 'Canal Street', near Brooklyn Bridge, takes its name from the canal dug there in 1811.

6 *the town of Poughkeepsie*: town on the east bank of the Hudson River, midway between New York City and Albany. James wrote a tale entitled 'Miss Gunton of Poughkeepsie', also first published in the *Cornhill*, though twenty years later, in 1900.

8 *as good as good bread, as the French say*: the French phrase is *être bon comme du bon pain*, 'to have a heart of gold'. Perhaps this is why Mrs Bread is so named in *The American* (1877), a novel set in France.

11 *twenty thousand dollars a year*: it is notoriously difficult to come up with accurate ways of measuring the modern value of figures like this. Using the Consumer Price Index alone, $20,000 in 1820 would according to some calculations be worth *c.* $380,000 at the time of writing (2009), but in terms of real buying power the equivalent figure would be very much higher.

In those days in New York . . . the temple of Republican simplicity: the austerity associated with the Roman Republic represented an important ideal of personal and public conduct to ruling-class Americans in the early decades of the nineteenth century. James is marking the distance of 'those days' from the unbridled money-making and rampant ostentation he believed to characterize the new era after the Civil War.

12 *a red satin gown trimmed with gold fringe*: Clair Hughes calls this 'one of the most startling colour notes in James's fiction' (*Henry James and the Art of Dress*, 29); see also note to p. 120. Lauren Berlant ('Fancy-Work and Fancy Foot-Work', 447) points out the possible reference to Hester Prynne's 'A' in Nathaniel Hawthorne's *The Scarlet Letter*, which is constructed of 'fine red cloth, surrounded with an elaborate embroidery and fantastic flourishes of gold thread' (*Hawthorne: Novels*, Library of America (Cambridge, 1983), 163).

the City Hall: constructed from 1803 to 1812 in French Renaissance style, the oldest City Hall in the USA stands between Broadway, Park Row, and Chambers Street in the Civic Center district of Lower Manhattan. James was touched to find in 1904–5 that 'the divine little City Hall' had survived 'that assault of vulgarity of which the innumerable mementos rise within view of it and tower, at a certain distance, over it' (*The American Scene*, ed. John F. Sears (Harmondsworth, 1994), 75).

13 *Washington Square*: a celebrated feature of the area known as Greenwich Village, the 'Square' stands at the foot of Fifth Avenue between Fourth and Seventh Streets, surrounding a handsome park, adopted by the city in 1827; the Arch and the Fountain are particularly notable. As James indicates the Square and its environs became fashionable in the 1830s and 1840s. Emily Kies Folpe writes: 'Nowadays these homes continue to impart an old-fashioned atmosphere, but early residents would have considered themselves to be very modern.' (*It Happened on Washington Square* (Baltimore, 2002), 24.) See Introduction, p. vii.

the tenderness of early associations: as will be evident, this is an autobiographical as well as a 'topographical' parenthesis. The second of five children born to Henry James Senior (1811–82) and his wife, Mary, née Walsh (1810–82), Henry ('Harry') James Junior was born on 15 April 1843 at 21 Washington Place, just round the corner from Washington Square; it is now the site of Kimball Hall, on the Washington Square Campus of New York University. Returning in 1904–5 after an absence of twenty years, the novelist was dismayed by the sharp snub to memory represented by 'the rudely, the ruthlessly suppressed birth-house'; the 'high, square, impersonal structure' that had replaced it so blocked his view of the past 'that the effect for me, in Washington Place, was of having been amputated of half my history' (*The American Scene*, 70–1).

it was here that your grandmother lived: Elizabeth Walsh, née Robertson (1781–1847), James's maternal grandmother, lived at 18, Washington Square North, from 1835 until her death.

the strange odour of the ailantus-trees: the ailant(h)us is a fast-growing deciduous tree native to south-east Asia, its (faux-Latin) name probably deriving from an Ambonese word meaning 'tree of heaven'. The odour has been compared to cat urine.

ferule: ruler or stick for punishing children.

14 *bugles*: ornamental glass-beads in tubular shape, usually black.

22 *Minnesota*: an outlandish destination in the 1840s, Minnesota was the thirty-second State to join the Union in 1858 and was not fully settled until the end of the Dakota War of 1862.

Excelsior!: the Latin title and refrain, meaning 'Ever higher!', of a popular poem of 1842 by Henry Wadsworth Longfellow (1807–82). The poet's standing in the James household was not high. Elizabeth Stevenson notes Henry James Senior describing Longfellow, privately, as 'good inoffensive comforting Longfellow' (*The Crooked Corridor: A Study of Henry James* (New York, 1961), 119). Looking back near the end of his life on a generation of eminent contributors to the *Atlantic Monthly*, the novelist described Longfellow as 'frequent and remarkably even, neither rising above nor falling below a level ruled as straight as a line for a copybook'— unlike Emerson, who was 'rare, but . . . sometimes surprising' ('Mr and Mrs Fields' (1915), in *The American Essays of Henry James*, ed. Leon Edel (Princeton, NJ, 1989), 269).

27 *Bellini and Donizetti*: Italian composers of *bel canto* opera, Vincenzo Bellini (1801–35) and Gaetano Donizetti (1797–1848) were less fashionable by the time James was writing this novel than they had been forty years ago, in the middle years of the century.

28 *Pasta and Rubini and Lablache*: Giuditta Pasta (1797–1865), Giovanni Battista Rubini (1794–1854), and Luigi Lablache (1794–1858), soprano, tenor, and bass respectively, all star singers of the 1830s and 40s.

29 *the elder of his sisters, Mrs Almond*: but on p. 6 Mrs Almond had been introduced as the younger sister. Perhaps the fact she is 'the Doctor's wiser sister' (p. 31)—the 'sense' to Lavinia Penniman's 'sensibility'—induced him into this inconsistency.

33 *something of a physiognomist*: adherent of the pseudo-science popularized in the nineteenth century by the Swiss pastor Johann Kaspar Lavater (1741–1801), and believed to enable the reading of personality through examination of the face, an idea congenial to novelists such as Balzac, Dickens, and many others.

35 *coxcomb*: a somewhat antiquated term of abuse (certainly by 1880) for someone with an excessively high opinion of himself and the manner to match.

49 *You will cleave to me?*: Morris may intend to invoke the solemnity of the King James Bible: 'Therefore shall a man leave his father and mother, and shall cleave unto his wife: and they shall be one flesh' (Genesis 2: 24), but 'cleave' also has an antiquated and sentimental ring to it, such as would appeal to Mrs Penniman.

58 *some proverb about a reformed rake?*: a proverb probably originating in the eighteenth century and a hardy perennial of the romantic novel ever since: 'A reformed rake makes the best husband.' In the Preface to *Clarissa* (1748) Samuel Richardson asserted that it was one of his purposes in writing the novel to warn children against this dangerous adage (reversing the conclusion to his own previous novel *Pamela* (1740)).

61 *Hasn't she made a scene?*: in *A Small Boy and Others* James recalls the momentous effect on his younger self, when he first heard a young cousin rebuked for protesting at being sent to bed: '"Come now, my dear; don't make a scene—I *insist* on your not making a scene!"' (*Autobiography*, ed. Frederick W. Dupee (London, 1956), 219.)

she thinks me very arbitrary: here 'arbitrary' does not mean what it mainly does now ('unpredictable', 'capricious'); it has the political sense, common in the nineteenth century, of 'authoritarian', 'tyrannical', and 'absolutist'. Note the reference to 'treason' just a few lines further, and compare the moment when Dr Sloper warns Mrs Penniman against 'high treason' (p. 91), and she calls his behaviour that of 'a great autocrat'.

62 *poplin*: fabric consisting of a silk warp with a weft of worsted yarn.

72 *referred to the skies the initiative, as the French say*: an awkward translation

of a French idiom designed to suggest Catherine's lack of familiarity with the language, in contrast to Morris's.

72 *duenna*: a chaperon.

73 *Greenwood Cemetery*: founded in 1838 as a rural cemetery in Kings County, New York, now in Brooklyn.

   an oyster saloon in the Seventh Avenue: oysters were cheap popular fare in the nineteenth century, and such saloons abounded in great city-ports such as New York and London.

82 *in the Bowery*: Mrs Penniman is venturing, or pretending to venture, into shady areas, but the Bowery (the name is derived from the old Dutch word for 'farm') had not yet descended into the squalor and violence for which it would soon become known in the 1850s, home turf of 'The Bowery Boys', one of 'The Gangs of New York' in Herbert Asbury's 1928 (non-fiction) book of that name, and the film derived from it by Martin Scorsese (2002). For James's own memories, see 'The Bowery and Thereabouts', in *The American Scene*, ch. 5.

89 *a farthing of money*: a very small, now obsolete coin, worth one-quarter of an English penny.

106 *hoisting your flag*: nautical metaphor, signifying the declaration of clear intentions.

108 *Raphael . . . the ruins of the Pantheon*: one of the most famous painters of the Italian Renaissance (1483–1520), but Mrs Penniman is on less sure footing with the Pantheon, which is the best preserved example of an ancient Roman monument. Originally a temple to 'all the gods' of Rome, as its name indicates, it was converted to a Roman Catholic Church in the seventh century AD. She may be thinking of the ruins of the Parthenon, a mistake repeated by her sister, Mrs Almond.

110 *vestals of old, tending the sacred flame*: in ancient Rome the 'vestal virgins' tended the fire sacred to Vesta, Goddess of the Hearth.

111 *castle of indolence*: the title of a poem (1748) by James Thomson that has passed into currency as a vaguely literary phrase for a state of luxurious idleness.

118 *posting roads*: route along which mail was carried by horse, hence 'smooth' (as opposed to rough ordinary roads).

119 *a commission-merchant*: a person who buys or sells on behalf of others, and takes a 'commission' for each successful transaction.

   an office in Duane Street: well south of the fashionable Washington Square in a downtown commercial district, Duane Street runs east–west between Chamber Street and Worth Street. Brian Lee suggests that James may have had in mind a well-known painting of *c*.1877 depicting this run-down area by Louis Tiffany (1848–1933), now in the Brooklyn Museum.

120 *a splendid cashmere shawl*: Catherine's European tour has brought her up

to speed with the latest French fashions, the cashmere shawl being 'the ultimate genteel fashion accessory around 1850' (Hughes, p. 37).

124 *the idea sticks in my crop*: or as we would now say, 'sticks in my throat'.

127 *sensorium*: the 'seat of sensation', where an organism perceives and interprets its environment.

129 *tables d'hôte*: fixed menus, not normally including wine, as Mrs Church is dismayed to find in 'The Pension Beaurepas'.

131 *reticule*: a small bag, usually of woven material (from the French).

132 *not an easy thing to bring out*: this is the reading in the *Cornhill* serial and *Harper's* book versions, but the 1881 Macmillan text oddly omits the 'not'. This must be an error; the 'difficulty' referred to in the second half of the sentence requires restoration of the 'not'.

138 *yellow fever*: in the 1820s the outbreak of 'yellow fever' in New York City had contributed to the migration uptown from lower Manhattan. New Orleans was seriously afflicted from 1853 to 1855.

140 *a dangler*: a man who hangs or hovers around women, with a view to shirking real work, 'a petticoat dangler'.

146 *the grief that does not speak!*: from a Shakespearian passage to which James was often drawn. Macduff has just received the news that Macbeth has had his family murdered. Malcolm says:

> What man, ne'er pull your hat upon your brows:
> Give sorrow words; the grief that does not speak
> Whispers the o'er-fraught heart, and bids it break.

> (*Macbeth*, 4.3.208–10)

156 *Il fait le mort*: he is 'playing dead'.

157 *aid-societies*: charity organizations assisting the poor.

with an even and noiseless step: 'with noiseless step' was a literary phrase popular with nineteenth-century writers in verse and prose (Scott, Irving, Cooper, Charlotte Brontë amongst many others). Like the 'castle of indolence' above (p. 111), it teeters on the edge of cliché.

159 *cicerone*: a guide.

160 *Bloomingdale*: this name acts as another historical marker insofar as its associations have radically altered. The Bloomingdale Mental Asylum was opened in 1821 on what is now the site of Columbia University's Morningside Heights Campus. The name ('Bloemendael') is derived from the era of Dutch rule, and has no connection with the Bavarian immigrant of the same name and his sons who gave their name to the still flourishing modern department store. The brothers started selling hoop-skirts on the Lower East Side in the 1860s and opened their first store in 1872, moving to the current location on 59th Street and Lexington Avenue in 1886. So their business was just getting under way as James was writing this novel.

buggy: a light four-wheel vehicle drawn by one or two horses.

162 *smaller dwellings, with brown stone fronts*: the 'brownstones' for which
New York is famous were built of brick faced with soft sandstone, pink
when first cut but weathering to a rich brown. Marcus Binney describes
the development of this new terraced housing as 'contemporary with the
great wave of speculative building that from the 1840s carried Manhattan
uptown from Washington Square' (*Town Houses: Urban Houses from 1200
to the Present Day* (New York and London 1998), 106).

163 *dressed in white . . . palmetto fan*: Hughes notes that Catherine finally gets
to wear 'the virginal white frock she so signally failed to wear at her début'
(see note to p. 12); it also signals 'the final stages of mourning for her
father's death a year before' (Hughes, p. 39). A species of palm-tree, a
'palmetto' provided leaves for fans and hats.

166 *morsel of fancy-work*: ornamental needlework. For the reminiscing James
'morsel' carried a welcome sense of nutrition: revisiting his childhood
haunts in 1904–5 he hailed 'the felt moral and social value of this
comparatively unimpaired morsel of the Fifth Avenue heritage', and
discerned in the shabby little red house on Waverley Place where he had
gone to dame's school 'as consummate a morsel of the old liquor-scented,
heated-looking city, the city of no pavements, but of such a plenty of
politics, as I could have desired' (*The American Scene*, 68, 70).

	Late Victorian Gothic Tales
JANE AUSTEN	Emma
	Mansfield Park
	Persuasion
	Pride and Prejudice
	Selected Letters
	Sense and Sensibility
MRS BEETON	Book of Household Management
MARY ELIZABETH BRADDON	Lady Audley's Secret
ANNE BRONTË	The Tenant of Wildfell Hall
CHARLOTTE BRONTË	Jane Eyre
	Shirley
	Villette
EMILY BRONTË	Wuthering Heights
ROBERT BROWNING	The Major Works
JOHN CLARE	The Major Works
SAMUEL TAYLOR COLERIDGE	The Major Works
WILKIE COLLINS	The Moonstone
	No Name
	The Woman in White
CHARLES DARWIN	The Origin of Species
THOMAS DE QUINCEY	The Confessions of an English Opium-Eater
	On Murder
CHARLES DICKENS	The Adventures of Oliver Twist
	Barnaby Rudge
	Bleak House
	David Copperfield
	Great Expectations
	Nicholas Nickleby
	The Old Curiosity Shop
	Our Mutual Friend
	The Pickwick Papers

WALTER SCOTT	**Rob Roy**
MARY SHELLEY	**Frankenstein** **The Last Man**
ROBERT LOUIS STEVENSON	**Strange Case of Dr Jekyll and** **Mr Hyde and Other Tales** **Treasure Island**
BRAM STOKER	**Dracula**
JOHN SUTHERLAND	**So You Think You Know Jane Austen?** **So You Think You Know Thomas Hardy?**
WILLIAM MAKEPEACE THACKERAY	**Vanity Fair**
OSCAR WILDE	**The Importance of Being Earnest and** **Other Plays** **The Major Works** **The Picture of Dorian Gray**
ELLEN WOOD	**East Lynne**
DOROTHY WORDSWORTH	**The Grasmere and Alfoxden Journals**
WILLIAM WORDSWORTH	**The Major Works**

ANTHONY TROLLOPE

The American Senator

An Autobiography

Barchester Towers

Can You Forgive Her?

The Claverings

Cousin Henry

The Duke's Children

The Eustace Diamonds

Framley Parsonage

He Knew He Was Right

Lady Anna

Orley Farm

Phineas Finn

Phineas Redux

The Prime Minister

Rachel Ray

The Small House at Allington

The Warden

The Way We Live Now